CHAPTER ONE

"Happy New Year, Chi Chi," Obi said, raising his glass towards his wife, Nkechi. "Welcome to 2012! Sadly, we will only live to see the 21st of December since the world will come to a sudden and apocalyptic end based on the prediction from the Mayan calendar."

Nkechi laughed and clicked her glass with Obi's before the two of them shared a light kiss. She and her husband had just watched the ball drop in Times Square on television.

"Honey, I think you might have drunk too much wine tonight," Nkechi said, teasing her husband. "You know that some wacko, or group of wackos, comes out every couple of years to say the world will end on a particular date. Do you now expect me to believe that this time is going to be the real deal?"

"Yea babe, but I have to admit that I used to listen to this late-night radio show a couple years back that talked about this whole Mayan stuff. I thought it was complete nonsense for the most part. But then they came out with the movie *2012* last year.

After I saw the movie, I had to admit that the whole thing was a little bit eerie."

Nkechi shook her head. "Well, I will let your ass wait for the apocalypse to happen then. But I do remember you telling me and Nnamdi back in law school about that radio show which talked about time travel, ghosts, and other crazy shit. We used to look at you thinking '*this is one weird Nigerian dude*'. It wasn't until you told us you grew up watching *Star Trek* that we understood where you were coming from. Luckily for you, I was able to look past your quirkiness to see how great of a guy you are."

"Well thanks for your ringing endorsement of me, Chi Chi," Obi said.

"No problem, honey," she giggled. Then she looked down at their sleeping son who was tucked between them on the couch and decided it was time to get him into his bed.

Nkechi smiled at her son and said to him, "Ike, are you ready to go to sleep now?"

Ikechukwu wiped his eyes with both of his hands and nodded his head.

"Our little man is growing so fast. I still can't believe that he is already 18 months old," Obi said to Nkechi

Nkechi flung Ike across her shoulder before responding. "Yes, you are definitely right about that. He is also starting to get too heavy to carry. Ike has such a big head which we both know he inherited from you."

"Chi Chi, you have to realize that we Ifeanyi men have above average brains and need larger heads to carry all the knowledge that has been bestowed upon us by our ancestors."

She burst out laughing, "Obi, you are a mess and I think you already know that about yourself by now," she said as she walked up the stairs with their son.

Obi turned off the television and began to clear the living room of all the food and wine bottles he and Nkechi used to celebrate the arrival of the New Year. He was in the middle of picking up the last glass when some picture frames caught his eye. He walked over to them. One contained a picture of them on their wedding day and the other was of them together, in their caps and gowns after their graduation from Howard Law School. He looked at the pictures sitting on the counter and smiled. Sometimes, he still had to pinch himself to be sure that this life that he had with Nkechi was not a dream. He had transitioned from living a single, carefree life, to being a husband and father with major responsibilities in just a couple of years.

He was still gazing lovingly at the pictures when Nkechi returned to the living room. She walked up behind him and wrapped her arms around his waist, resting her head against his back. "Are you ready to call it a night?"

Obi shook his head in disbelief and turned around to face his wife. "I was just thinking about how we partied till damn near the break of dawn every night, during Obama's inauguration three years ago. Now we can barely stay up past 1 a.m. on New Year's Eve."

Nkechi sighed, then laughed. "Yea, those now seem like the good old days. I was thirty years old, and I was in great shape and didn't have any baby weight on me. I remember people would mistake me for Lauryn Hill from time to time. But I think we have both seen that having a little child to care for takes a lot out of you. I still remember how I broke you off on the dance floor at the Beenie Man and Sean Paul concert. You couldn't hang with me that night."

"I still contend that I slipped on a wet spot on the dance floor or something," Obi said in his defense. "Anyway, I do remember you being drunk as hell and I had to nurse you back to health the next day."

Nkechi smiled. "Well, that was such a magical weekend for the country as well as it was for us." She traced a finger down the side of his face and continued, "That was also when we took our friendship to the next level."

"We can recreate that moment right here in the living room if you want to," Obi said, eagerly. "I just have to get my iPod out real quick and then we can get it popping." He attempted to go and get the iPod by wiggling out of Nkechi's embrace.

But Nkechi was quick to stop him. "Obi, maybe we can do that another time. I am tired now." Seeing the look of disappointment on Obi's face, she quickly added, "don't forget that I have to wake up early to prepare food for the New Year's Day dinner at your parents' house tomorrow.

Obi struggled to get over his disappointment as they turned out the lights in the living room and headed to the bedroom. He still held out hope that he could get some sex to start off the night, but when he saw Nkechi change into some big t-shirt and sweatpants, he knew that nothing was about to happen. Thirty minutes after they entered the bedroom, Nkechi was fast asleep. Obi, on the other hand, struggled to fall asleep. He found himself wide awake and thinking about what 2012 had in store for him and his family.

The last two years had been busy, to say the least. Nkechi's pregnancy and subsequent birth to Ike, their wedding; it all seemed to have happened in the blink of an eye. But despite the triumphs, he had also suffered some setbacks as well. The recession had caused him to close his uncle's downtown law office and layoff the two paralegals who worked for him. He had moved some of the existing files to a storage facility and was now operating the firm's business out of his townhouse. On top of that, collecting outstanding debts from his clients for services already rendered had become an issue he was still trying to solve. While he tried to collect what was owed the firm, he had resorted to taking on contract and temporary projects for other law firms to keep up with the piling bills. His only saving grace was that he had expanded his tax services beyond the normal tax season and was getting more clients on that end.

Nkechi, on the other hand, was on track to finishing up her Master's degree in Public Policy from The University of Houston in 2011, but she had been forced to push her graduation to the following May to enable her to adjust to life as a new mother.

In the meantime, she had taken on some part-time work here and there. For the most part, however, Obi was the primary breadwinner in the household. Obi's mother had retired from teaching last year which allowed her to see her grandson every day. Having his mother watch Ike during the day, cut out the cost of paying one-fifty to two hundred dollars in childcare costs every week, an expense Obi and Nkechi really couldn't afford to pay. In addition to everything they had going on at the time, Obi had to deal with his health insurance premium going up once he added his wife and son to his policy, forcing him to consider going to work in corporate America. It meant working longer hours, but at least he would have a steady paycheck, more money, plus bonuses and cheaper health insurance premiums than what he had from buying on the individual market.

2012 was also an election year which meant that President Obama would be up for re-election as well. It was crazy how Obama had entered his presidency in 2009 with so much momentum and steam that no one had ever seen before. But now with the economy still stagnant and most Americans weary of his policies, the chances of Obama winning a second term went from an almost certainty to now being a coin flip at best. There was even talk among people in his own party that his current Secretary of State and 2008 Democratic primary challenger, Hillary Clinton, should be inserted as vice president instead of Joe Biden to give a boost to the ticket going into the general election.

Obi lay in bed thinking about everything that had transpired the year before when a thought came to him and he laughed. It was the sound of his Uncle Ugo's voice saying, "Obi, Rome wasn't built in a day and your problems won't be changed in that period either. Relax and just take life one day at a time." It was a reassuring thought that caused Obi to take a deep breath and fall asleep.

When he opened his eyes, it was daylight. Nkechi was lying beside him fully awake. She leaned across the bed and gave him a kiss on the lips.

"Happy New Year, my sweet Obi. I hope that you slept well and that all your wishes and desires for this year come true for you. Also, I want you to remember that we are in this thing together and you will always have my full love and support."

Obi rolled on his side to face her. "Thanks, Chi Chi. You know that my feelings and sentiments for you are the same." He kissed her on her lips and then on her neck.

"Damn, babe. I see that you woke up with all types of sexual energy," she teased him. "The year isn't more than a few hours old and I see the way you want to bring it in."

"I am just trying to bring in 2012 with a bang," he whispered against her neck. He brought his lips back to hers and captured them in a fiery kiss. The thought of sleeping with his wife filled Obi with an intense excitement. Between work, Ike, and the holidays, it seemed like it had been almost a month since they had sex. The fact that this was about to happen was cause for celebration.

Obi run his hands down Nkechi's body, feeling the curve of her hips, before finding the band of her pants and attempting to pull it off. Just then, a loud cry came drifting in from the other room.

Nkechi placed her hand on his and stopped him from going further. "I see that our son is awake. Let me go and see what is up with him."

Obi could have groaned loudly right there and then as he saw the moment slipping away from him. "Chi Chi, all I need is about five minutes," he begged instead. 'Ike will be ok, he cries all of the time anyway."

Nkechi, who was now sitting on the edge of the bed, seemed to consider Obi's request for a few minutes, but her maternal instinct kicked in and she stood up. "Sorry, Obi, but I have to go and check on Ike. We will get back to where we were when I am done with him."

Obi grunted and rolled back to his side of the bed as Nkechi left the room. After about ten minutes, Obi got out of the bed and went to Ike's room where he found Nkechi breastfeeding their son.

Obi smirked. "Ike sees more of your breasts lately than I do."

Nkechi laughed. "Obi, stop being so selfish. This isn't a competition between you and Ike. Ike is a baby and he needs my breasts to get his nutrients. You, on the other hand, only want them for your pleasure."

Obi knew he was being unreasonable, so he dropped the matter even though he still felt slightly neglected by his wife. After Nkechi finished feeding Ike, perhaps he could try again from where they left off.

He was sadly mistaken. It was the New Year, and well-wishers had begun a persistent avalanche of calls before either one of them could get dressed and head out the door to meet his parents.

By the time they were ready to head out, there was no time to slow down. They had to make a stop at the grocery store to pick up a few things before making it to his parents' house across town.

It was in the wine aisle of the grocery store where he heard a very familiar sultry voice sing out his name. He turned towards the sound of the voice and came face-to-face with his ex-girlfriend, Tamika. By the time he could react, she had her arms around him in an intimate and seductive hug.

Time had passed since their last physical encounter, but Obi still found himself thoroughly enjoying the sense of her touch; being next to her and having her skin rub against his. Just when he felt himself begin to relax in the warmth of her embrace, he quickly backed away and cleared his throat.

"Happy New Year, Obi," Tamika said, breaking the uncomfortable silence that followed. "How have you been doing? I haven't seen you in a long time."

"I'm doing well," Obi responded, looking at the woman he had once dated. She still looked fine as hell. Childbirth had been kind to her, her breasts were bigger and her body was still in great shape.

"I see you are still looking great, too," he added, not thinking his words through. Once the words had rolled off his tongue, however, he wanted to have them back. He didn't want to give her any type of compliment at all. Tamika had a big ego and he knew she would start to get full of herself. But it was too late to take back the compliment because Tamika basked in it right away.

"Thanks for noticing, Obi. I had to work very hard to get the baby weight off. I hired a personal trainer and I now go to the gym about four to five times a week."

"Hey, that is good for you," he said and tried to turn his attention back to the wine rack. But Tamika was obviously not done and was not going anywhere anytime soon.

"So, how is married life going so far?"

"I and Nkechi are doing great. She is somewhere in the store with my son, Ike. We're picking up a few things to take to my parents' house."

If he hoped his newest revelation would make Tamika back off and want to leave, it didn't. But he did not expect her next statement either.

"Wow, that is awesome," she exclaimed. "I really would like to see her and your son."

Obi did not have a chance to respond, Nkechi was walking down the aisle towards them carrying a basket in one hand and holding their son in the other. His heart began to race as Nkechi approached. Once she was standing close to him, he took Ike from her while she kissed him on his cheek.

"Hey babe," he said to Nkechi, his eyes shifting restlessly from one woman to the other, "this is Tamika, my ex-girlfriend from college."

Nkechi's eyes widened. "Oh, it is so great to finally meet you," she said, extending a hand out to Tamika. "Obi has told me so much about you."

"It is good to meet you as well," Tamika said, taking Nkechi's hand in a delicate handshake. "Just wanted to tell you that you have a great man here. I know that you are lucky to have him."

Nkechi could not hide the smirk on her face. "Thanks for letting me know that. He is a great husband and father. I would never dream of letting him slip through my fingers." She sat the basket down on the floor and looped her arm through her husband's.

Obi could sense the tension building. He tried to direct his attention away from the women and towards Ike. Tamika did the same.

"So, who is this handsome little man?" She asked, touching her palm to the baby's face. Ike tried to shield his face with his small hands.

"I see he is a little shy," Tamika said, redirecting her attention to Nkechi and Obi. Nkechi simply smiled tightly.

"Do you guys mind if I carry him for a little bit?" She asked, reaching her arms out towards Obi. Obi was a little uncomfortable with the whole situation and looked to Nkechi for guidance, but got none. Instead, Nkechi avoided making eye contact with him. Obi knew he would have to make this call on his own.

With a half-smile on his face, he handed the baby over to Tamika. "Yea that is not a problem at all. But be careful with him, he isn't as light as you think he might be."

Tamika took Ike in her arms effortlessly and began tickling his nose. Ike giggled in response as Obi and Nkechi looked on, amazed at how quickly he had warmed up to Tamika.

"Your son is so cute," Tamika said to Nkechi, while still tickling the baby's nose. "He looks so much like Obi and even has some of his mannerisms."

Nkechi smiled and looked at Obi but did not say anything.

"Maybe we can set up a lunch or play date with Ike and my son, Jamal. How old is Ike by the way?"

"He is about 18 months old," Nkechi said.

"That is just perfect. My son is about three months older than him," Tamika responded gleefully. "I know Obi still has my number, but I will take yours down as well."

Obi was a little bit bewildered at the sight of Tamika putting Nkechi's phone number and email address into her cell phone. Then to make matters weirder, Tamika said to Nkechi, "Are you on Facebook? If so, I will send you a friend request. I post pics of Jamal all the time and can see some of your pics as a family and of Ike."

Ten minutes later, they were finally able to break free of Tamika. While they waited in the checkout line, Obi could only imagine the conversation they would have in the car on the drive to his parents' house. He was not looking forward to it.

So he turned on the radio as quickly as he could, the moment they were in the car and Ike was safely strapped into his infant car seat. Nkechi smiled to herself.

They drove along in silence for about five minutes before Nkechi reached over and turned down the music.

"Well, that was a pretty interesting turn of events back there," she started, "all I can say is that was one hell of a way to start the first day of the year."

Obi nodded. It seemed this conversation was unavoidable.

Nkechi continued. "Honestly, Tamika isn't anything like I imagined her to be. She has such a bubbly personality and you can tell she has good maternal instincts in the way she handled Ike." Obi kept his eyes on the road as Nkechi continued. "I know he is usually very shy around people he doesn't know, but for some reason, he was very much at ease in her presence. She kind of threw me for a loop with that whole trying to have our kids hang out and stuff. But I guess she was just trying to be nice and friendly."

"So, did you pick up all the things that we need for dinner at my parents'?" he asked, trying to change the topic.

Nkechi paused and looked at Obi before responding. "Yes, I did honey. When did you become so concerned about groceries?"

"I just don't want us to get there only for me to have to go back to the store because we forgot something. You know my mom is very particular about cooking with certain foods."

Nkechi began to sense that Obi had been subdued since they got in the car. She wondered if it had anything to do with seeing Tamika.

"So, how did you feel about seeing Tamika today?" she asked to be sure.

Obi hesitated for a few seconds before he responded. "It was good to see her and catch up for a bit. I haven't seen her in a couple of years."

Nkechi decided to delve a little deeper. "Yea, she is a very attractive woman. I can see why you dated her. I can't even lie, even with her jeans and blouse on, she looked toned. And she has a firm booty. I would love to have her body."

Obi started to feel uncomfortable. He tightened his grip on the steering wheel. "Tamika has always been in pretty good shape for as long as I have known her."

Nkechi threw one last monkey wrench at him. "So, do you think she looks better than me?"

Obi shook his head vigorously. That's not what he meant. She had to know that's not what he meant. He wiped his hand across his forehead and Nkechi watched him struggle a little more before bursting out in laughter.

"Babe, you know I am just fucking with you, right? I know that Tamika was your first love and you guys had a long history together. She will always have a special place in your heart."

Obi was relieved. "Chi Chi, you know you're the only woman I love."

Nkechi smiled. "Obi, I know that is true. But, I have to admit that it was funny seeing you sweat when I was asking you those questions." Then she leaned over and kissed him on the cheek and told him how much she loved him.

To the outside world, Nkechi was a strong and assertive woman, but, she was a very sensitive and insecure person. Even though she had been married to Obi for close to two years, she still wondered if he was completely satisfied with her.

They arrived at Obi's parents' house about ten minutes later. They pulled into the driveway and were met by Obi's father and mother before they could even get out of the car. Obi's father was the first to greet them as soon as they both got out. With a jovial laugh, he belted out a hearty "Happy New Year to you guys. We are very happy that you have arrived."

Then taking turns, they each embraced Nkechi before going over to see their grandson who was still in his car seat. Obi greeted his father and mother and headed into the house with the grocery bags while his mother was reaching into the back seat to unbuckle Ike from his seat.

"My boy, how are you doing?" Uncle Ugo said, hugging Obi when he walked into the living room.

"Uncle, I am doing well. How are you?"

"I'm doing well, my son."

"Good, good. Good to hear. Auntie Nkiru, good morning," Obi responded also greeting his uncle's wife. Without waiting for her response, he walked into the kitchen to put down the grocery bags. They were getting heavy.

When Obi walked back into the living room, his uncle was now seated on the sofa next to his wife, and his parents were still outside chatting with Nkechi and playing with Ike. Obi sat in the love seat next to his uncle.

"So, how is your health, uncle?" he asked uncle Ugo.

"I am well, my son. Same since the last time you saw me."

After a brief pause, uncle Ugo asked, "where are your wife and the baby?"

"They are outside with mom and dad," Obi responded, looking out of the window at his father having some sort of discussion with Nkechi while his mother held Ike in her arms and swung him from side to side while the baby giggled excitedly.

Uncle Ugo's eyes followed Obi's. "I hope that you realize you now rank third in importance in your household, behind your son and wife," he said with a laugh. "Everybody will always ask about how they are doing and almost forget about you. Welcome to the club."

Obi smiled and nodded in agreement. Thinking about everything that had happened that morning before they left the house, he could not argue with that. Ever since Ike was born, things had been different at home. Obi knew what to expect, and he even thought he had prepared himself for everything when Nkechi was pregnant, but now that things were playing out in real time, he realized how unprepared he was forever going to be.

About five minutes later, Obi watched as his wife, parents, and son came walking into the house. Nkechi was the first to enter the living room, she had Ike with her. She greeted Uncle Ugo and Auntie Nkiru before heading over to sit on the armrest of the sofa where Obi was sitting.

"Bring Lil Barack to me," Uncle Ugo said to Nkechi, referring to Ike by his middle name. He moved his walking cane to the side to make room for the baby as Nkechi walked Ike over. Since his heart attack in 2009, Uncle Ugo's health had changed. A year later, he had suffered a stroke that left the right side of his body paralyzed. Although he had recovered from the stroke, he now got around with the use of a cane.

"Lil Barack, I hope all is well with you," Uncle Ugo said to the baby while bouncing him on his knee. "You are in a safe position unlike your older namesake over there in the White House who has to deal with the crazy Republicans, the Tea Party, and a bad economy. I pray that *Chineke* will allow him to win another term."

"Amen!" said everyone gathered in the living room.

Uncle Ugo smiled before turning his attention back to his grandnephew. Auntie Nkiru and Nkechi were engaged in a discussion of some sort about breastfeeding and motherhood, while Obi tried not to hear them, his eyes trained on the television set.

"I hate to interrupt everybody's good time, but I need my sister-in-law and my second daughter to come help me in the kitchen," Obi's mother said, stepping into the living room a few minutes later."

Aunt Nkiru and Nkechi got up and headed to the kitchen while Obi's father joined uncle Ugo on the sofa. Now, the two men had their attention fixed on Ike. There was a college football game on television that no one was really glued to. Obi watched his father's interaction with his son and noticed how playful and affectionate he was with Ike. He found it odd, especially since his father had never shown that type of affection towards his own son growing up. Nevertheless, he had to smile, watching the old men play with the cooing baby.

"So," Uncle Ugo said to Obi, "how is everything going on with you? And don't give me that 'everything is fine' bullshit."

"Uncle, I can't lie to you. Things are a little bit tough," Obi responded. "I am going to start applying for permanent full-time work at some corporate law firms. I tried the small business entrepreneur route, but with a wife and child, I am tired of barely making it every month."

Uncle Ugo simply nodded while Obi spoke. "I am sorry that I couldn't keep the firm going after you passed it on to me," Obi concluded.

"Obi, don't worry about it at all. All good things come to an end eventually. Being able to provide you with your first job after law school was a joy. It was a pleasure working with you and getting to know you as a colleague, aside from you being my nephew."

"Uncle, I don't know how to ever repay you. Thanks for giving me the opportunity and for all the advice you have given me throughout the years. It has made me a better man."

"Obi, at the end of the day, if anything that I have done has helped you grow as a man, then I have done my job and you owe me nothing. The only thing you have to do now is to try and be a good father to your son."

"I will, Uncle, thank you."

Right then, Obi's sister Chinwe, came bouncing into the living room from the kitchen. She greeted the older men and took Ike from Uncle Ugo and began to tickle and kiss on him.

"Hey, big bro," she finally said to Obi, as if she was now realizing his presence. At that moment, Obi looked over at Uncle Ugo who was already laughing at him. He no longer existed. He smiled at that knowledge.

"Ike is getting big," Chinwe continued, obliviously. "I don't know how often I can be picking him up anymore before my back gives out."

"So, are you going to come and help us in the kitchen or not?" Their mother said, interrupting their little chat.

"Mama, I am a twenty-first-century woman. I don't feel that women must cook all the time. Why can't the men ever help out in the kitchen?" Chinwe said to her mother.

Their mother laughed. "My dear, I agree with your assessment that we live in a different time where men and women should both share in domestic responsibilities. Unfortunately, most Nigerian men will not marry a woman who doesn't want to cook."

"And who says I am going to marry a Naija man anyway? I am open to dating men of different races and ethnicities."

"Chinwe, I am not going to have this conversation with you on the first day of the year. If you want to help, fine, if not too, it is ok." Then she stormed back into the kitchen.

Obi's father, Chukwuemeka, could tell that his wife was upset. He glared at Chinwe disapprovingly. Without having to say a word, Chinwe knew what to do.

She took a deep breath and handed Ike back to Uncle Ugo. "Fine, daddy, I will go and help them out."

Obi's father nodded. "Thank you, my little angel." He felt proud that even at twenty-nine, his daughter still revered him.

After she was gone, Uncle Ugo said to the men, "Even though I am old, I would not want to be dating in this day and time. The women of today are more educated than their mothers' generation, but many of them lack the wisdom of knowing what it takes to be a great woman."

"My brother, I agree with you wholeheartedly," Obi's father nodded in agreement. "I blame the so-called feminist movement for deceiving these women into believing that they can have it all. A woman should learn that you can't be the CEO of a company, mother of the year, and satisfy a husband's wants all at the same time. You have to decide what is important to you and focus on that."

"So, are you saying that there is a double-standard when it comes to the way society views men and women?" Obi asked his father.

"My son, I have to admit that there is one. Let us examine your own situation for a minute. Your wife, Nkechi, gave up a very powerful career to move and be with you. If she had kept up her same trajectory, she surely would have moved into a higher-level position, but she probably wouldn't be married or have a child. Men just don't have to make those same type of sacrifices that women have to make to have the life that they want."

Obi was still chewing on what his father had just said when his mother called out to them from the kitchen saying that the food was ready to be served.

Everyone gathered around the dinner table to eat. Obi's mother led them in prayer. "*Chineke,* we thank you again for bringing us out of 2011 and into 2012. I hope that you continue to give protection to our relatives across the world. Also, thank you for this meal that we have prepared in hopes that it gives us nourishment and strength." She paused briefly before continuing, "Finally, my God, I have one special request for you. I pray that you send my only daughter, Chinwe, a husband, with this year marking her thirtieth year of life. My God, if you know my heart, you won't send an *Oyinbo, Akat*a, or Mexican, but a good Igbo man. If you can grant me this wish my God, I will eternally be grateful to you. Amen."

There was laughter all around as everyone opened their eyes. Uncle Ugo stood up and said to his sister-in-law: "Ijeoma since you have said it, it shall be done." Then he looked in Chinwe's direction and said sarcastically, "This was a very strong prayer your mama just prayed to *Chineke.* Don't be surprised if you have many marriage proposals come your way this year."

Obi's father jumped in and, with a smile, said to his wife: "My dear, I think you might have stumbled yourself into your next career as a TV evangelist. All we need is to find a building and start with a small congregation. If these impostors who know nothing about the Bible can start a church, why can't you, with the anointed power of God, have one?"

There was more laughter around the table. When the laughter died down, Chinwe spoke. "Mama, thank you for your prayers and concern, but finding a husband isn't as easy as you make it out to be. I have met a lot of *Naija* men, and they either fall into two categories; traditional or Americanized. The traditional ones are the ones usually born in Nigeria who moved to the States in their twenties and thirties. They are very rigid in their views and, for the most part, are boring. The Americanized ones are only Nigerian in name. They either don't know or don't care about their culture.

Most of the Americanized Nigerians were born and raised in the States."

Aunt Nkiru had a puzzled looked on her face. "So my dear, what is it that you are actually looking for in a man then?" She asked Chinwe.

Before Chinwe could respond, Nkechi intervened, "Chinwe, I understand the predicament you are in. You want a *Naija* man who enjoys the music of both P-Square and Jay-Z. Someone who knows and can talk about the current events and trends in this country, but who also knows what is going on in Nigeria."

Chinwe nodded her head in agreement.

"Chinwe, then why don't you find a man like your brother, Obi over here?" uncle Ugo said, looking over at Obi. "I think he encompasses the traits that Nkechi has just described."

Chinwe rolled her eyes. "Yes, you are right, uncle. Obinna represents the gold standard for young Nigerian American men everywhere. If only we could clone him a lot of single *Naija* women like myself wouldn't have to remain man-less for too long."

Obi laughed. "Chinwe, don't hate the playa, hate the game."

Everyone joined in the laughter. The laughter was soon followed by silence as everyone around the table concentrated on dishing out portions and eating their food.

Uncle Ugo looked at his plate and shook his head. It did not escape the eyes of his wife, Nkiru.

"Ugo is everything ok with you," she asked him, looking concerned.

"Oh yes, everything is okay. It's just…I have to add some salt to give this stew some kick. It doesn't have any taste at all."

"Ugo!" Auntie Nkiru admonished him, but got up and walked to the kitchen. When she came back to the dining room, she handed Uncle Ugo the salt substitute shaker.

"Do you remember what your doctor told you?" she asked, pulling out her chair and sitting down to her meal. "You have to reduce your salt intake."

Uncle Ugo did not respond. Instead, he vigorously sprinkled the contents of the shaker into his food. As if it was not enough that he had to give up his favorite Nigerian staples, Moi, and farina with egusi or pepper soup. Now, he had to sit and watch others enjoying these very staples under his nose while he was stuck sitting there eating tasteless brown rice with tasteless meatless stew, plantain, and broccoli.

Obi's father looked at Uncle Ugo as he sprinkled his food, and he shook his head. "You know, this life we live is very cruel at times," he said. "The same foods that a person ate and enjoyed when they were young can no longer be eaten as they grow old."

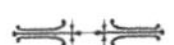

After dinner, everyone gathered in the living room to unwind and talk. It began with some mundane topic and quickly veered into politics. This is what Obi loved about these family visits. Listening to his family laugh and talk about the things happening around them.

"So, what do you think about this 2012 election and how do you see any of these Republican candidates stacking up against Obama?" Uncle Ugo asked Nkechi.

"Honestly, I guess we will have to wait and see who wins their primary first. If someone like our radical home state governor, Rick Perry, wins, then Obama shouldn't have a tough time in the general election. But if Mitt Romney wins, I see things being a bit tighter because he is a moderate and will appeal to independent voters in a way that Perry cannot."

Uncle Ugo nodded in agreement.

Nkechi continued. "Even though the economy is bad and his approval rating is below fifty percent, Obama is still favored to win in November."

"I think the true question will be if people will come out to vote for Obama in the record numbers we saw in 2008," Obi's father said, jumping into the conversation. "In my opinion, his presidency has been a little bit above average so far. He wasted his first two years trying to make deals with the Republicans instead of forging ahead with his agenda."

"I agree with you, dad," Obi said. "Just look at how he handled the healthcare law. He knew the Republicans weren't going to vote for it, but he was still trying to make overtures to them. He could have gone for a public option which would have allowed people to buy health insurance from the government. Instead, he settled for people now having to buy insurance from private insurance companies."

"This summer, we will see if the U.S. Supreme Court will strike down the healthcare law as unconstitutional," Nkechi added.

"I don't see how people can support these Republicans," Chinwe piped in. "I know that in 2011, the Republicans in this state cut over $5 billion dollars towards education spending. For people like me in the educational field, that had a huge effect on us. A lot of teachers were laid off here in Texas and the class sizes ballooned for those who were retained. Now, these guys are mad because Obama wants to make health insurance accessible to people who don't have any and can't afford it."

Auntie Nkiru, who had been observing the flow of discussion up to this point, chimed in. "I am going to tell you guys the truth. They are giving Obama all these problems because he is black. I have never seen this level of opposition to an American president in all my time in this country. I know it is having a huge effect on the man. He came into office with black hair and now it has turned mostly grey. Ah, the man now has to color his hair to bring back his natural hair color. At just 50 years old, he shouldn't have to be going through this process yet."

Everybody chuckled. Chukwuemeka looked at his wife who had not uttered a word. She was busy playing with her grandson and probably had not even been listening to them.

"Ijeoma, you have not added your two cents to our discussion," he said to her.

"You know that I am not really into politics," she responded. "But it is always good to have everyone here just talking about different topics."

Obi looked at his watch, an hour had gone by already. He could not believe it was already 9:30 p.m.

"Well, this was fun as usual," he said, addressing his family, "but some of us have to go. It is getting late and I have to work in the morning."

Before long, everyone was saying their goodbyes. Obi's mother helped Nkechi pack some leftovers to take home with her. Auntie Nkiru and Uncle Ugo took turns carrying Ike before it was time to go. And Chinwe cleared the glasses from the living room table.

Just as Obi was about to head toward the door, his father said they needed to talk. Obi looked at his watch again but followed his father into his home office. Obi's father closed the door behind him.

"My son," he said, as soon as the door was closed, "I really appreciate you guys coming over to spend the New Year with us. It was a really good time."

"It was fun for us too, dad."

"Eh, I overheard you telling your uncle that things were kind of tight for you and Nkechi..."

"Na, dad, it isn't too bad," Obi said, nonchalantly. "You know unexpected money stuff comes up here and there. It is no biggie at all."

Obi's father looked at his son sternly. "Obi, I know you are trying to have pride and I respect that. Both I and your mother have seen you grow into a family man these last couple of years and we are very proud of you, but you must accept help when it is offered to you."

Then he pulled out a check and handed it to Obi. At first, Obi was too stunned to take it. Then he glanced at the amount of $2,000 dollars and he could not believe his eyes.

"Thank you very much, dad. But I don't know if or when I can repay you the money."

Obi's father laughed. "My son, this is not a loan. You don't have to pay anything back to me or your mother. God has blessed us with good health and a little money as well. Let us know if you guys are ever in a tough spot and we will try and help as much as we can."

Obi leaned close to his father and gave him a big hug. Such generosity had overwhelmed him. His father hugged him back and patted him on the back before opening the door and letting them out.

On the drive home, Obi replayed what had happened with his father and admitted that the whole thing had surprised him. The thought of it all caused him to smile. He felt a sort of relief knowing that he had $2000 to help take care of some of their financial struggles.

"Well, it is never a dull moment with the Ifeanyi clan," Nkechi said, cutting through Obi's thoughts. "Your family always keeps it interesting."

"They surely do, babe. And you won't guess what my father did when we went into his office."

"Why, what happened? Are you in trouble?"

Obi chuckled. "No, I'm not. My father handed me a check for $2,000, and I didn't even ask him for it."

Nkechi's mouth and eyes widened. "Well, that was nice of him to do that. I know our savings account isn't looking too hot right about now."

"Yea, but my father has rarely given me any money my whole life. As a matter of fact, he was always telling me that a man must earn his money and shouldn't ask for handouts from anybody, even his own family."

"Well, honey, people do change you know. Your father now has his first grandchild maybe that has had some emotional effect on him. He probably wants you to know that he is here to help us when we need it."

That could have been it. Obi thought about what Nkechi had just said and decided to just accept the generosity of his father for what it was. If today was indicative of how 2012 would play out, then he felt good about it already because it was playing out to be a very interesting year already.

CHAPTER TWO

The New Year seemed to drag on as everybody tried to get back into their regular routine after the holidays. It was always a struggle. Nkechi didn't go back to school until the third week of January, she decided to use the time between now and then to spend as much time as possible with Ike. In the meantime, she also decided that now was a good time to start submitting job applications. She had a little over for months until graduation, it was never too early to get the process started.

She sat at the kitchen table watching Ike play with the cheerios she had scattered on his high chair tray, and smiled. She loved being a wife and mother, but she could not help but think that she had lost some of her fire and ambition along the way. After high school, then college, and then law school, she had a plan for what came next at each stage along the way. But now, she was beginning to feel unsure about how her career would pan out.

She thought back to the time when she was applying for her Master's degree in Public Policy, she had such a burning desire to be fully entrenched in political and social causes. Now, she was not so sure anymore. She hardly even engaged in any activities that would expose her to any of that, like networking or volunteering to work with any public policy organizations or political campaigns like she had planned on doing after graduation.

She was no longer even sure if she wanted to sit for the Texas state bar exam. The idea of practicing law no longer thrilled her like it used to. However, she knew that she had to do something that would earn her a decent income. Obi needed help with the finances and she could no longer sit back and watch him carry that weight alone.

Ike picked up a cheerio and threw it across the table and giggled. Nkechi picked it up and popped it into her mouth before tickling her son's nose and nudging him to finish eating. Then she went back to her thoughts which had now shifted to the characters in one of her favorite TV shows, *Girlfriends.* Nkechi had once seen herself through the lens of Joan. Joan was a successful, independent lawyer who had everything going for her except for a man in her life. But now, she was beginning to feel like a Lynn. Lynn was a free spirit with multiple degrees and passions, but no true direction in life.

At thirty-three, Nkechi was already rethinking the idea of having another child. Even though she loved motherhood, she didn't know if she could really move up in her career, have multiple kids, be a good wife, and achieve her own personal happiness, all at the same time.

Sometimes, when Nkechi talked with her friends and heard them talking about getting promotions and advancing in their companies, she got a bit envious of them. But then she would think about the life that she shared with Ike and Obi, and those feelings would disappear for a while. She shook her head to clear the thoughts swimming inside and got up to clean Ike.

By the time she was done giving her son a bath and taking one herself, half the morning was already gone. She took some time between playing with Ike before his nap time, to send out a few job applications and respond to emails. One such email was from a friend in one of her classes. The email was an invitation to attend a meeting with a woman in her friend's sorority. The woman was running for city council of Houston and her friend thought she could use the networking opportunity. Nkechi accepted the invitation.

⸻

Obi came home from work later that day to a nice meal of jollof rice and chicken. Before he sat down to join his wife and son at the dinner table, he headed straight for the refrigerator.

"Babe," Nkechi said, stopping him in his tracks, "There are two bottles of Heineken for you on the dining table."

Obi smiled, walked over to her, leaned over and gave her a peck on the cheek and then one on her lips.

"Chi Chi, you know me too well. It is almost scary sometimes."

"We have been married for almost two years, Obi. I just know your tendencies. But thanks for the compliment."

Obi sat down at the table and reached across the table for a chilled bottle of Heineken.

"On a serious note though, you need to slow down on your beer drinking. I have noticed a little pudge in your stomach. When we got married you were tall and lanky and that is the size I intend to keep you at."

Obi laughed. Ike cooed in response to his father's laughter which caused both Nkechi and Obi to laugh together.

Obi looked at his son with pride. "Chi Chi, I didn't think we would ever get this whole parenting thing down. I can't believe how well-behaved Ike is most of the time."

Nkechi smirked. "Honey, you aren't here during the daytime. Your son is usually tearing up shit in this house. I can't get him to calm down until about an hour before you come home from work so that's what you see."

Obi looked sternly at his son who had put his hands over his eyes and was shaking his head.

"Well, I guess we will have to shoot for a girl next time."

Nkechi did not respond.

"Babe, you didn't respond to my comment. Did you hear what I said?"

"Oh, I am sorry about that Obi. I didn't know you were looking for a response. Well, the man determines the sex of the baby, so we will have to see what happens."

Obi was a bit puzzled by Nkechi's response but decided not to pursue it any further.

"So, anything interesting going on in the news?" Nkechi asked after a few minutes of silence. Obi's eyes had been trained on the television that was on in the living room.

"Not really, just seeing these Republicans fight over who will be their nominee to go against Obama. I am not a conservative, but I don't hear any new ideas these guys are formulating beyond cutting taxes for the rich guys and companies and reducing government spending to help the everyday folks trying to make it. It feels like I have heard them keep regurgitating the same terrible economic policies for the last 20 years or so."

"You are definitely right, but Americans don't punish Republicans enough during elections to make them change their ways. Anyway, let us talk about something else besides politics."

"As a matter of fact, I do have something new to introduce to you. I was on this music blog a few days ago and they were discussing a new album called Black Radio, from a jazz pianist and producer named Robert Glasper. So, I decided to check out some tracks that were on YouTube. Chi Chi, when I say this album is jamming...you can play it the whole way through without skipping to another song."

"Wow, I haven't heard you this excited about new music in a long time. So, who is featured on this album?"

Obi spoke to her with a lot of excitement in his voice.

"The true question should be who isn't on this album. He has Musiq Soulchild, Lupe Fiasco, Mos Def, and Lelah Hathaway, just to name a few. But my favorite song on the album is Afro Blue, which features Erykah Badu."

Nkechi raised her eyebrows. "Damn, I am definitely going to have to cop that album. I am really interested in seeing how Robert Glasper remixed Afro Blue by adding his own sound and vocals in comparison to the original track by John Coltrane."

"I didn't know Coltrane composed the track Afro Blue first. Anyway, I forgot to add that Glasper and his band made a rendition to the Nirvana song, *Smells Like Teen Spirit.*"

Nkechi laughed. "Obi, what do you know about Nirvana. I always assumed that you just listened to R&B and hip-hop."

Obi smirked. "Chi Chi, your man knows a little something-something about a whole lot of things."

Nkechi shook her head and sighed. "Just when I was trying to give you some credit for knowing something, I see you took it completely to your head."

Obi struggled for a response to that so Nkechi jumped in and continued. "I also wanted to clarify that I was referring to the head which contains your bigger brain. I know how your mind wanders into all types of nasty thoughts."

"Babe, why are you trying to play me like that. I have more on my mind than just sex."

"Obi, first, stop trying to lie in front of me and Ike. Secondly, you have that pre-existing condition that afflicts all Nigerian men. It consists of being extremely cocky and arrogant. Finally, you are an Igbo man, which means that these levels are twice as high as the average non-Igbo Nigerian guy."

They both laughed.

Obi later washed the dishes and put the food away while Nkechi gave Ike a bath and got him ready for bed. Then they settled on the couch in the living room to watch television.

Nkechi was the first to reach for the remote.

"Chi Chi, I was still watching the highlights on ESPN," Obi lamented.

Nkechi rolled her eyes. Not again. "I have taken care of our son all day and made dinner. If nothing at all, let me relax for the rest of the evening."

Obi didn't feel like fighting. "No problem, honey, you can watch whatever you want to watch."

Nkechi kissed him on the cheek and went back to flipping through the channels. She settled on the Bravo TV channel which was showing *Real Housewives of Atlanta.*

"Obi shook his head. "Damn, an hour worth of fake bullshit reality show drama," he sneered. Nkechi laughed at him. She knew how much he hated those reality shows, but they were what helped her unwind after a long day of go-go-go.

"Obi, don't do me like that," she pleaded. "I watch these shows strictly for entertainment. I admit the ratchetness is a little over the top, but it is an escape from the daily monotony of my regular life," she tried to explain to him. "Anyway, I don't say anything about your obsession with sports."

Obi laughed. "Chi Chi, what are you talking about? I think you are mistaking the passion that I display for my teams with obsession, which are two separate things."

"I know the difference between the two, and you are obsessed. You spend all day Sunday glued to the TV watching football for hours on end. Then you are in all these fantasy football leagues which makes no damn sense to me at all. Also, you are so emotionally invested in your team that when they lose, you become a grouch for the rest of the day like you play on the team or something. That is an obsession, not passion."

"Babe, these games are real. They are not staged for fake fights and outrage like these shows you watch."

"Honey, you watch grown ass men hit each other all day over a leather oval-shaped ball. Then the other sport you watch has another set of grown ass men try and see how many times they can put a leather circle-shaped ball into a twelve-foot net. So please, spare me the mess about what is real or not."

Obi opened his mouth to speak but Nkechi put up her hand to stop him. "Oh no, I know you want to debate this topic to the end, but I really just want to watch this show right now. So, I am going to need you to be quiet for now. I know that is hard for you to do, but please try."

Obi laughed and stood up. "I can take a hint, and right now, I am sensing that someone wants me to leave." He kissed her on her forehead and walked towards the bedroom he had converted into an office. "I need to check my email and take care of some things anyway."

"Thanks, babe, I will see you in about an hour or so," Nkechi said without taking her eyes off the TV.

Once he was behind the computer, Obi logged into his laptop and went through his email. He was hoping to see a request or two for interviews from the various positions he had applied for. Unfortunately, all he got were a lot of automated responses from employers saying that he wasn't a match for their position. He needed to find something soon or things were going to get tougher financially.

Getting online, he proceeded to fill out a few more applications. His current job was going well, but he wasn't sure if the company would bring him back after the project was completed at the end of February. Even his tax business was struggling. He had lost a few small business clients who had themselves given up their companies to look for full-time jobs. Adding all these things together, he knew that it was going to be a long road ahead, but he was still optimistic.

After filling out the job applications, Obi decided to check out Facebook. He rarely logged onto the site anymore, but now, he needed something light and fun to take his mind off business and the uncertainty of his job. He scrolled through his newsfeed, catching up on the lives of friends, family, and even some complete strangers. It did not take long for him to notice the barrage of weddings, babies and kids' pictures on his friends' pages.

Times had surely changed since he and millions of others joined Facebook back in 2004. He was 24 years old and had just graduated from college back then. Facebook was the cool site to join at that time. It was a place to catch up with people from your past. Later, it evolved into a place where people came to discuss topics ranging from what women really wanted in a man, LeBron James surpassing Kobe Bryant and Michael Jordan as the greatest basketball player in history, and a whole multitude of topics.

Obi remembered when the site hit its peak during the 2008 Democratic primary. Supporters of Barack Obama and Hillary Clinton used the site as their own debate stage. There was talk back then that Facebook would revolutionize the way people would communicate and get the word out about things, which is true today. Unfortunately, the site also became a place where people could tell you whether they were at the store or at the airport. Some even used the site to post pictures of their crazy nights at the club, and some guys even got caught up by having their girlfriend or wife and the side chick as friends.

Due to its decline, Obi began to log into the site less and less, until he realized that it had been six months since he had been there. On this night, he decided to create a post for some of his friends to think about. He wrote, "Are we living the American Dream or the American Scheme? Because I honestly don't know which one we are supposed to be going after. But I know one thing, paying these student loans damn sure isn't a dream for me." A few people liked what he had written, and there were even a few comments.

One was from his homeboy, Nnamdi: "It is good to see that you are gracing us with your words of wisdom this evening. How are you, Chi Chi, and Ike doing?"

Obi smiled at the comment. "Thanks, man, everybody is doing well," he responded. "Ike is sleeping and Chi Chi is watching *Real Housewives of Atlanta*. How are things on your end?"

"I am doing well. LOL," came Nnamdi's response. "Ogechi is watching the same thing too."

Obi grabbed his phone and called Nnamdi. "My nigga, Nnamdi, what's been up with you. It has been a minute since we talked," Obi said when Nnamdi answered the phone.

"I know, it has been a while, my brother, it is good to hear your voice."

"So how are you guys coping up there? I heard on the news that the D.C. area got hit with ten inches of snow in the last couple of days."

Nnamdi sighed. "Yea, bro, this weather up here is a muthafucka. I don't know how much more of this shit I can take, and it is only January. We have at least two and a half more months of winter left. What was the temperature in H-town today?"

Obi smiled and said, "Don't get mad Zik but it was like 70 degrees."

Nnamdi shook his head. "Obi, I gotta get my ass out there as soon as possible. I will make it a goal of mine that I need to work on pursuing."

"Zik, have these automatic budget cuts enacted by Congress started to affect jobs at your company yet?" Obi asked Nnamdi.

Nnamdi paused for a little bit before he responded. "All I can say, my brotha, is that shit is getting real than a muthafucka out here. We get most of our contracts from the U.S. Defense Department, so we are all bracing for layoffs or reduction in work hours."

"Damn, Zik, I am sorry to hear that. Hopefully, you can transition into another job soon. I know people hating Obama thinking he is the cause of this."

"Thanks, man," Nnamdi said solemnly. "It is a little more nuanced than blaming just Obama. The deficit has been a problem for over ten years, and this financial crisis just brought everything to a head."

Obi was still on the phone with Nnamdi when Nkechi popped her head through the half-closed door.

"Who is that?" she whispered, not wanting to disturb the call.

"Nnamdi," Obi mouthed back to her.

Nkechi's eyes lit up and without warning, she burst into the room and grabbed the phone from him.

"Zik, *nwannem nwoke,* how are you doing, my brother?" she sang excitedly into the phone.

Nnamdi laughed at the sound of her voice. "Chi Chi, *nwannem nwanyi,* I am doing well, my sister. It is always a pleasure to hear your voice. How is my little man doing?"

Nkechi smirked. "Ike is doing well, beyond trying to destroy everything in the house. He is starting to resemble Obi as each day passes."

Nnamdi laughed. "I can only imagine seeing a two-year-old version of him with a skinny body and big ass head running around."

"Zik, you are a complete fool, I hope that you know that. So how is everything going between you and your girl, Ogechi? The both of us were texting each other while we were watching *Real Housewives of Atlanta* a few minutes ago."

"She is actually right here. We are both doing fine, just trying to make it."

"So Zik, do you plan on proposing to Ogechi anytime soon?" Nkechi's asked Nnamdi bluntly. "My brother, you guys have been dating for over three years. Like Beyoncé says, *'if you like it then you should put a ring on it.'*

Obi looked at her and shook his head. Nnamdi, on the other hand, was not surprised about the way Nkechi had come at him.

"We have talked about the whole marriage thing," he said, calmly. "We are just trying to iron out a few things." Nnamdi paused, as if he was done talking, but then he asked, "Did she mention to you that something was wrong?"

"Honestly, she hasn't told me anything. But as a woman, I can tell that she is ready for you to ask her."

Nnamdi sighed in relief.

Nkechi continued. "Zik, I hope that you aren't stringing this beautiful, smart woman along without any intention of getting married to her."

Nnamdi laughed. "Chi Chi, you don't have anything to worry about. Once I decide to make that decision, you and Obi will be one of the first people that I will tell."

Seemingly satisfied with his response, Nkechi bade Nnamdi good night and handed the phone back to Obi and walked out of the room.

The two men resumed their conversation after she was gone.

"Damn, Zik, I am sorry about that interrogation. She was giving you the ultimate third degree."

Nnamdi laughed. "My sister Chi Chi always gives her two cents about an issue and then some."

"Yea, my honey can be a handful at times," Obi said in response. "The one thing I have learned is that loving someone all the time is hard. Tolerance is more important in keeping a marriage together than love."

"Damn, bro you have been married for two years and you are sounding like the honeymoon phase is over already?"

"Nnamdi, I am not trying to say that things between me and Nkechi are bad. I still enjoy her presence in my life. But know that you are going to be dealing with a lot more bullshit than you initially signed up for. Enjoy what you have now, because the minute you put that ring on Ogechi's finger and y'all get married, shit will change quickly."

"I hear you, bro. Anyway, I have to shut it down for the evening. It was great catching up with you and Chi Chi, and I will talk with you guys later."

Obi made his way to the bedroom a few minutes after he got off the phone with Nnamdi. Nkechi was in bed reading a book. He was getting settled into bed beside her when she asked him, "do you think Zik is fucking with another woman?"

Obi was taken aback, he quickly sat up. "Chi Chi, what are you talking about right now? Zik isn't messing with anybody besides Ogechi."

"But if he were doing some dirt on the side, I know you wouldn't even snitch on him. Men always turn a blind eye to their friends' transgressions, but if their homeboy's girl messes up, they are the first ones to tell him to dump her."

Obi chuckled. "Chi Chi, I think all of those Real Housewives of Atlanta episodes are messing with your head.

"Honey, please, that show has no effect on my way of thinking. I am serious about Zik though. For the life of me, I don't understand why he hasn't proposed to Ogechi yet."

"Babe, you know he is an engineer at heart and most of those guys are sometimes too analytical in their decision-making. I know he probably will do something within the next six months or so."

Nkechi shrugged her shoulders. "Well, it's his decision at the end of the day. I give Ogechi her props because I know I couldn't be the one doing all this waiting around on a man."

Obi looked at her. "So, you wouldn't have waited that long for me, honey?"

Nkechi smiled and patted him on his leg. "I love you babe, but you were on the clock. You had 18 months from the time I moved out here to put a ring on my finger."

Obi shook his head. "Damn, Chi Chi you don't play around, for real."

"Obi, for as long as you have known me when was there ever a time when I didn't mean business?"

He thought about her comment carefully before responding. "Yea, you are right on that one."

Having gotten that out of the way, they turned off the bedside lamps and laid back in bed. There was a moment of silence. Then Obi inched closer to Nkechi's side of the bed. He kissed her on her neck and her shoulders, but when he began to undo her bra, she stopped him.

"So what are you trying to do?" she asked him, sitting up.

Obi looked confused. "I was trying to have sex with my wife if that is ok with you. Is it that time of the month already?"

Nkechi was a little put off by his comment. "No, honey, I am not on my period right now if you must know."

"So what is the problem then?"

Nkechi hesitated for a minute as she thought of a good way to answer that question. Nothing came to mind, so she threw caution to the wind. "It is about our sex life."

"What about our sex life? What is wrong with it?"

"Obi, right now, I want us to plan for our next child."

Her response did not completely surprise Obi. She was four months away from finishing up her master's degree, and he knew that she wanted to get serious about her career. But did that have to mean that they couldn't have spontaneous sex?

"So what are you suggesting? That we don't have sex at all? Because I know that is not something I am willing to go without."

"No. I was thinking more along the lines of using condoms."

Obi shook his head but said nothing.

"Well, I guess it's safe to say that you aren't happy with my proposition," Nkechi said, noting his silence.

"Well, let's just say that I never thought I would be 32 years-old with a wife and a son, and still have to worry about getting condoms from Walgreens to have sex."

"I see how self-centered you are. Everything is about you just trying to get yours. Did you even take the time to consider how I feel about this whole situation? I just assumed that you cared about my happiness and well-being as well."

The last thing Obi wanted right before bed was to see his wife angry, so although he wanted to keep the discussion going, he decided against it.

"I am sorry. That's not how I meant it," he said instead. "But I guess was being a bit selfish about how this whole thing would affect me." He hugged her. "We will figure out this situation together like we always do. My only request is that you put the condom on for me. You know I hate how trying to put them on messes up my concentration."

"Honey, you have no swag at all," Nkechi said, laughing at him. "But I still love you."

They laid in the darkness engulfed by silence until Obi decided to give it another go before they absolutely had to use condoms. He reached over to touch her and found her asleep.

He rolled over and tried to fall asleep, but his mind was thrown in multiple directions. He was thinking about sex and kids. He always thought he and Nkechi were on the same page when it came to having multiple children, but tonight had been a wakeup call. It seemed he did not know his wife as well as he thought he did. He began to wonder if this was just a phase she was going through or if she was dead set against having any more kids. In the end, he decided not to add this issue to the list of problems already on his plate. He wasn't going to fight Nkechi on this issue just yet. It would have to wait until it's the appropriate time.

CHAPTER THREE

"So, when do y'all want to try and meet up on this court again?" That was the group text message Obi received from Lamar on Monday afternoon.

Obi replied to the text indicating that he was available to meet up that weekend. It had been six months since he, Lamar, Chike, and the rest of the guys had met on the basketball court and, he was looking forward to being active again. The rest of the text messages suggested that they meet on Saturday afternoon to play a couple of pick-up games. He needed the distraction. The last month and a half had been very stressful for him with increased demands at his job, his seasonal tax work, along with juggling his family life.

After a long morning, Obi decided to leave the office for lunch. He usually ate lunch he brought from home, at his desk. But today, he felt the need to break away from the usual and order out. He chose Chick-Fil-A. On the drive there, he called Nkechi to see how her day was going.

"Hey, Chi Chi, how is everything going with you?"

"I am doing great, just finishing up some school work."

"Ok, that's cool. How is little Barack doing?"

"He is acting up as usual. It seems the closer he gets to turning two, the harder he is to deal with. I think we are going to have to start whipping him now."

Obi chuckled. "I am happy that you have finally come around to my way of discipline. I told you timeout doesn't work."

"We can talk about it more when you come home from work. So how is your lunch going so far?" Nkechi said, changing the topic.

"It is going well. I decided to grab something outside of the office today," Obi said as he turned into the Chick-Fil-A drive-thru.

"Oh, okay. So where are you heading to right now?"

Obi was silent. Nkechi was not big on eating at Chick-Fil-A because she had heard that they injected steroids into their chickens. In his opinion, that was better than eating a burger, but she did not buy that argument.

"I am going to just grab a sandwich from Subway," he finally said to her.

She smiled on the other end of the line. "That's a nice healthy move, honey. Just remember to ask for multigrain whole wheat bread and no soda."

Obi laughed. "Thanks for reminding me, babe, you are the greatest."

"No problem, I am happy to be helpful even though your comment had a hint of sarcasm in it."

"I was being serious," Obi said, laughing again.

"Yeah, I'm sure you were," Nkechi said, still sounding skeptical. "Anyway, I will let you go so you can enjoy the rest of your lunch."

"Okay, well I will text you when I get back to the office."

After he got off the phone with Nkechi, Obi got his food and went back to the office. He was in the middle of lunch at his desk when his phone notified him of a text message. It was from Tamika. He was a little surprised to hear from her. He hadn't heard from her since their meeting in the grocery store on New Year's Day. Obi thought about sending her a text message that day but never got around to doing so.

He read the message she had just sent.

"Hey, it was great seeing you the other day. You have been in my thoughts lately. Anyway, I hope everything is good with you and your family. Maybe we can chat sometime."

Obi was not sure how to respond. He wanted to be careful not to lead Tamika on. This was just two friends catching up. Finally, he found a way to respond:

"Thanks for checking up on me. I hope everything is good on your end as well. Shit has been hectic with work, but it's all good though. Yea, I can call you later this week after I get off from work."

He was not expecting her next response. He looked at his phone and his heart almost stopped.

"I took these pictures a couple of days ago when you were on my mind. I know you haven't seen me naked in a while, so I decided to spoil you a little bit. Hopefully, this will get you through your workday," was written beneath a picture of her in a black bra and panties.

Obi felt enticed. He had to admit that her body still looked right. It was almost the same as it had been since the last time they had sex. He sent her back a simple response.

"SMH, thanks. I will talk with you later."

"No problem, I hope you don't let your wife see them. I can send them to your personal email if you need me to."

Obi smiled and assured her that he won't, and hung up the phone. Obi couldn't get his mind off Tamika, and the image of her in her panties, out of his mind, for the rest of the day. As great as his sex life had gotten with Nkechi, it still wasn't the same as what he had once shared with Tamika. It seemed that over the years, he and Tamika had developed this sexual connection with their bodies that was like magic. They knew how to fulfill each other's needs without having to say or do anything extra.

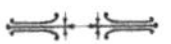

The rest of the week went by without anything out of the ordinary happening. On Friday, he informed Nkechi about his plans to meet with his friends for a game of basketball on Saturday. The hardest part of married life for Obi was coming to grips with having to ask Nkechi if it was cool to go out and do stuff. He did not have a problem with letting Nkechi know his plans, it had more to do with trying to gauge how she would react to it.

They were eating dinner when Nkechi asked him about his plans for the weekend. And that was when he told her about his plans to meet with Lamar and Chike the next day.

"Oh ok," she responded, a little surprised that he already had plans. "I know that the Children's Museum is free this weekend, I was hoping that we could spend tomorrow afternoon there. But I don't want to disrupt your plans with your 'boys.'"

Obi put down his fork. "Chi Chi, don't try and place some type of guilt trip on me right now. It's been a long week and I am just trying to relax and catch up with the fellas for a bit."

Nkechi took and deep breathe. "Obi, sometimes you can be so damn selfish! Don't you think that I want to meet up with my girls for some brunch and mimosas on a Saturday afternoon after a long week of taking care of our son while trying to study as well? All I wanted was for us to spend a little bit of quality time with each other."

Obi could not stand the disappointment in Nkechi's voice, so he tried to appease her. "I guess I do feel where you are coming from. Do you think we can hit the museum on Sunday afternoon instead?"

Nkechi was a bit disappointed that Obi wasn't willing to change his plans, but she also realized that she didn't want to fight with him, so she agreed to his plan.

"Sure babe, we can definitely go on Sunday," she said to him, half-smiling.

Later, after dinner, Nkechi performed her usual routine of getting Ike ready for bed. When she was done, she poured herself a glass of wine and did some research on her laptop in the bedroom. Meanwhile, Obi watched CNN and ESPN in the living room. He wasn't sure what type of mood Nkechi was in after their discussion during dinner, so he tried to give them some space. After about an hour or so, he decided to check on her.

"How is everything going with you?" he asked her, while he stood in the doorway.

"Fine."

That one-worded response only meant one thing – she was pretty pissed off. He learned this from having a mother and a sister, and from having come across a lot of women in his life. But Obi was not deterred, he decided to push back a little.

"So, what are you working on right now?"

It took about thirty seconds for her to respond. "Well, if you must know, I am checking out some information about a candidate who is running for city council."

Obi was intrigued. "Who is the candidate?"

"Her name is Folosade Olufemi. Does that name ring a bell to you?"

"Yeah, I know Sade. She was the president of the Houston Young Black Lawyer's Association when I first came back from Howard."

"Yeah, she does have that on here as well," Nkechi said, pointing to the screen in front of her. "Her father is Nigerian and her mother is black American. They met each other at Yale. She comes from a great pedigree, but do you think she has a chance to win the race."

"It's possible," Obi said. "Her dad is a federal appellate court judge and her mom is the assistant superintendent for Houston Independent School District. I also know that her grandfather was a Texas state representative for many years. She has name recognition and money on her side. Plus, I'm sure the Nigerian community will get behind her as well. Sade has always been a very ambitious and driven woman, so I have no doubts she can win and be a great public official."

Nkechi nodded her head at the ringing endorsement Obi had given to Sade.

"Well, I guess I don't need to go and hear what she has to say since you have taken on the role as her press secretary."

Obi laughed. "Chi Chi, when you are around certain people, you just pick up things about them, that is all."

But she was not done. How well did Obi really know this Sade woman? "Obi, I am looking at the pictures of your girl and she is very attractive, I am surprised you guys were never romantically involved."

Obi sensed where this was going, and he was not going to have this conversation. "We were just good friends, Nkechi," he said simply.

"That's cool, honey. Anyway, I think it's time for me to get ready for bed."

She placed the laptop on her bedside stand and turned out the light. Obi shook his head and walked into the bathroom to take a shower. He figured that by the time he came out, Nkechi would have cooled down a little. But by the time he was finished showering, Nkechi was already asleep.

Obi got into bed and tried to fall asleep, but his thoughts kept floating to his situation with Sade. He hated lying to Nkechi, but he knew he couldn't tell her about him and Sade, just seeing how she reacted to his relationship with Tamika and her funny behavior the day they had run into her on New Year's Day.

⟿

The following morning, Obi woke up to that special feeling he had every Saturday morning. That feeling he had when it hit him that he did not have to follow his monotonous regimen that defined the work week.

Before Ike was born, he celebrated Saturdays by lying in bed until noon. Now, he was thankful if he could sleep till 9 a.m.

He got out of bed and stretched loudly. Knowing he would be spending substantial time away from home with the fellas, Obi decided the least he could do was help around the house before he left. He made his way downstairs to make breakfast while Nkechi was getting Ike ready.

"I thought your mom or Chinwe had stopped over to cook," Nkechi said, walking into the kitchen a few minutes later, with Ike on her hip.

Obi laughed. "Dang, Chi Chi, you forgot that your man got some skills in the kitchen."

She looked at him with astonishment and said, "Honey, since when have you cooked anything beyond breakfast in this house?"

"I have made spaghetti plenty of times," Obi said in protest.

Nkechi shook her head and laughed. "If you call pouring a bottle of Ragu sauce into a pot, and adding some salt and pepper, cooking, then I guess so. The only real cooking that you did was boiling the noodles, which, remarkably, you have never burned."

Obi sighed. "Babe, all I can do is try to the best of my ability."

"Obi, you know I just be giving you a hard time," she said, noticing his bruised ego. "I really appreciate you being thoughtful enough to make breakfast for the family." She followed up her compliment with a kiss on his lips. That seemed to do the trick because he broke out into a very broad smile.

After breakfast, the three of them went into the living room to relax. Nkechi turned the channel to Nickelodeon for Ike, while she and Obi just sat back and relaxed. Obi looked at his son glued to the television screen and began to reminisce about what Saturday mornings meant to him when he was a kid.

"I remember waking up early on Saturdays as a kid and making myself a bowl of cereal and watching cartoons all morning and into the beginning of the afternoon. That's when Soul Train would come on. Chinwe, Okey, and I would try hard to mimic those dances, it was so hilarious. Heck, we even got my mom and dad to bust a few moves from time to time. Man, I had some good times as a kid."

Nkechi chimed in. "I agree with you, honey. Me and my brothers used to do the same thing. I remember how much they used to get on my nerves, but as you get older you reflect on those times and start to cherish them more and more."

Obi wondered if his son would have the same childhood he had experienced with his siblings growing up.

Around noon, Obi thought it was time to start getting ready for his time with the boys. Ike had since fallen asleep, and he was thinking that perhaps he could sneak in a quickie with Nkechi before he left. He leaned over to try and make his move on her, but she too had started to doze off. Obi turned off the TV and went to the bedroom to get ready.

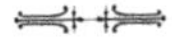

It was during the drive to the gym that Obi began to think about Tamika and the picture she had sent him the day before. He began to think about having sex with her and how it would feel to have her body next to his one more time. Society made people believe that when you get married, you get to have this over-abundance of love for your spouse which is far greater than any other love you have ever known. But the reality is that most people don't marry the person they love the most. They usually end up with the person who is ready to get married when they are.

It wasn't that Obi didn't love Nkechi or feel like he had made the wrong decision in marrying her, but sometimes, he thought, why should a man be limited to having just one woman to love for the rest of his life?

These thoughts were still in his mind when Obi pulled up in front of the gym. He went inside to warm up before everybody else showed up. Which they did, after about 20 minutes. Lamar and Chike were the first to arrive.

"Damn, I better go play the lottery tonight. Obi Ifeanyi arrived to an event on time," Lamar said, teasing Obi. "I guess wifey gave you a little booty to get your motor going this afternoon."

Both Chike and Obi burst out laughing while Obi shook his head. "I see this nigga Lamar already talking shit and we haven't even started hooping yet."

The three of them dabbed each other up and started taking turns shooting the basketball. After some time, Obi looked perplexed and asked Chike and Lamar, "I thought a couple of your homeboys were falling thru as well.'

Chike smiled and shot the ball. "Obi, they had to cancel at the last minute."

"Oh ok, I hope everything is all right with them."

Lamar shook his head. "The only thing wrong with those guys is that their women run them. Plain and simple."

Obi interjected. "Lamar, it isn't always as black and white as you make it seem. I have learned that sometimes you have to make some compromises to keep the peace with your wife."

"Obi, I understand that in relationships you can't always get what you want. But as a man, you gotta draw a line in the sand about something. A man will run himself into the ground if he thinks he can make his woman happy all of the time."

Chike chimed in. "So, I guess Lamar doesn't buy into the phrase, *Happy wife, Happy life* I presume?"

"Why can't a man be happy too? I'm not getting married to see if I can get permission from my wife to go anywhere. I am not about that life." Lamar stated seriously.

"So, I guess it's safe to say that you aren't ready to get married then?" Obi said, looking to Lamar for a response.

"I definitely want to get married one day. But right now, life couldn't be any better for me. I'm currently juggling between a 23-year-old senior at U of H, who is still young and impressionable, and a 40-year-old college professor. All I can say is that having a cougar on the team is the real deal. She can cook her ass off, and the sex is so good that she literally makes my toes curl."

"Doesn't Lamar remind you of Quentin from The Best Man?" Chike asked Obi. "I keep telling him you can't have sex with every woman in the world even if you tried."

Lamar laughed. "Damn, Chike, you can't be mad at a nigga for trying though. I need to consider getting some Viagra to keep up my stamina. Especially with my old-school chick, her sexual energy be off the charts at times."

"Don't listen to him, Chike," Obi said. "Don't buy into this cool playa life that Lamar is trying to portray to everybody. I remember when this dude was so lovey-dovey over his ex-girlfriend, Tanya. Your boy used to write poetry for her and send her flowers like every other week."

"Dang, Lamar, it sounds like you were pretty deep in love with her, what happened?" Chike asked Lamar, who acted as if he didn't hear what Chike had said and continued to shoot the basketball.

Finally. Lamar sighed and said, "There you go, Obi, trying to bring up some old shit. But on the real Chike, I did cut for Tanya hard back when we were in college. But the problem is that she wanted to get married right after we graduated and I wasn't ready for all that at the time. We tried to make it work, but eventually, we broke up. Maybe about six months after that, she called and told me she was dating somebody else and was pregnant."

"I am sorry to hear that, Lamar, life can be cruel sometimes."

"Thanks, bro, but it is all good. Tanya called me about a month ago and said that she was going through a divorce. We have hung out a few times here and there."

Obi was surprised to hear this because Lamar had not mentioned any of this to him in any of their previous conversations.

"So, are you thinking about rekindling y'all's romance?" Obi asked Lamar.

Lamar laughed as if Obi had asked him something crazy. "Na, my nigga, I am not going down that road. We are just at two different places in our lives. She has two kids now and is just trying to figure out what she wants out of life. But if she is talking about having sex, I am down for that on the real."

Chike laughed. "Just when I thought Lamar was getting soft and sentimental on us, dude reverts back to his old self."

"I think love is cool and everything, but it always has to be about the pussy," Lamar said.

"Fellas, can we move past discussing relationships. I thought we came out here to escape all of that for at least a few hours or so," Obi said, jumping in.

Lamar chuckled. "You are right bro. It is time for me to pull my Lebron moves on you guys."

"So which Lebron are you going to be?" Chike asked, teasing Lamar. I hope it's not the guy who choked against the Dallas Mavericks in the NBA Finals last season. I am happy that Miami lost that series, especially after the way Lebron announced leaving Cleveland with The Decision."

"Chike, why are you being a hater for bro. I still don't see how you can be mad at dude for going to play in Miami with one of his close friends, Dwayne Wade" Lamar said. "Anyway, I would rather be on South Beach, drinking Mai Tais and looking at beautiful women all day than to stay in cold and boring ass Cleveland."

About an hour later, the three of them were ready to leave the gym. In the parking lot, Obi asked the guys what their plans were for the rest of the day since he himself was not ready to head home just yet

After a bit of back and forth, they decided to go to one of their old spots called The Chill Spot. They got there to find that The Chill Spot was not what it used to be. There was construction going on around the building, and the parking lot looked almost empty.

Inside, they were seated almost immediately.

"Dang, what is going on over here," Obi asked aloud, as soon as the waitress left with their drink orders. "It seems like they are either doing renovations in this place or it's about to get closed down."

"Honestly, Obi, word on the street is that some real estate developers are trying to buy out The Chill Spot, along with other surrounding businesses," Lamar explained to Obi and Chike.

Chike was puzzled. "That is crazy!" he exclaimed. "What are they going to do with the land?"

"Probably put up some high-end condos and restaurants," Obi said. "I see that they are trying to gentrify this part of town."

"So what does that mean?" Chike asked.

"Well, in layman terms, bro, it means they're kicking out all the low-income black folks who have been here all their lives, so some yuppie white folks can live closer to downtown," Lamar said with a smirk on his face.

The subject obviously hit close to home for him since he had a lot of family living in the area. He had seen firsthand how the area had changed since he was a kid.

"So do you have a problem with white people wanting to live in this area?" Chike asked Lamar.

Lamar sighed. "Chike, I don't have any problem with anybody deciding to live anywhere they want to. But before white folks were talking about moving over here, I didn't hear anybody in the city of Houston talk about revitalizing this part of town. It is just sad that they continue to tell us that black folks are equal to white folks, but why doesn't anybody care that our neighborhoods are always more depressed than theirs."

Obi was a little surprised to hear Lamar have such an extensive take on the issue. Most of the time, Lamar steered clear of engaging in any type of political or social talk.

By the time the waitress brought their food, the discussion had moved back to a more familiar subject matter.

"Hey, I ran into Tamika and a couple of her homegirls last week during happy hour," Lamar said to Obi. "When is the last time you guys talked?"

Obi shook his head. He reached into his pocket and brought out his phone and passed it to Lamar and Chike.

"I think this should answer your question," Obi said to them, laughing.

The two of them looked at the pictures Tamika had sent to Obi and shook their heads.

"Do you think it is right for a married man to have these types of pics of his ex-girlfriend on his phone?" Chike said, not particularly asking for a response.

But Lamar jumped in with one anyway. "Chike, let a nigga have a little excitement in his life. It isn't like he is having sex with Tamika yet. Have you been messing with Tamika, Obi?"

"Na man, it definitely hasn't gotten to that point yet," Obi said defensively. "The pics are just some tease shit to keep a nigga alert at the job. I have a real dilemma on my hands right now. Nkechi is trying to go a meet and greet with Sade. She is having a kickoff for her campaign for city council."

"Dang, I almost forgot that you guys used to mess around back in the day. Have you told Nkechi about y'all's past?"

Obi seemed to be doing a lot of squirming before answering the question. Lamar started laughing. "Chike, the way this nigga is trying to dodge the question I take it the answer is not really," Lamar said.

"I have told her that we are cool, but I didn't tell her about our sexual history together," Obi tried to explain to the guys. "Nkechi is still trying to cope with Tamika, adding Sade to the mix doesn't seem like such a good idea."

"Obi, I know that when you guys were dating, you tried to hide things, but now that you guys are married, isn't it good for you to share that type of information with your spouse? Isn't your wife supposed to be your best friend?"

Lamar and Obi burst out laughing at Chike's statement. "Chike, what you said sounds good in a romance novel or Hallmark card, but that isn't how things actually go down in real life," Lamar said. "The thing you have to learn about women is that you can't tell them everything. You give them enough information to act like you are sharing your feelings and thoughts. Would you tell your wife that you went to the strip club or that you slipped up and had sex with a woman from your past? The answer to that question for most husbands would be no."

"Fellas, this marriage shit is way harder than I thought it would be," Obi chimed in. "I mean, the notion of only being with one person for the rest of your life sounds good when you are at the altar, but it is so damn hard to actually practice in real life."

"Marriage isn't the same as it used to be during our parents' generation," Chike said. "People aren't as loyal as they once were."

"Honestly, some men have always stepped out on their wives. But a lot of the women put up with that stuff because the man was the breadwinner in the home. Now, a lot of women are more educated than men and have their own money before they enter a relationship," Lamar began. "As a result, most of them are no longer willing to stay in a bad marriage because they are worried about how to care for themselves financially."

On the drive home, later that evening, Obi felt good having been able to catch up with his homeboys. They had agreed to get together at least once or twice a month, if possible. But now, his mind was preoccupied with thoughts of Sade. He remembered the first time they had sex was at the National Black Lawyer's Association Conference in Atlanta. Sade was sharing a room with one of her homegirls, but her friend had informed her that she would be having somebody over for the night. So Obi had invited Sade over to stay in his room. Then the two of them had gone out and gotten drunk before heading back to his hotel room.

Obi used to think that Sade was uptight and conservative because she talked real proper and went to Stanford for undergrad and Yale for law school. He almost thought that she didn't even mess with black dudes. But that night, he saw a different side of her. Their sexual relationship had continued when they got back to Houston. He still remembered going by her job one day while she was working late on a project and having sex with her in her office. They only stopped when they heard the cleaning crew coming by.

Obi enjoyed Sade's company on a physical and mental level, but once Sade was promoted to junior partner in her law firm, her work became more demanding and that left very little time for her to enjoy a social life. Eventually, they went their separate ways. Obi used to wonder what could have been, but he knew that life was crazy like that sometimes. He had met Sade's parents and they both took a strong liking to him. From what he had heard, they were upset when things didn't work out with Sade.

Obi got home to find Ike asleep beside Nkechi while she watched television. Seeing the image of his family, the one he had consciously created, made it crystal clear to him that these two people were his main priority in life. This was his wife and his son, and he had chosen them.

CHAPTER FOUR

"Hey Obi, how are you doing? It has been a minute since we have talked."

Obi was reading a text message from Sade on his way home from work. It had been a few weeks since Nkechi had attended the meet and greet to introduce Sade's city council campaign.

"I am doing well, just living life," was Obi's response to her.

"That is great to hear, I was hoping we could meet up sometime in the coming weeks to grab drinks or dinner if that is at all possible."

Obi thought about it for a minute and then responded.

"Yea that is not a problem, what day is good for you?"

Sade texted back indicating that she would get back to him by the end of the week. She also mentioned how great it was to meet his wife, Nkechi. Of course, Nkechi had raved about Sade after meeting her, it was almost as if she had just made a new friend. Naturally, this made Obi nervous, especially since he had not told Nkechi about his history with Sade, and he was not sure how much she knew now that the two of them had met. After all, women talk, who knows what they might have talked about?

He pulled into his driveway to find his sister's car parked outside.

"Hey bro, what's going on with you?" Chinwe greeted him as soon as he walked through the door."

"Another day, another dollar at work my sister. I can't imagine having to look forward to this for the next 30 years of my life." He flopped onto the sofa and turned on the television while kicking off his shoes. Chinwe and Nkechi were in the kitchen drinking wine and cooking plantain and spaghetti with meatballs. The aroma that drifted into the living room from the kitchen made his stomach growl loudly. He had skipped lunch earlier because of his workload and was now starving.

"I hear you, my brother," Chinwe said, from the kitchen, in response to his earlier comment, "unless one of us wins the lottery, I guess we will just have to make do with our jobs. I am stressing out over this STAR testing which starts district-wide next week."

"Yea, I have been hearing about it on the local news lately," Nkechi said. "I get the feeling that it is a big deal from the way everybody is talking about it."

"Big deal would be an understatement, Chi Chi," Chinwe replied. These standardized tests can determine how much funding a school gets and whether a principal or teacher will be fired or not."

In the living room, Obi shook his head. "I guess we can thank our former president, George W. Bush for his great initiative, No Child Left Behind, for ushering in this era of making kids test takers instead of actually learning anything in school."

Nkechi chuckled. "I guess you can throw this, along with the economy and foreign policy, in as one of the things Obama is still trying to fix three years after Bush has left office."

When dinner was ready, they all gathered around the dining table to eat. Obi was glad that Chinwe had joined them, she always brought an atmosphere of fun and intelligent conversation along with her.

"Obi, your sister and I were discussing her dating life before you came back home," Nkechi said between bites of plantain.

Obi smirked. "Chi Chi, I thought I was going to be able to eat my food in peace tonight. We may need to get Chinwe on Dr. Phil's show to help with her man issues."

Chinwe, who was sitting next to Ike, helping him with his food, said, "Bro, don't make me come over there and slap you silly in front of your wife and son right now."

Obi tried to put on a serious face. "So, sis, what do you think your main problem is in dating?"

Chinwe looked at him resolutely and replied, "Honestly, I think I am going to start dating only white men. I have given too many brothers a chance and they continuously keep playing games and never have their shit together."

Obi shook his head. "Here we go again with the bashing of the black man. It seems that we are to blame for everything wrong with the black race."

"Obi, can you stop this pity party you are trying to have for black men? Most black dudes don't even want to date someone like me. I am going to scream if I hear another guy tell me how pretty I am for a dark-skinned chick. I don't know why people act like that is some sort of compliment. If we can keep it all the way real, most black dudes want to get with a white girl and if they can't get that, they settle for the next best thing, a light-skinned black woman."

"Honey, the dating game is way harder for an educated black woman versus an educated black man," Nkechi said, throwing in her two cents. "Before we started dating, I had gone out with a couple of European guys. I never thought I would marry a black or Nigerian guy, but I started contemplating the idea, so I can understand what your sister is talking about and going through."

Obi was a little stunned to hear his wife's comment. She had never told him that she was ever into white dudes. Chinwe looked at the blank stare on her brother's face and said, "I guess you didn't know that your wife flirted with the idea of some jungle fever."

"So, have you given up on Nigerian guys as well?" Obi asked Chinwe.

"They are on very thin ice with me," she responded. "Honestly, the pickings with them aren't that much better. You either deal with the guys who are "fresh off the boat" and who only want to talk about being in love and marrying you after going on one date, or you deal with the Americanized Nigerian guys who usually just date black or white women. Heck, look at our own brother, Okey. He dates women from all over the rainbow, but I never hear him talk about dating a Nigerian girl. My question to you, bro, is, why can't Nigerian women keep Nigerian guys interested in them?"

Obi could feel Nkechi's and Chinwe's eyes glued to his face waiting for an answer. He wanted to say something that wasn't too harsh but still wanted to be honest at the same time.

"I think it's because of the way Nigerian women are raised, they come across as possibly too conservative."

"Can you provide us with an example of what you mean?" Nkechi asked him.

"Sis, I know exactly what he is trying to say. Black and white women give up the booty after like one or two weeks, and Nigerian women try and make you wait a minute before they give a dude some ass. Am I right bro?"

Obi knew she was spot on with her answer and nodded his head in agreement. Nkechi sighed as she got up to get some more food.

While she was gone, Chinwe smiled at Obi and said, "Bro, your wife was telling me how much she enjoyed meeting Sade."

Chinwe knew that this would make her brother uncomfortable, but for her, this was payback for him trying to make light of her dating woes. She sarcastically blew a kiss his way before Nkechi came back to join them.

"I see you guys are talking about my new favorite person," Nkechi said, sitting down. Chinwe looked at Obi and smiled mischievously.

"Obi, you were definitely right," Nkechi continued. "Sade has that natural ability to just connect with people. As the meeting was clearing out, I went up to her and introduced myself. We talked about her stances on a variety of policy issues and then discussed how the both of us grew up. Sade talked about how her dad and your Uncle Ugo have been good friends for over 30 years."

Chinwe jumped in. "I think my uncle also helped her dad in his first campaign as a municipal judge. Isn't that right bro?"

Obi just nodded his head in agreement.

"Is everything ok with you honey? You seem like there is something on your mind," Nkechi asked him, sensing that something was bothering him.

"I'm good, I guess I am just a little tired after a long day at the office."

Nkechi looked at the time. "Yea, it is starting to get late and I need to give Ike a bath and get him ready for bed."

"I guess that is my cue to go," Chinwe said, pushing back her chair. "I need to leave anyway, I have some tests that I haven't started grading yet. Anyway, Chi Chi, thanks for letting me come over and vent to you. It feels good to finally have a sister to talk to."

Nkechi stood up to take Ike from Chinwe and they hugged goodbye. Obi then walked his sister outside to her car. Once outside, Chinwe laughed and said, "This has been a fun night. Did you enjoy the evening, bro?"

"Sis, you were trying me for real in there."

"That is what you get for trying to make fun of me for not having a man. You know that I am sensitive about that stuff. I took it from your body language that you haven't told Chi Chi about your past with Sade."

Obi leaned on Chinwe's car casually. "I just told her we were cool."

"Well, the ending of your situation with Sade was very awkward anyway. I think you eventually have to let her know about it."

Obi sighed. "You are right, I just have to find the right way to tell her. Anyway, how is everything going at home?"

Chinwe laughed and said, "It is going well. Just tired of mom asking me when I am going to get married. Dad too has been acting strange lately, he is showing some interest in what's going on in my life beyond seeing if I have found a husband or not. The other day, he asked me about school and if I was still trying to get my non-profit idea off the ground."

Obi looked amazed. "Either he has some incurable disease and is trying to make up for lost time, or he is, dare I say it, changing."

They both laughed.

"Well, whatever it is, I am happy to see it," Chinwe said. "I have realized that he and mom have been fussing a lot more than usual though. I guess that is to be expected from two people who have been married to each other for over 30 years."

"Yea, I can definitely see how that can happen. Marriage is really tough, sis, I am not even going to lie to you."

"Obi, all I can say is that I hope you don't mess over Nkechi. If you do, I will have to cut you for real."

Obi started to laugh, but his sister maintained a stern look, so he stopped laughing.

"Bro, I am just playing with you. Anyway, if you and Nkechi need a night out together, let me know. I won't mind taking care of Ike for you guys. I guess my life is pretty bad when my nephew is the most interesting man in my life."

Obi thanked her and they embraced before she got into her car and drove off. Back in the house, Nkechi was sitting on the sofa with her laptop on her lap while she drank some wine. He sat down next to her.

"So, my wife has a thing for white dudes on the low. The things you find out about people the longer you stay married to them."

Nkechi gently pushed him and said, "Honey, do I detect a bit of jealousy from you. I didn't take you for being the sensitive type."

His eyebrows raised up and he said, "Chi Chi, I have the utmost confidence in myself. Anyway, I have always proclaimed my unbinding love for the physique and intellect of the black women."

Nkechi laughed and said, "That's funny to hear that from you when I see you get glossy eyes every time you see Kim Kardashian on television."

Obi responded, "Even though she is Armenian, she got the booty of a black woman. So technically, my previous statement is correct."

"Anyway, let's talk about some more pressing matters at hand," Nkechi said, changing the topic. "I wanted to let you know that I was thinking of taking Sade's offer to work on her campaign. She thinks I can help her out with some of her policy proposals. I wanted to run it by you before I gave her my answer."

Obi was thrown completely off guard. He did not see that one coming. What was he supposed to tell her? He didn't really want her working too closely with Sade, but he also didn't want to tell Nkechi about him and Sade without giving her the opportunity to work for her campaign.

"Well, if you think that is something you can handle, I am in full support of you doing it."

She hugged him tightly. "Thanks, honey, I really appreciate it. Sade said that you would be fine with it."

As the weeks that followed went by, Obi saw the effects being part of Sade's campaign had on Nkechi. She seemed to have that fervor that had been missing since she left her corporate law job in Washington, D.C. For the past two years, her relevancy as a woman had revolved around the lives of her son and her husband. But now, even though she wasn't getting paid a lot of money, a part of Nkechi felt a sense of renewal and self-worth. To have her opinions and perspectives desired by others, helped to boost her self-confidence.

One day on a nice spring evening Obi was driving home from work when he received a text message from Nnamdi. It was a picture of an engagement ring with the caption: *"My playa card has been turned in bro."*

Obi was so excited that he could not wait to share the news with Nkechi when he got home. He walked through the doorway to find Nkechi already on the phone with Ogechi. He kissed Nkechi and said congrats to Ogechi.

"Thank you for your well-wishes, Obi," Ogechi said excitedly over the speakerphone. "I was starting to wonder if your boy was ever going to come around and propose to me. But I am glad that he finally did."

"Obi, me and you both know how Zik takes like a million years to make a decision on anything," Nkechi chimed in. "Sometimes he is so much into his own world that he forgets about reality. Ogechi, that is what you should look forward to for the rest of your life. Aren't you such a lucky woman to have him?"

Ogechi sighed. "My babe can be a challenge at times, but I love him regardless."

Obi wanted to get some rest and wasn't ready to listen to the women talking for too much longer. "Anyway, I will let you guys finish up your conversation," he said. He went upstairs to check on Ike before heading to their bedroom to lie down.

Just when he was about to fall into a deep sleep, his phone notified him of an incoming text message. It was from Sade. She was confirming which day he was available to meet up. Obi laid there with the phone in his hand, thinking about whether it was a good idea to still meet up with Sade. He finally decided that he wanted to see her, so he texted her back to say that they could meet up at The Chill Spot on Friday for happy hour if that was cool with her. Sade said it was fine.

He tried to go back to sleep after that but found it difficult to do so. He was unsure about the whole thing. Was meeting with her a good idea? He didn't know about Sade's feelings for him, but he wanted to at least chop it up with her about her campaign and other things going on in her life.

As these thoughts were going through his mind, Nkechi came into the room to call him for dinner. Obi got up and went downstairs to join Nkechi for dinner.

"It is still weird to think that in about a year, Zik will be somebody's husband. That dude has gone through so many girlfriends since we have known him," Nkechi said to Obi.

"Yea, he finally realized that you can't find a woman who will look like Beyoncé, be smart and sophisticated like Michelle Obama, cook like your mother, and fuck you like a porn star, all in the same person."

"Yea women have unrealistic expectations as well. I think the one thing you must learn is how to accept people for who they are. People think that marriage is this magical remedy that will make people change into the person their spouse wants them to be," Nkechi responded.

Obi nodded, chewing his food. Nkechi continued. "I forgot to mention that Ogechi asked me to be a bridesmaid. So now, I have to help with the bridal shower and bachelorette party. I love these events, but trying to coordinate them with women is always a struggle. Ogechi told me that Zik has you and his brother as his best men. What do you have planned for the bachelor party, honey?"

Obi smiled. "Well, Chi Chi, I haven't talked with Zik yet. But once I do, you will definitely not know what the plan will be."

"Obi, I know that you guys will get some big booty strippers who will give y'all lap dances all night. All I care about is that you and Zik don't partake in any extracurricular stuff with them chicks. Having brothers made me realize that all you guys think alike when it comes to bachelor parties."

After they finished eating, Obi watched TV for a little while and before deciding to call Nnamdi.

"Oga, many congrats to you on your engagement. How are you feeling right now?"

"I am good, bro. But I can't lie, shit got real when I put that ring on her finger. In my mind, I could see all the women that have passed through my life to get me to this moment. It has been one hell of a ride, but now I can honestly say that Ogechi is my queen."

Obi took a moment to respond. "Dang, Zik, that might be one of the deepest things you have ever said. I see that your mind is ready for this marriage thing. I am happy for you bro. Now on to the only part of the wedding process that you control, how do you want your bachelor party to go down?"

Nnamdi laughed. "Obi, you ain't never lied about that. But back to your question, I am thinking about either doing a Vegas or Atlanta blast. I will shoot you the numbers of my groomsmen so you guys can get to know each other and start planning this thing."

"That is cool man. But I wanted to ask you, how was it when you had to ask Ogechi's dad for her hand in marriage? I remember when I had to ask Chi Chi's dad, I was a little shook. I knew he was going to give me his blessings, but it was still a daunting task in my opinion."

"Yea, Ogechi's stepfather is real chill, so it wasn't a problem."

"Oh ok, so does Ogechi have any type of communication with her biological father at all?"

"Well, it's a complicated situation. Her biological father was married to another woman when he was messing around with Ogechi's mother. I think she told me that she has only talked to him a handful of times in her life, and only met him last year for the first time. But she recently talked to him and informed him that I had proposed to her. He told her that he wanted to come to the wedding if that was fine with her and her mom."

"Damn, that is a whole lot of stuff to deal with while planning a wedding. Anyway, have you guys set a date yet?"

"Yea, it will actually be on the third weekend of January 2013."

"Ok, that's what's up. I am pretty sure that will be the same weekend as the inauguration."

"Wow, I totally forgot about it. Hopefully, we won't be witnessing Romney getting sworn in. Do Mormons even use the same bibles as Christians? Regardless, even if Obama gets re-elected, I can't see him drawing the same crowd as 2009. That was such a magical moment that you just can't duplicate."

Obi nodded in agreement. "Zik, unfortunately, your assessment is correct. The unemployment rate is like 9% and Obama isn't the new sensation anymore. He went from being the anti-establishment guy to now being part of the establishment. Sometimes, he doesn't even look like he even wants to be president anymore."

Nnamdi laughed. "My brotha, it is hard for any man to change the system. It is easy for these politicians to say they will bring change and all this other stuff. But the bottom line is that there are a lot of interest groups with big pockets who want to keep things status quo. The symbolism of Obama has been a good thing for the people of color in this country, but beyond that, I don't care too much for the Republicans or Democrats."

Nnamdi promised to contact Obi in the coming days to pass on some wedding information before they got off the phone. Obi went to find Nkechi right afterward. He found her in the bedroom.

When he told her about what he had just heard about Ogechi's biological father, Nkechi shook her head in disbelief.

"Wow, that is some deep stuff, honey. Ogechi only told me that her folks weren't together, but I never dug too much deeper than that. I figured if she wanted to tell me more, she would. But unfortunately, I am not all that surprised to hear about her circumstance. Some of our men have a family in the States and then have their mistress or another wife back in Nigeria. The sad thing is that this secret can go on for years before any of the women find out about each other." Bn

"I agree with you, honey. It seems like there is a stigma out there that somehow says that Africans are fine with polygamy."

Nkechi tried to keep a straight face but then began to laugh.

"Obi, let's be honest with ourselves. Most African men wouldn't have a problem having multiple wives if Western society thought it was an acceptable practice. Wouldn't you have another wife if you could have one?"

"Chi Chi, you are the only woman for me."

"You are so sweet, honey. Unfortunately, those lesbian porn sites on your laptop tell me another story."

If Obi was surprised by her statement, he tried to hide it.

"Why, are you trying to come up with an explanation to my statement?" Nkechi prodded. "I am going to jump in the shower."

After about 15 minutes, Obi heard Nkechi screaming. He rushed to the bathroom to see what the problem was. "Is everything ok with you honey?"

Nkechi was frantic. "I found a gray hair."

Obi looked at her with a smirk on his face. "Babe, we are getting older. It isn't a big deal to have a couple strands of gray hair on your head."

Nkechi was shaking her head. "The gray hair isn't on my head." Obi followed the direction of her finger, she was pointing toward her pubic area. Obi's eyes widened while he was trying to hold himself from laughing.

"I hope that doesn't signify that your vagina is dying off. Because then I would really need to get a second wife."

Nkechi grabbed a towel to cover her body. "I see you got jokes. When you don't get any ass tonight, you will know the reason why."

On Friday, the day when Obi and Sade were supposed to meet up, Obi found himself spending the whole day feeling anxious. He told Nkechi that he would be hanging out with some of his co-workers for happy hour. He did not like to lie, but he couldn't tell Nkechi the truth - that he would be seeing Sade.

Later that evening, Obi pulled into the parking lot of The Chill Spot and saw Sade's grey BMW 3 series was already there. He knew it was her car because she had her name on the license plate. He parked his car, sweat gathering on his hands and forehead. Obi found a napkin and wiped down both areas of his body. He also sprayed on some cologne, and once he was satisfied with how he looked and smelled, he got out of the car and walked towards the restaurant. He had jitters that felt like he was on a first date rather just meeting up an old friend.

He paused in the doorway and looked around. Then he saw her, she was waving at him and trying to get his attention. Obi waved back and inhaled before walking towards her. It was a long walk, or, at least, it seemed like it was. Once he was standing within a few feet of her, Sade stood up and hugged Obi. It was a tight, intimate hug. Obi started to notice that he was aroused and tried to pull back. But Sade wanted to hold onto him for a little bit longer.

"Obi, I see that somebody else is excited to see me. Let him know that I have missed him as well."

Obi realized what she meant and scrambled to find a way to respond. Sade started laughing and said, "Hey, you know I am just fucking with you right?"

Obi laughed too, but he knew that there was some truth to her comment. After they finally sat down, he started to size her up. He noticed that she had added some thickness to her five feet ten inches honey brown-skinned athletic frame. He also realized that she had gone natural and was rocking some sister locks. But the wrinkles under her eyes and the strands of gray in her hair showed that she had aged as well.

"Do I still look the same way you remember me, Obi?"

"Yea, you still look great. I see you gave up your creamy crack addiction."

Sade laughed hysterically and patted her head. "Yea, I decided to change it up. But it's not because I was trying to be some type of soul sista though. Honestly, it costs more money to keep your hair natural than it does to get it permed every two weeks or so."

Right then the waiter came over to hand them their menus. After he left, Sade continued, "I forgot to tell you that I absolutely love your wife, Nkechi. She has so much passion about a variety of progressive issues. I can see why you guys are together. I also see you guys as some Nigerian hippies and I mean that in a good way. Y'all aren't caught up in all this social status bullshit that most Nigerians consume themselves with."

Obi shrugged his shoulders. "Thanks for the compliment."

She took a sip of the margarita the waiter had just placed in front of her before speaking again. "No problem," she said.

Obi was about to take another sip of his drink, when Sade asked out of nowhere, "So have you told Nkechi about us having sex in the past and the other thing that happened?"

"Not exactly, I just told her that we were good friends."

Sade looked a little bit disappointed by his answer. Obi decided this topic was a delicate one and he wanted to ask her about her professional life, so he switched the topic.

"What made you give up your position at the firm? I know you were working very hard to become a partner."

Sade hesitated for a minute before answering the question. She said, "I realized that I wasn't interested in that lifestyle anymore. Don't get me wrong, I enjoyed the perks of traveling, money, and having access to corporate suites for sporting and music events. But everything just revolved around how many billable hours we charged to our clients. It didn't help that I was working seventy to eighty hours a week. All in all, it wasn't the life for a woman about to be 35 years old and trying to get married and have kids one day."

He nodded. "I remember Chi Chi telling me the same thing about her life when she was living in D.C. So how has the dating scene been for you? I know that you got a bunch of guys lining up to get at you."

She laughed and said, "If you want to count old white men in their 50s who want to be with a black woman to fulfill some exotic fantasy of theirs, then I guess so. Most of the black men on the same level as me are either not ready to settle down or want to date petite and submissive white women."

"That is funny, my sister says the same thing."

"Unfortunately, there aren't a lot of Obi Ifeanyis running around to choose from. My dad is trying to set me up with these old school Nigerian guys but I don't have chemistry with any of them. At least I have my battery-operated boyfriend to help me out from time to time."

They laughed.

"First of all, I am flattered that you think that highly of me, but I'm just a regular guy," Obi said, in response to her compliment. "I know that dating is hard, but I think you will find a good guy soon."

By this time, an hour had passed and Obi had started looking at his watch. Sade noticed.

"Wifey got you on a curfew or something?" she asked.

"Na, it is definitely not like that."

"Ok, good to know. So, why did you want to meet up with me?" Obi asked her.

"Well, I just wanted to make sure there wouldn't be any problems with Nkechi working on my campaign from your side of things."

"Obi, I know how to separate personal and business matters. Regardless of our past, I respect the relationship between you and your wife. Anyway, it is starting to get late and I have a bunch of things to take care of in the morning," she said, reaching for her purse while Obi signed the receipt the waiter had placed in front of him.

They walked outside together. Sade fought the urge to grab a hold of Obi's hand as they walked and talked. Once they got to her car, Obi told her he had a wonderful time with her. Then as if he did not want the night to end, he asked about her folks.

Sade smiled and leaned against the open car door.

"My folks are doing well. My dad asks if I have talked to you from time to time. He says if you are ever interested in working for the district attorney's office or as a federal attorney let him know and he will help you out. He also told me about your Uncle's health issues, is he doing better?"

Obi laughed, "Your pops is always looking out. I haven't seen him since my wedding day. Uncle Ugo is doing well, he is just monitoring what he eats now."

Sade was silently observing Obi as he talked. Then she said, "Obi, I have to be totally honest with you. I am kind of scared of this whole political office thing. For white candidates, going to Ivy League schools and working for a big law firm is a plus for them. But in dealing with black people, it can make you come across as being out of touch with the community. Also, in a weird way, have to defend my own blackness to black people simply because I am half Nigerian."

"That is why you have to respect President Obama even more for how he got to where he is. But I think you will be fine. Once people get to know who you are and where you stand on the issues that affect them, I know they will come around and warm up to you."

"Thanks, Obi. You always know how to make me feel good about any situation."

Before she got into her car, Sade gave Obi a goodbye hug and kiss on his cheek. She held his face in the palm of her hands for a minute and then let go. Before Obi could shut her car door, however, she began to talk again. "I was thinking about the picture of your son that Nkechi showed me when we met. It made me think about Adaorah. You know we would have been celebrating her fifth birthday this year? Do you ever wonder what our lives could have been like right now? I know I am bringing up a touchy subject, but I just had to put that out there."

Obi hesitated to respond for a minute. And when he did, his voice was somber.

"Sade, first, you should never feel like you can't talk about what happened with our daughter. I am thankful that God allowed me to be a parent again by having Ike, and I pray that he also grants you that opportunity. Sometimes I do think about what we could have been doing together, but unfortunately, our lives move on and we must follow suit. But I will always have a place in my heart for you."

By this time, tears had started to flow from Sade's eyes. As she was wiping the tears from her face, Sade hugged Obi. Before he could react, her lips were on his and she was kissing him. Obi was surprised, but he did not try to stop her. The kissing got intense and Sade started to unzip Obi's pants, grabbing onto his penis. Then out of the blue, she just stopped. A second later, she became frantic.

"Obi, I am so sorry for putting you in this situation. I guess my emotions and the margaritas got the best of me."

"Don't be so hard on yourself. We both were complicit in doing what we did."

Obi straightened up his shirt and bade Sade goodbye before walking over to his car. Once he got in his car, Obi took a moment to collect his thoughts. Everything between him and Sade had happened so quickly. As much as he knew what they did was wrong, he still enjoyed having that intimacy again for a little bit. But then, he began to think about what happened to his daughter. He thought about her from time to time, however, seeing Sade again had brought back all the emotions from that time.

Later that night, he was at home when he received a text message from Sade showing a picture of Obi holding Adaorah in the delivery room. He smiled. "*Thank you, I really appreciate that,*" he wrote back. "*No problem at all, for my first baby daddy lol,*" she replied. "*You are funny. Good night and we will chat later,*" was all he could say.

CHAPTER FIVE

"Wow, I can't believe Easter Sunday is coming up so quickly, this year is moving so fast," Obi said to Nkechi. They had just finished clearing up the table after lunch when Obi said this.

Nkechi nodded her head in agreement.

Obi continued, "So I know we really don't go to church much, but my folks really want all of us to go to church that day."

"Ok, that is definitely not a problem with me."

"Ok, cool."

Nkechi noticed his hesitation after that. "I get the feeling that there is something else you want to tell me, so whatever it is, just say it."

Obi thought about dodging the question, but when he saw the stern look on her face, he knew he had to be straight with Nkechi. He sighed. "Well, my mother was asking when we were going to get Ike baptized."

"And what did you tell her?"

"I told her that we were thinking about doing it soon."

Nkechi shook her head and walked to the living room. Obi decided to give her a few minutes to cool down before he went over to talk to her. About ten minutes later, he approached the couch and tried to put his hand on her thigh but she pushed his hand away.

Obi laughed. “So how long are you going to be mad at me for?”

Nkechi was not having any of it. “I am happy you think that playing with my feelings is a joke. I don’t know why you couldn’t just tell your mom the truth.”

“Babe, you know how my mom is, what was I supposed to tell her>”

“You could have just told her our plan is not to get Ike baptized until he is older, and that we want him to make that decision himself!” Nkechi said, growing increasingly irritated with Obi.

He rubbed his hands on his face in frustration. “Chi Chi, you know my folks are die-hard Catholics. If I told my mother what you just said, she would think that you converted me to atheism.”

Nkechi stood up. “Babe, you know that I am nowhere close to not believing in God. I do acknowledge though that I don’t feel like being boxed into practicing a particular religion. In my perspective, God’s love isn’t limited to Christians, Jews, or Muslims, but to all of the people who inhabit this planet.”

Obi knew where Nkechi was coming from. He didn’t think that pouring some holy water on his child’s head would bring him any closer to God or Jesus than the next person, but it was a good symbol and, at the very least, would appease his folks in the meantime. He decided to change the subject and talk about something else with her.

“So, are you excited about graduation coming up in the next month or so?”

Nkechi was put off. Why was he trying to change the topic? Although it did not sit well with her, she took the hint and decided to reluctantly go along with the diversion. “This will be my third one in the last 10 years, so I guess I am ready to get it over with. I admit that getting my bachelor's degree was the most refreshing moment in my life to that point. I thought if I could survive those four years, then everything else in life would be a breeze. Boy, I was very naïve back then."

Obi laughed. "Don't feel too bad, everybody felt like that after finishing undergrad."

"I feel that this time will be more rewarding because I will have my husband and son to share this experience with."

Suddenly, Nkechi started contemplating her job prospects. She was still working on Sade's campaign on a part-time basis. But with a crowded field of ten candidates running for the at-large city council seat, it wasn't a sure bet that Sade would win the election. Even though Nkechi felt that being involved with this campaign was great, she needed to find a good paying job that would help with the household bills along with her student loan payments.

Obi, on the other hand, was also weighing his job prospects. Things were okay now because it was almost the end of the tax season, so he was happy about that. But Obi's mind and energy were mostly focused on his full-time job. He had been at the company for nine months and was hoping that he would be offered a permanent position. His performance review was coming up at the end of April and he was hoping to get a lot of positive grades from his supervisor. The firm was majority white along with everybody there being conservative Republicans. He was surprised when he was offered the job. As part of preparing him for working there, Nkechi and Nnamdi had even advised him to try and avoid any discussions of religion or politics at work. Both topics were considered off limits in corporate America.

For the most part, Obi heeded their warnings and stuck with talking about sports. They thought of him as a sports guru of some sort when he told his coworkers that he used to play basketball in high school. There were two other black lawyers who worked for the firm. One of them was Byron Washington, a brown noser to the tenth power. Obi remembered asking him for some advice about the do's and don'ts about the company, and Byron telling him to learn how to play golf and go hunting to make his coworkers feel more comfortable with him. According to Byron, once everyone realized that he wasn't some scary black guy trying to take over their company and mess with their women, they would let him into their circle of trust.

After that conversation, Obi saw the depths a person would be willing to go to in order to be accepted by his colleagues. But Obi did not knock Byron's hustle. He just knew he wasn't going to become someone he wasn't so he could move up in the company. The other black lawyer was Keisha Moore. She had gone to Howard University for her undergraduate studies, so they had hit it off from the start.

Keisha had a thing for Nigerian guys and was intrigued by Obi when she first met him. But once she found out he was married, she limited herself to just playfully flirting with him. They would go out to lunch from time to time, but their conversations were restricted to office politics and how much everybody disliked President Obama. Obi was physically attracted to Keisha and she knew it. She was close to five feet six inches in height, with a slim body frame, along with a light skin tone, with hazel eyes. Keisha had caught him glancing at her behind a few times, but she never said anything to him about it. She knew that regardless of how refined and educate Obi was, he was still a man. And with the sea of white men at the job, in some respects, she didn't mind being desired by one of her own.

"Are you ready to eat dinner, honey?"

Obi snapped back to the present at the sound of Nkechi's voice. He got up from the living room sofa and made his way to the dining room. Just then his phone buzzed with a text message notification. He checked it, it was Tamika. He decided to wait until after dinner to read it.

He was about to dig into the food when Nkechi started to pray. "God, thank you for this food you have given us in the hopes that it nourishes our bodies and minds. Amen."

They rarely said grace before dinner. Obi knew Nkechi was only trying to show him up based on their conversation from earlier in the day. To confirm his suspicions, she sarcastically added, "I hope that my prayer was Godly enough for you and your family. Let me know if it isn't."

Obi shook his head and said simply, "It was perfect, Chi Chi."

After dinner, Obi went into his office to read Tamika's text. She wanted to know when they could set up some time to meet up and possibly have a play date. In his mind, Obi knew that her plan wasn't going to happen. There would be no way in hell that Nkechi would sign off on that or go along with him having any type of alone time with Tamika.

> *"Schedule is busy right now, will get back with you about it later,"* Obi wrote back.

He hoped she would get the hint and drop trying to meet up, but ten minutes later, he got a response from her.

> *"Ok."*

And right following that "ok,"

> *"I hear that when people get married, they have a whole bunch of sex. Is that the case with you and your wife?"*

Obi shook his head and laughed. He always found it interesting that Tamika was so intrigued about his sex life. But he also realized that women had an ego when it came to sexual experiences just like men did. Even when you are no longer with your ex, they still want to know how they measure up to the person you are with.

"We have a healthy sex life."

She laughed. *"LOL, I thought your delay was you trying to make up something to say. Anyway, I would love to hear about it?"*

"Yea, that is definitely not going to happen."

"Well, hopefully, you are pleasuring her the way you used to do me. Anyway, let me get off this phone, my mind is starting to go to places it doesn't need to when it comes to you. Good night."

"SMH, you are a trip for real. Take care of yourself."

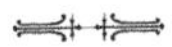

Easter weekend came quickly. Obi, Nkechi, and Ike were meeting up with his family at St. Xavier Catholic Church on Easter Sunday morning. It was going to be an interesting Sunday since part of the service was going to be done in Igbo.

Nkechi wore her traditional Nigerian clothing along with a very elaborate head-tie. When she came out to the living room, Obi started singing, *"She's my queen to be, a queen to be forever, a queen who will do whatever her husband desires."* He was about to sing the second verse when she started laughing.

"Obi, you are an absolute fool. I remember when kids found out I was African, they would sing that song to me. It used to upset me all the time. Thanks for bringing up old wounds from my middle school days, honey."

"Chi Chi, you need to stop fronting. You, me, and Nnamdi would always watch *Coming to America* on DVD and imitate the characters."

She laughed. "I was trying to be a bit extra and play the victim role for a minute. Anyway, thanks for your attempt to serenade me. It was kinda weird, but it made me feel special for some type of reason."

Obi looked at his watch. They were running late as usual. He quickly ushered his wife and son out of the house and sped to the church, where the service had already begun. They walked in hoping to sit with his family only to realize that there was no room in that pew.

After church service, everybody met up to talk and take pictures with one another. That was when Obi spotted his younger brother, Okey. He did not know that he was in town, so it was quite a pleasant surprise. Okey was currently working overseas as a project engineer for an oil and gas company.

Obi embraced his brother, excited to see him. "Little brother, it's great to see you. I see that you have picked up some weight. I guess things are going well for you."

"I am doing well, bro," Okey responded with a broad smile. "I got so many stories to tell you. These European and Arab women be loving some black men."

Before he could continue saying what he was saying, Obi stopped him. "Alright, big timer. We will discuss all the details later. I don't want anyone overhearing your exploits and making you give up that squeaky-clean image everyone has of you. Because I know in some crazy way, mom will blame me for you going astray."

They both laughed because it was true. The family congregated outside of the church for another 20 minutes before heading out to Obi's parents' house. Once they arrived there, Obi's mother headed straight to the kitchen to start preparing Easter dinner. She was followed by her sister-in-law and her daughter-in-law. The men headed to the living room to watch a basketball game on TV. Chinwe went into her room to change, but she was taking her time because she didn't want to help the women with the cooking.

Eventually, she slipped into the living room and started watching TV with the men. They were about fifteen minutes into the game when their mom shouted from the kitchen, "Chinwe, come into this kitchen and help us out!"

Chinwe did not respond. She kept her eyes glued to the television. Obi and Okey laughed, then Okey said, "Chinwe, you better go in there before mom comes out here and starts tripping."

Chinwe had a sense that her mother would come and grab her at any minute, so she started a conversation with Uncle Ugo.

"Uncle, I forgot to mention to you that the Fela musical will be coming here next month.

Uncle Ugo's eyes lit up upon hearing her say that. "My niece, are you serious? I have heard it was on Broadway in 2009 and 2010 and I knew they would be touring in different cities, but I wasn't sure if they would make it down to Houston."

Chukwuemeka laughed and jumped into the conversation. "Brother, have you forgotten that we live in the capital of Nigeria in the United States. There would be no way that something dealing with Fela wouldn't plant its feet in here. If they didn't come it would be an abomination."

Uncle Ugo nodded in agreement.

"Jay-Z and Will Smith helped with financing the production of the musical. I heard they put up 5 million dollars of their own money."

Uncle Ugo was amazed to hear that. "Hmmm, we as Nigerians always criticize black Americans for not caring about or respecting African culture, but I must salute them for their efforts on this project."

"I can't wait to check it out," Obi chipped in. "I heard that some Nigerians were upset that they had a guy from Senegal playing Fela instead of a Nigerian."

Uncle Ugo laughed. "Our people are wonderful. I never heard anybody trying to do anything to commemorate Fela, but now we are trying to dictate to others about who should play him. Let those guys go and sit down."

"If they have an African playing Fela, then I am fine. I am not sure if a black American actor can capture that energy of him," Chukwuemeka said.

Obi walked over to the entertainment center and put in his uncle's favorite Fela song, *Teacher Don't Teach Me Nonsense.* Even though he was now using a cane to walk around more than ever, Uncle Ugo stood up and started swaying his body to the music.

Chike and Chukwuemeka tried to hold on to him, but he waved them off. "Let me be now. Regardless of my health, I am still a man."

As Uncle Ugo was soaking in the music, he started to feel nostalgic. A few minutes into the song, Nkechi, Aunt Nkiru, and Ijeoma came out of the kitchen to see what all the commotion was about. Aunt Nkiru laughed and shook her head when she saw her husband up and dancing. "Old Man, what are you trying to do, don't hurt yourself out there." She said to Uncle Ugo, who laughed and said, "My dear, I am trying to show these youngsters how to get down as they say."

Chike, Chinwe, Obi, and Okey started to laugh at Ugo's attempt to use slang.

Ijeoma chimed in and said, "Why do you immortalize that crazy man, Fela? He lived a very reckless life as we all know."

Chukwuemeka sneered. "Kids, your mother doesn't like Fela because one of her sisters tried to run away and become one of his twenty-eight wives."

"Which of her sisters?" Obi asked his father.

His father was about to say something but looked at his wife and saw the stony expression on her face. He stopped. He knew that was his sign not to say anything. "I will let your mother tell you who it is," he said instead.

Now all the attention was on Ijeoma. At first, it looked as if she was not going to say anything either, but then she softened up and said with a laugh that it was Auntie Chioma. Obi and Chinwe were very surprised to hear that. Auntie Chioma, as they remembered from their childhood back in Nigeria, always had a rosary bead around her neck while carrying the Holy Bible wherever she went.

"Auntie would always tell us that we had to pray to Chineke three times a day or he wouldn't be pleased with us. I don't think she ever missed a Sunday of service at The Holy Redeemer Church," Chinwe said, remembering the auntie she knew.

Their mother laughed. "Well, you can say she became a bit too religious as she got older. But she was such a wild child as a teenager. I remember my mother writing letters to me saying how she was obsessed and in love with Fela."

Uncle Ugo responded, "In those days, Fela's lifestyle of smoking marijuana and having women around him wearing next to nothing clashed with the traditional Nigerian culture. He was loved by radicals like myself and surprisingly by some young Europeans."

Aunt Nkiru said, "Well enough about the trials and tribulations of Fela. The food is ready for us to eat"

With that, they all headed to the dining room to eat. They blessed the food before they began to eat. With everyone's concentration on their food, Ijeoma said, "Easter Sunday always renews my spirit. We can do all things through our savior, Jesus Christ."

Everybody nodded their heads in agreement. She looked at her grandson as he sat on his mother's lap trying to use his fork to eat his food. Then she turned her attention to Obi and said, "So when will you and Chi Chi be getting Ike baptized?"

Obi finished chewing his food and drank a big gulp of water. "Honestly mama, Chi Chi and I were discussing this matter just a few days ago. We are leaning towards waiting until Ike is a little bit older so he can understand and appreciate what the whole process means."

Nkechi patted Obi's thigh to show her approval of his answer. His parents looked at each other in astonishment. His mother sighed and said, "Well you kids have to do what you think is right for your family. But always remember, human beings are nothing without following the teachings of Jesus Christ. If you feel you want to try and circumvent that process, that is your choice. But all I know is that I have raised my kids the proper way."

Obi wasn't surprised at the comment that his mother had made. When she felt a certain way about something, she did not mince her words. Even though he let it roll off his back, Nkechi was a bit more upset at what her mother-in-law had just said.

"Mama, me and your son want Ike to have a spiritual relationship with God. Whether a pastor pours holy water on his forehead or not shouldn't determine whether he is saved, in my opinion. I think a lot of people are tired of the dogma of religious practices as some type of acknowledgment for being an obedient follower of God."

Chinwe and Okey widened their eyes in amazement to Nkechi's boldness. They had never seen anybody challenge their mother in that type of way. There was a moment of silence before Uncle Ugo said, "Nkechi, I agree with you. The African man has been tricked by the Europeans into believing that they had no religion and that all our ancestors did was worship trees and other objects. It wasn't until about 20 years ago that I began reading books about various African tribes and their religious practices. I started to realize that our people were more sophisticated than we were ever led on to believe. All our Igbo names refer to God and our love and appreciation for him. I honestly can say that I never really embraced all of Christianity because I didn't want to dismiss the role that my ancestors play in providing protection over me and my family."

"So, Uncle Emeka what is your opinion on this matter?" Chike asked Obi's father who had been quiet this whole time. Now, he could feel all eyes on him in anticipation of what he would say.

He hesitated before answering. "Well, I think everybody should do what they feel is right for them on their journey of enlightenment towards finding what the meaning of God is for them."

Everybody nodded their heads in agreement and the controversy was over for now. Ijeoma wished that her husband had been on her side, but she knew that he was trying to be fair and impartial to everybody's views. For Obi, this wasn't the conversation he wanted to have on Easter Sunday, but he was happy that his uncle had jumped in to support them.

After dinner, everybody headed back to the living room to talk some more, all except Obi's mother and aunt. Both women spent time putting the food away. Aunt Nkiru could tell that Ijeoma was still fuming about everything that had just happened during dinner. She asked her with a smile, "Ijeoma, are you going to tell me what is bothering you or will I have to drag it out of you by force?"

Ijeoma put down the towel she was using to dry her hands with before responding. "It is that girl, Nkechi. She has a very sharp tongue on her and doesn't know how to respect her elders. Just because these kids were raised in this country, they now feel they have the authority to talk to us like we are equals. That is utter nonsense to me. Then to add further insult, Obi is there moping his head like a sheep as his wife is upstaging me at my dinner table."

Aunt Nkiru stood next to her with her arms folded just shaking her head. Ijeoma said to her, "So what do you think my sister?"

Aunt Nkiru took a moment to collect her thoughts before responding. "It is funny to me that my nephew married a woman who is just like his mother."

Ijeoma was taken aback. "Nkiru, have you lost your mind? The only thing me and Nkechi share is our love for Obi."

"Both of you are very strong-willed women and are very opinionated and outspoken. I still remember when I first met you with Emeka and I told Ugo that his brother's fiancé might be a little too aggressive for him. But three kids and over 30 years later, you guys have made it work."

Ijeoma started getting irritated and said to her, "So what is your point?"

Aunt Nkiru came over and wrapped her arm around Ijeoma's shoulder. "Just because we gave birth to our children doesn't mean that we own them or that they will follow the same path that we did. Obi and Nkechi will have to do what is best for themselves and for their own family. We, as parents, should give our kids advice when they request it from us, but we can't get mad or upset if they don't take it the way we want them to."

Ijeoma thought about what Aunt Nkiru had said and had to admit that it made sense. "You are right, Nkiru, thank you for telling me what I needed to hear and not what I wanted to hear."

Both women finished up in the kitchen and went to join the others in the living room. As Ijeoma approached, everybody was tense and not sure what she was going to say or do. But as she came into the room with laughter in her voice and a smile on her face, everybody breathed a sigh of relief. Obi was even more relieved because he didn't want to deal with the tension between his wife and his mother. As Aunt Nkiru was sitting down, she asked, "So what are you guys discussing right now?"

Chike responded, "Well mama, we were asking dad and Uncle Emeka why Nigerians still want to build homes back in Nigeria even though they spend 95% of their time overseas."

"Well Chike, when everything is said and done, it boils down to pride. If a man can come back to his village and build a house, his family will be able to see the fruits of his labor from his time living in the white man's country." Obi's father said.

Uncle Ugo laughed. "Brother, your reason is correct on a multitude of levels. But I have experienced building a house back home and honestly, it was not worth the stress and money. In the end, your own family will say that the house isn't bigger than their neighbors who also have a relative overseas. I have also witnessed seeing people build houses in under a year. Sometimes I have to ask myself what are they doing that I am not."

"Ugo, we all know that some Nigerians have dabbled their hands into selling drugs and engaging in Medicare fraud to gain this money. But it is hard to explain this notion to our people back home who don't know or care about how your wealth was earned," Ijeoma stated.

"Let us not forget about your family members who have financial problems or are just plain lazy who want to live in one of the rooms in the house. You think that you are doing them a favor, but that notion turns into a nightmare when they are constantly calling you every month asking for money. Your family begins to believe that just because you guys share the same blood that they should profit equally from your success," Aunt Nkiru said, adding to what Ijeoma had said. She was pretty much summing up the experiences that Uncle Ugo was going through and he abruptly said, "That is why I had to throw everybody out of the house and lock up the place. I had to learn the hard way that you have to be harsh with your family to get them to respect you."

Ijeoma looked at Chinwe playing with Ike and said to her, "My daughter, when will we see you with your own baby to be carrying around?"

Chinwe stopped what she was doing and said, "Mama, can you not let this conversation rest for at least one day now? Why don't you ever ask Okey about his love life?"

Ijeoma turned her attention on Okey. "Okey, I hope you aren't talking with any of these Arab women in Dubai and the next time we hear you have converted to Islam?"

Everybody laughed. "Mama, you don't have to worry about that. I can't give up my pork chops and Heineken for their religion," Okey said to his mother.

The family continued to talk for the next hour or so before everyone started to leave. Nkechi went into the kitchen to grab some plates of food to take home with her. Chinwe came behind her not too long after that. Nkechi noticed by her sister-in-law's body language and facial expressions that she had something she wanted to get off her chest, so she said to her, "Chinwe, are you good right now? You look mad giddy about something."

Chinwe smiled and said, "You are my new hero. The way that you spoke up against my mom was classic. I love her with all of my heart, but she can come across as a bully at times."

Nkechi responded, "Actually I wasn't trying to come across like that, but I felt that what she said was kind of condescending towards me and Obi. I have a lot of respect for your mother, but I can't let anybody try and do me like that."

Chinwe laughed. "I forgot that you were born and raised in Brooklyn, which means you have a little bit of an edge to you. Honestly, my mom is scared of you because of your independence and unorthodox views about life. You have this aura about you that I think is very liberating. I wish some of that would rub off on me."

"Sis, we all have our own way of doing things. Hell, I'm still trying to figure some stuff out in my life right now," Nkechi replied.

Ike came running into the kitchen and Chinwe picked him up. "Chi Chi, when will Ike be having another brother or sister to play with? And selfishly, for me, I need another nephew or niece to spoil. Unfortunately, with my bad luck with men, and Okey still living a playboy lifestyle, Obi might be the only hope for our family for the immediate future," Chinwe said.

Nkechi was a bit hesitant in responding to the question. "Well, sister I don't know right now. At this moment, I am trying to reestablish my career and having another child isn't in my plans."

Chinwe was shocked to hear that. "Wow, I never knew that you felt that way about it. What does Obi think about it?"

"We really haven't had a full-blown discussion about it, I don't know how he will take it. I know he wants to have at least two more kids."

"Chi Chi, to be a woman is a tough job o," Chinwe said. "We are supposed to be so many things to everybody in our lives, but in the end, we are nothing to ourselves. I think you should do what is best for you now. If I know my brother the way that I do, he will be resistant to the idea at first, but eventually, with time, he will come around to your way of thinking. Obi and my father are very similar in that point of view."

Nkechi reached out and hugged Chinwe. "Thanks, sister, for your understanding and support. I really need it now."

"Well, I will keep this conversation just between the two of us. God forbid if my mother finds out about the possibility that you don't want more kids. She will probably advise Obi that he needs to marry another wife."

Both women laughed. "Chinwe, what you said is funny and painfully honest all at the same time," Nkechi said.

They finally left the kitchen and headed outside to catch up with the other family members. Nkechi was putting Ike into his car seat when she looked at Obi's face and saw that something was bothering him. She decided she would wait until they started driving before asking him any questions. Once they got on the road it was total silence for the first five minutes. Then Nkechi finally said, "Is everything ok with you honey? Since we left your parents' house, I could tell that something was on your mind."

"It is just that my mom started asking me when we are going to have more kids. She keeps saying that since you never talk about having any more kids that maybe that isn't in your plans. But I have told her that simply isn't true at all. We both want to have more children, but it's all about planning everything out."

Nkechi felt a lump develop in her throat. She finally said with a fake laugh, "Obi, you know how cynical your mom is about everything. She feels that there is only one way to do things."

"Yea, my mom can be a drama queen at times," Obi said, agreeing with her. "Anyway, I could tell that she was upset with my dad about something. Every time he got a text message on his phone, she would be glued into what he was doing. After a while, she said to him, *"I guess your mistress doesn't know that this is your family time."* Everybody was a little bit taken aback by her comment until she started laughing and we knew it was just a joke."

"That would be funny as hell. Your dad has that quiet old-school playa demeanor to him. Unfortunately, that trait didn't get passed down to his two sons."

Obi laughed. "Chi Chi, I see that you got jokes right now. I know one thing, Ike is going to break some women's hearts as he gets older."

"I know one thing for sure is that my son will not be a womanizer, he is going to be a feminist. I don't want him thinking that women are just pieces of meat."

Obi shook his head and said, "Hell no, my son is a man and that is the bottom line. I am going to teach him to respect and treat women fairly. But at the end of the day, he is a hunter and the woman is his prey."

"Obi, you are acting a little extra and dramatic right now. Men always get scared when you talk about feminism and their sons and quickly equate it to being gay. Also, if you had a daughter, would you tell her that her purpose in life is to be some man's play toy?"

Obi was silent after that and didn't respond to her comment.

"I guess that silence means you are acknowledging that I am right. But I know that your pride won't let you admit it to me."

Obi laughed. "Chi Chi, I hate your sarcasm sometimes."

She laughed. "I hate some of your outdated perspectives on the roles of men and women, but I still love you regardless of that." Chi Chi leaned over and gave him a peck on the cheek.

When they arrived home, it was already late. Nkechi took Ike to his room and got him ready for bed. Obi went to the living room and started watching TV. While he was sitting, he started contemplating if he would be about the idea of him and Nkechi not having any more kids. At first, he thought that maybe Nkechi was just having fatigue about dealing with Ike all the time. But then he realized that their continued use of condoms and her not ever bringing up the issue was a sign that they weren't on the same page anymore. Their sex life had become so mechanical and boring that Obi had to resort to watching porn and masturbating to keep himself sexually fulfilled at times. After another hour or so, he went to his bedroom and saw that Nkechi had already fallen asleep. Obi took a cold shower and climbed into the bed. He was about to close his eyes when he came to grips that the honeymoon phase was over and the rest of their marriage was about to begin.

CHAPTER SIX

"*Do you want to hit Atlanta or Las Vegas for your bachelor party, bro.?"* That was the text message Obi sent to Nnamdi. He felt relieved that he could partake in his best man duties. Since the beginning of the year, he had been bogged down with never-ending deadlines at his full-time job, along with contending with the clients he was preparing taxes for in the evenings and on weekends.

"Damn nigga, that is a tough choice to make. Both spots will go down regardless of which one we choose. Have you asked my groomsmen where they would be inclined to hit up?" Nnamdi finally responded.

"It is a split. Some want Vegas and others want ATL."

Nnamdi called Obi.

"If you were me, what would you do?" Nnamdi asked Obi as soon as Obi answered the phone.

"Nnamdi, you just put my ass on the hot seat for real." Obi paused for a minute before answering the question. "Hmmm, I would pick Atlanta strictly just to check out the strip club, Magic City. I always hear all the rappers talk in their songs about this spot. I also heard they got chicks built like Serena Williams and Beyoncé stripping in there all the time."

Nnamdi responded, "Yea, I have cousins in ATL and they have been trying to get me to come down there for a minute. They've been telling me that the woman to man ratio out there is like sixteen to one. I definitely want to hit up some lounges and clubs to see how the nightlife is as well."

Obi laughed and said, "Yea, you had better soak up all that stuff when we are out there because once you get married, there is no way in the world that your wife will let you go to ATL by yourself with all of those available single black women. Nnamdi, you better not pull a Murch move from The Best Man and fall in love with one of these strippers."

Nnamdi responded, "Obi, don't be wishing that one for your boy. I am a sucka for a thick woman with a big booty. Anyway, I wanted to let you know that me and Ogechi are planning to fly down there for Chi Chi's graduation."

Obi was excited to hear that. "Oh, for real? She will be very excited to see you guys come and celebrate with her. I know we haven't seen each other since our wedding two years ago."

"Yea, man," Nnamdi said. "I am ready to come to Houston and get away from everything for a minute. I always thought that studying for the bar exam was the most stressful point in my life, but this wedding planning shit takes the cake. It's crazy that you must spend all types of money for a thirty-minute ceremony and feed like five hundred friends and family. If it wasn't for my folks, I would have gone to the Justice of the Peace in a heartbeat."

Obi shook his head and said, "Zik, welcome to the club, my nigga. I hate to add insult to injury, but you forgot to throw in the traditional wedding."

Nnamdi sighed and said, "Obi, you just made my head hurt again by reminding me of that shit. All this makes you really think long and hard about marrying a Nigerian woman, on da real."

Obi laughed. "Nnamdi, you are sounding delusional right now. You need to just grab you a Heineken and watch some basketball to get your mind off this stuff."

"Yea, you are right bro. Thanks for allowing me to vent real quick. I will be in touch with you in the coming days once we finalize our travel plans to come out there."

Once Obi got off the phone with Nnamdi, he began to reflect on him and Nkechi's crazy wedding experience. He remembered how hard it was for him to deal with her mood swings from her being pregnant along with her being a bridezilla.

About thirty minutes after ending the call with Nnamdi, Nkechi came into the kitchen.

"Hey, how is the studying going?" Obi shouted out to her from the living room. Nkechi slammed the refrigerator door after grabbing a bottle of water. Obi could tell that his wife wasn't in a good mood.

"This final project is kicking my ass. I don't think this professor knows this is my last semester of grad school and I need to pass this class. Hell, this shit is stressing me out so much that I feel the need to smoke a blunt to put my mind at ease."

Obi said to her sarcastically, "Chi Chi, I forgot that you were a weed head when we met in law school. You tried to keep that shit on the low, but me and Nnamdi finally caught on to your late-night case of the munchies."

Nkechi laughed and said, "I admit smoking weed pretty strong back in the day, but it never affected me getting my work done. It really just helped me clear my mind and gather my thoughts."

"Well, I might have something that can help relieve some of your tension," Obi said while grabbing Nkechi's right hand and guiding it towards his penis.

She pulled her hand away and laughed. "As tempting as your offer is, I am going to have to pass on it right now."

"We can just do a fifteen-minute quickie if you want to."

Nkechi rubbed her hands on his chest and said, "Honey, I need one hour plus to fully satisfy my needs along with yours."

All Obi could do was shrug his shoulders and say, "Well Chi Chi suit yourself, but my offer still stands whenever you want to entertain the idea. Anyway, I just got off the phone with Nnamdi and he said that he and Ogechi are planning to come down here for your graduation."

"Oh wow, that will be so awesome," Nkechi said. "Even though Ogechi sent me a pic of her engagement ring, it will be nice to see how big it is in person."

Obi sighed. "You women kill me with all this obsessing over an engagement ring. I think I am going to start a petition for men to get a gift from their woman after he proposes to her. It seems like a reasonable request in my opinion."

Nkechi looked dumbfounded by his comment. "Babe, a man gets a lovely woman he will spend the rest of his life with. Why would you need anything more than that?"

"Everything you are saying is correct, Chi Chi, but can a brotha get a big screen TV, nice watch, or something like that? Can a man get pampered and spoiled as well?"

Nkechi just stared at him for about thirty seconds without saying a word. She finally said to him, "On that note, I am going back to finish up what I was working on. I am not going to let you get me pissed off over this nonsense theory you are trying to perpetuate to me."

She walked up to their bedroom. A few minutes later, she returned. "I forgot to mention this to you earlier in our conversation, but do you think you can attend this fundraiser Sade is having this weekend? I would go, but I am swamped with finals. It would really mean a lot to me if you could go. It will also give you guys a chance to catch up as well."

Obi hesitated for a moment as he was trying to gather his thoughts and he finally mumbled out, "Sure, it's no problem at all."

"Thanks, honey, you are the best. I will give you the information about the time and location tomorrow. Also, I forgot to mention that my parents will be flying in for my graduation as well. Do you think your folks would mind if they stayed at their place? I would love for them to stay over here, but we don't have a whole lot of space."

"I will talk with my folks and see what they say. But I don't think they will have a problem putting them up. How long do your parents plan to visit for?"

"Hmmm, I am not exactly sure. Since they are both retired now, maybe they can stay for two weeks or so. I know they would love to spend time with me and Ike."

"I know your dad can't wait to see me," Obi said, sarcastically.

Nkechi responded, "Obi, my dad likes you. I know he wasn't too happy about us shacking up together when I first moved out here, but he eventually got over it. A father might know that his daughter is having sex, but when she is living with a dude it is all but confirmed that they are fucking."

Obi responded, "Yea, I know my dad was like that with my sister. It would be funny how we all knew that she had spent the night at one of her boyfriend's place at the time, but she would always tell my dad she was tired and crashed at her homegirl's apartment. I guess daughters' always want to maintain that pure and innocent image for their fathers."

Nkechi responded, "Yea, you are definitely right about that. Anyway, let me stop procrastinating and get back to my project before I have to take you up on that offer you proposed earlier."

After they both had a good laugh about the matter, Nkechi went back to her room for the second time. Obi picked up his phone and saw that his mom had called him. By this time, it was already after eight o'clock so he decided he would give her a call later in the week.

A few days later while at work, Obi's mother sent him a text message. *"How are you doing, I hope you and your family are well. I need for you to have a talk with Chinwe. I think she has gone mad."* The text message read.

Obi responded, *"Mama, all of us are doing fine. I talked to her last week and she seemed fine to me. What is the problem?"*

Ijeoma was a bit irritated with the way her son answered her question and responded back, *"Son, just give her a call, please. I don't feel like going into full detail on this text message. Have a great rest of your day."*

Obi shook his head in dismay and responded, *"Ok mama, we will talk soon."*

As he got settled back into his work, Obi knew that his mom was probably tripping over something minor that Chinwe had done. He sent his sister a text to try and see what was going on. When Chinwe finally got back to him, he was heading home from work.

Chinwe wrote: *"Bro, what's good with you?"*

Obi wrote back to tell her that he was in the elevator leaving work and would call her when he got to his car.

Once Obi got situated in his car, he called his sister. "Weezy, how far now. What is going on with you and mom, she texted me this morning saying that you have gone mad."

Chinwe burst out laughing. "All I did was cut my hair a little bit shorter than I normally do."

Obi was puzzled for a minute and then he said, "Oh ok, but it seems like it has to be more than that to get mom all fired up."

"Mom always overreacts to everything. I will text you a pic and then you can let me know what you think after that. So how is the family man doing?"

"I am in grind mode with work, Chi Chi's graduation and planning Zik's bachelor party," Obi responded. "I also found out Nnamdi and his fiancé are coming out here, along with Chi Chi's parents. It should be an entertaining time, to say the least. Did I mention that Chi Chi wants me to ask mom and dad if her folks can stay at their house?"

"Hmmm, good luck with that one. You know our folks like their privacy, and secondly, they will be upset that her father didn't call dad with a formal invite. They will say that Chi Chi's dad didn't follow the proper protocol or something like that, knowing full well that our dad is a "Chief".

Obi sighed. "Oh well, I guess we will figure something out before they arrive."

"So, on to the important news," Chinwe said, "where are y'all going for the bachelor party?"

"We are leaning towards heading down to Atlanta right now."

She shook her head and said, "The black man's adult paradise. All I can say is don't bring any STD's or mistresses back home with you guys. I know how it goes down in ATL."

"Dang, Weezy, how are you going to put dudes out on front street like that. It ain't going down the way you think it will."

Chinwe laughed. "Bro, this is your sister that you are talking to right now. I know how niggas revert to playa mode when they are away from wifey for a few days. Dudes want to try and relive their single years and play that who can get the most numbers game. Next thing you know, it is 2 a.m. and you are having sex with some random woman in your hotel room."

"Weezy, you are in rare form right now. Which one of these guys cheated on you? Me, Chike, and Okey will deal with him as soon as possible."

She chuckled. "I see you got jokes, bro. The last thing I am going to tell you is that I am on Chi Chi's side if you get caught up doing any dirt out there."

Obi said, "Man, I guess blood ain't thicker than water."

"It isn't if you are the one causing the problems." They both chuckled. "Anyway, I have to get ready for my date tonight. Let me know what you think of the pic when you get home."

"Who is my little sister going out on a date with? You forgot that I have to pre-screen these guys to give them my seal of approval,"

Chinwe said. "Bro, none of your damn business. Goodbye."

Obi arrived at home shortly after that. He did his usual routine of watching television, eating dinner, and then playing with Ike. It wasn't until later that night that he remembered to check out the picture that Chinwe had sent him. When he did, he was shocked. He showed Chi Chi the picture, but she did not seem shocked at all.

"What is the big deal, honey?"

"Weezy's taper fade looks better than mine right now. All I know is that when a woman cuts her hair this low, it can only be because of two things; she is either going through some deep depression or she is considering becoming a lesbian."

"Obi, you are sounding pretty idiotic right now," she said, looking at him ridiculously. "Your sister is becoming natural. Some women cut off all their hair so that they can regrow it without the chemicals. She discussed it with me because I went through the same process to grow my own natural hair."

Obi was at a loss for words. "Oh ok," he said, letting it sink in.

But Nkechi was not done, she wanted to dig deeper into the matter "So how did this topic come up between you and Chinwe?"

Obi responded, "My mom hit me up about it this morning and expressed her frustration about her hair. This was before I saw the pic, so I wasn't too sure what it was all about."

Nkechi sighed. "Yea, I knew that your mother would have something to say about it. Let me guess, she told you that this will harm your sister's chances of finding a man, right?"

Obi knew that this topic hit close to home with his wife since she had been rocking a natural hairstyle for as long as he had known her. She continued, "It is crazy to think that in 2012, in this country, where we have a black man as the president, that some black people will be denied access to a job or promotion because of wearing their hair the way God gave it to them. If that is not bad enough, don't get me started on black and African men who won't date a black woman because she has a natural hairstyle."

Obi decided to change the topic, so instead, he asked Nkechi about their plans for graduation.

"I have finished one of my projects, but still have two more finals to study for. I am ready to let loose. Hell, you might even get yourself some ass tonight."

They both laughed. "If I can quote the great Marvin Gaye, I need some *'sexual healing'* from you," Obi said, leaning in to kiss Nkechi on her neck. Then he attempted to take off her clothes. He had off her shirt and her bra and was about to take off his pants when Ike appeared out of nowhere just staring at them and laughing.

Obi shook his head and said, "Well I guess little man will get to witness the process in how he was created."

He continued to kiss her, but Nkechi pushed him off her and put her NYU t-shirt back on.

"Damn, Obi, we can't have sex in front of our son, it might traumatize him for life. It could cause him to be hypersexual or something like that."

"The only person who is going to be traumatized is me if I don't get some ass soon."

Nkechi looked at him with a smirk on her face and said, "Stop being overly dramatic. You will survive, I promise you that."

As Nkechi was picking up Ike, she said to Obi, "Once I get him cleaned up and ready for bed, we will pick back up where we left off at."

She walked past Obi and he slapped her on her behind, "Don't take too long. I am about to drink a Red Bull, so I can bring my A game tonight."

She shook her head and said, "You are talking a lot of noise right now. I hope you can back it up later."

Obi walked back to the living room and noticed that he had received a text message from Chinwe. She was asking what he thought of the picture. Obi thought about the conversation he had earlier with Nkechi and texted back, *"Weezy, it is definitely a different look for you, but I will get used to it as time goes by. What made you want to change your hairstyle?"*

She paused for a moment and texted back, *"I have always heard how some young folks were going through a quarter-life crisis. The whole notion seemed like some psycho mumbo jumbo until I realized that I was experiencing it myself. I guess the whole idea of turning 30 this year is a little frightening to me. In the end, I just wanted to take on a new look to redefine the next phase of my life."*

Obi could relate to her fears because he had the same feeling about three and a half years ago. He replied: *"LOL, I definitely can relate to how you are feeling. At the end of the day, you must realize that your age doesn't define who you are. We will just have to live our lives to the fullest for as long as we have air in our lungs to breath."*

She texted him back, *"I see you dropping knowledge, brother. You got me snapping my fingers over here the way people be doing it at those spoken word spots."*

"Well, I try to do what I can when I can if you know what I mean."

"SMH, I tried to give you a small compliment and you take it like you should have been on Def Poetry Jam or something like that."

"I am the jack of all trades. I am a lawyer, CPA, and a philosopher."

"I can't go there with you tonight. Anyway, "Mr. Renaissance Man", I am about to call it a night. Tell Chi Chi I said hello and give my nephew a kiss on the forehead from me if you can."

"No problem, so how did your date go tonight?"

Chinwe texted back, *"SMH. Good night again my overly nosey brother. LOL."*

"So, you are going to leave me hanging like that? You ain't right for that one, Weezy. Anyway, we will catch up later. Take care."

Obi watched television for another hour or so after that. At about 11 p.m., he decided it was time to call it a night. Nkechi was still in the bathroom when he got upstairs. He climbed into bed quietly and pretended to be asleep. Nkechi finally came out of the bathroom and got into bed, about twenty minutes later. She nudged him to see if he was still awake. When he did not respond, she laid back on her side with a big smile on her face. Just as Obi started to finally get into sleep mode, Nkechi started kissing on his neck, then his chest, and continued to go lower down on his body. By the time he knew it, Nkechi had grabbed his penis and put it in her mouth.

His eyes flew open, he was a bit shocked. He usually had to convince her to give him oral sex. But this time she was acting very aggressive. As he tried to sit up, Nkechi pushed him back down on the bed and said, "I got this honey. Just lay down and enjoy the show."

Obi was turned on by Nkechi's assertiveness. As he began to relax, he could feel his toes curling. He was in awe of the intensity of Nkechi's head game. Obi grabbed a pillow to hide his facial expressions.

Nkechi laughed, "I can stop doing it if you want me to."

Obi almost panicked. "Na, I'm good, keep it going," he said with such urgency.

For about five more minutes, Nkechi continued until Obi finally orgasmed. The two of them laid next to each other on the bed in silence for several minutes after that. Finally, Nkechi asked, "So did you enjoy what I did for you?"

"It was off da chains. You really brought your 'A' game this time around."

"Thanks for the words of encouragement. I have to admit that I was watching porn for some tips on improving my skills while using bananas for extra practice."

Obi shook his head. "I see you have entered the dark side. Once you enter, there is no going back."

"Anyway, before you go to sleep," Nkechi said, "I was going to tell you that I sent a text to Sade about her coming to my graduation."

Obi hesitated for a while before responding. "Oh ok, I know she is pretty busy with campaigning and stuff, what was her response?"

"Yea, I thought she would say no, but she said she would be thrilled to come. I think it is kind of her to come and show me her support. Now the next thing I have to do is try and hook her up with a good man."

Obi laughed. "Chi Chi, did Sade ask you for your help in that department?"

She responded, "No, she didn't ask me directly. But let's just say that I have this womanly instinct that senses she is longing for the company of a man. I know it has to be lonely with all of her focus on running for office."

"Honey, Sade is fine, if you ask me. She is a very driven and ambitious woman. I don't know if she is into the whole having a family thing like most women are. But I could be wrong about that."

Nkechi responded, "Well, I am not buying that theory if you ask me. You guys used to be pretty cool, what type of guys is she into?"

Obi thought about it for a minute and said, "I never got involved in Sade's love life, so I am the wrong person to answer your question."

Nkechi shook her head and said sarcastically, "Thanks, honey, you have been such a big help to me."

Obi laughed. "No problem, Chi Chi. As much as I have enjoyed the activity and conversation that we had, I need to get a couple hours of sleep to be at least half productive at work in the morning."

Obi leaned over and gave Nkechi a kiss on her forehead and then laid back on his side of the bed. Even though Obi had fallen asleep, Nkechi was still up thinking. Her mind began to wonder about the true relationship between Obi and Sade. She started to notice that every time she brought up Sade's name, Obi would get disoriented like he was trying to conceal something. She often wondered if Obi could resist Sade's sophistication and good looks back in the day. Nkechi found it hard enough having to deal with

Tamika here and there, but it was even more difficult when it came to Sade.

Nkechi looked at Obi while he slept and realized that she couldn't worry herself about his past. If she was going to be real with herself, she had never told Obi about her threesome with a guy she once dated and one of her homegirls. It was an adventurous six-month streak that Nkechi had chalked up to youthful exuberance after finishing law school.

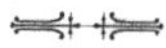

As the time of the fundraiser was fast approaching, Obi began to think more and more about trying to back out of going. But he didn't want Nkechi to begin to suspect anything.

On that Friday evening, he attended the fundraiser after work. Once he got there, he was surprised to see a lot of familiar faces at the fundraiser. They were mostly from the Young Lawyers' Association. Obi walked around the room for a couple of minutes, and then he locked eyes with Sade. She was talking with a group of people across the room from him. She waved towards him and he could see her lips saying thanks for coming.

He was heading past the donation stand to say hello to Sade when he ran into Ron Jones, who had once been the vice president of the Houston Young Black Lawyers organization.

"Damn, I think I must have run into a ghost. Obi Ifeanyi, how are you doing, my brother?"

They dabbed each other and Obi responded. "I am doing well man. Just coming to give support to our girl, Sade."

"Yea, man, you already know what it is. Sade has always been a classic overachiever to the tenth power. Anything that she puts her mind to, she usually gets."

Obi nodded his head in agreement and Ron continued, "I know that this is old news right now, but why didn't you and Sade ever take it to the next level. I remember that you guys were always flirting with each other and had pretty good chemistry. Everybody in the group felt that you guys were having sex on the low or something like that."

Obi laughed. "Bro, you know how things work out sometimes. Anyway, Sade was working so hard to try and make junior partner at her firm, she wasn't going to divert her attention from attaining that title."

Ron thought about it for a minute and said, "Well, at least she had the opportunity to be in play for a position like that. Most young college-educated black folks have been bamboozled into buying into this corporate dream bullshit. It is especially hard for black men in corporate America."

"Ron, preach my brotha. It is almost like these companies feel like they did us a favor by giving us a job. If you ever open your mouth and say you want to get into a management or leadership role, they nod their heads in agreement with you, all the while knowing that your ass ain't going to get to that level."

"You hit the nail right on the head, man. I guess we were all naïve to think that having a black man in the highest office in the land would change some people's minds."

Obi chuckled. "Some of these people still think Obama was born in Kenya and is a practicing Islam. Dude has Osama Bin Laden killed, saved the country from a depression, and passed universal health care and people still critique him like he hasn't done anything. He can't win for losing."

As Obi and Ron were still talking, Sade made her way towards them. "I knew that I would find my two pro black friends over here. I hope you guys didn't scare the white folks away with all of your talking."

Ron said, "I actually want them to hear what we are talking about. The real problem in my view is these so-called white liberals. But that is a discussion for a different day. How is your event going so far?"

Sade sarcastically said, "Ron, you already know how I feel about that topic. But I need to play this political role right now. To your question, we are very close to our money goal which is the most important thing." Sade turned her attention towards Obi and said, "Well, I am happy that you could make it out to one of my events. Where is Nkechi?"

"She is trying to put the finishing touches on her final projects before graduation...and along with Ike being sick."

Ron looked at both of their eyes and could tell that they needed some space to talk so he said to Obi, "Obi, it was good catching up with you. We need to grab some drinks one of these days."

"No problem, we will definitely do that."

They exchanged business cards and Ron walked away. Obi sipped on his wine while trying to think of something to say to Sade. Finally, she said, "So, I know that Chi Chi is ready to graduate and get back into the working world, right?"

Obi nodded his head in agreement. "Yea, as much as she loves spending time with Ike, I think she is ready to get back into the rat race. Speaking of rat races, how is everything coming along with the campaign so far?"

Sade sighed. "It is the most demanding thing I have ever done. I knew you had to meet with all different types of constituents, but sometimes this shit can get overwhelming. Politics is a messy game. All that buttery shit everybody hears from the politicians isn't how stuff really gets done. Sometimes, I have doubts about what real change anybody can give to the residents of this city, especially the low-income folks."

Obi looked at her and said, "Sade, what you said might be the realest thing I have ever heard anybody running for office say. Now don't repeat what you just said to me to anybody else."

They both burst out laughing after that.

"Obi, only you know how to bring a sense of levity to a fucked-up situation. Anyway, we are about to wrap this thing up and I need to talk to a few people before they leave. Do you have time to wait around to talk for a bit after everybody goes?" she asked Obi.

Obi responded with caution. "Yea, I don't think that would be a big deal."

Sade smiled. "That is good, I don't want to get you into trouble with wifey for staying out past your curfew."

"Even though we are married, I am still a grown ass man."

"Ok, bro, I hear you. I hope you tell her what you told me when you are sleeping on the couch tonight."

Obi responded, "Sade, maybe instead of you trying to be a politician, you need to try and be a comedian."

"I see somebody is a little sensitive about this topic," she teased. "Hopefully, you will calm down by the time I get back to you. So how did you like that come back?"

Obi smiled, "It was pretty weak, but I will let you make it though." He watched her walk away to mingle with her guests. Obi did the same.

About thirty minutes later, Sade came back to him and they walked outside to his car. By this time, it was nightfall. Sade stared at the stars in the sky. "I always thought I would be the one helping you on your political campaign," she said. "You had so much passion for a multitude of issues, back when we were messing around."

Obi sighed and said, "I guess life just happened. My uncle got sick and I had to run the law firm by myself, and then Nkechi moved down here and got pregnant shortly after that. Everything just happened so quickly."

"You aren't having any sort of buyer's remorse or anything like that, are you?"

"Not really. I always wanted to be with Chi Chi, but maybe we could have taken things a little bit slower." Obi paused. "But then again, that's life. In the end, you just have to deal with the cards that you have and try to make the best of a complicated situation."

Obi felt his phone vibrate and pulled it out to check who it was.

"I see wifey is checking to see where you are at," Sade said with a hint of sarcasm.

"Here we go with this conversation again," Obi said, throwing his head back in exasperation. "No, it is not. My sister just hit me up on text."

"Oh ok, I guess I was wrong this time. Anyway, how is Weezy doing?"

"She is doing well. Just trying to find Mister Right, like yourself, and all the other single Naija women in this city."

Sade laughed. "The great thing about this whole campaign is that I can block my mind from that dilemma for now."

Then suddenly, Sade blurted out, "Do you think we should tell Chi Chi about our past? She is such a great person, and at times I feel bad about withholding this information from her. If I was in her position, I would totally want to know everything."

Obi looked at her. "I had a feeling that this conversation was bound to come up eventually. Sade, I see where you are coming from, but it isn't as easy as you make it out to be. I know this will come out as a little crazy, but even though women say that they want to know the truth, in reality, they don't. Most women want to live in this pretend fantasy world where their man gives them the answers they want to hear and not the answer which they need to or don't want to hear."

Sade was silent for a moment and then she said, "I really want to challenge everything you just said, but sadly you are 100% correct. I never took you as the cynical type though, but I guess time changes everyone I see."

Obi let out a half smile and said, "I guess you can put that on the way I have seen Obama fumble away some missed opportunities during his first term so far."

Sade responded, "Don't get me started on that topic. We would have to head to Starbucks to have an in-depth conversation about that and I don't have the energy, nor am I currently in the mood for that right now."

"Yea, I remember the heated debates we would get into with the folks from the Young Lawyer's Assn back then. I remember the one time that it got so bad that they kicked us out of there and we kept the discussion going in the parking lot for a couple more hours. We had some fun times back then. Anyway, it's getting late and I need to start heading home."

"Yea, I need to go back inside and help with cleaning everything up," Sade said, embracing Obi.

After they disentangled from the embrace, Obi said, "So I guess the next time we see each other again will be at Chi Chi's graduation in a couple of weeks?"

Sade responded reluctantly, "Yea, that is true. It should be a very joyous day for her family and yours. Thanks again for coming to support me today. I really enjoyed reminiscing about the past with you. It felt good to take my mind to another place for a little bit."

Sade kissed Obi on his cheek before he got into his car and drove home.

Nkechi was on the couch with her laptop watching television when he walked into the house. She looked up at Obi when he walked into the living room. "So how did it go?"

"Everything went well, I ran into some old acquaintances that I haven't seen in a couple of years. Sade had a really good turnout."

"That is good to hear," she responded blandly.

Obi wasn't sure what was bothering her, but he didn't feel like trying to find out at this hour of the night. Eventually, Nkechi went to bed, leaving him the living room to watch TV. He decided to also listen to music on his iPod. As he listened, one of his favorite John Coltrane song's *In a Sentimental Mood,* began to play. He drank some red wine and listened to the song, it made him realize how music was really the soundtrack of people's lives. It was funny how listening to a song could make you remember an epic night you had with your homeboys at a frat party during your freshman year of college. While another song could make you remember the time when you were in love with someone. Obi started to think about how human beings spend so much time trying to reach specific goals and accomplishments that they never enjoy being in the moment. But the irony is that when folks get to the place they've wanted to get to for so long, it never feels the way they thought it would.

He remembered the quote his Uncle Ugo always told him when he would go off on a tirade about changing the world, "Obi, you expect too much out of life." At first, he thought his uncle was trying to diminish his dreams, but he came to realize that he was just trying to let him know that in life the illusion is sometimes better than reality. By the time he knew it, Obi had fallen asleep on the couch with the music still playing in his headphones.

CHAPTER SEVEN

Nnamdi emerged from the arrival terminal about twenty minutes after Obi got to the airport. Obi stood outside his car and honked his horn to get his attention. Nnamdi spotted him and walked over, a broad smile on his face. They embraced and got into the car after exchanging greetings and the usual male pleasantries, before getting into the car.

"Damn, bro, I knew that drinking all of those Heinekens would eventually catch up to you. Look at your beer belly." Nnamdi said to Obi who laughed heartily at what Nnamdi had just said.

"Nnamdi, you ain't been in my city for over an hour and you are already trying to cap on folks. I was going to wait to tell you that your hairline is worse than Lebron's right now. I didn't want to take it there, but you pushed me."

"Bro, you really hitting below the belt right now. If Ike wasn't my godson I would slash at you even harder."

They both laughed at each other.

"I am happy to be out here to catch up with you and Chi Chi though. All this wedding planning is draining my time and money. I can't wait till it is over and done with."

"Bro, I definitely understand where you are coming from. You guys can always go to the Justice of the Peace and get everything knocked out for a hundred bucks."

Nnamdi laughed and said, "Obi, at this point, that would-be music to my ears. But you know that if we ever did that it would be an abomination within the Nigerian community."

Obi responded, "Yea, that is true. So, what's up with Ogechi, is she going to make it out here for the weekend?"

"Na, man. She really wanted to come, but she got tied up with some last-minute stuff."

Obi was surprised that she wouldn't be coming, but he decided not to press Nnamdi on exactly what situation had come up. "I hope you are ready for this bachelor party in ATL," he said instead, shifting the focus. "This will be your last chance to sow your oats before you get married."

Nnamdi shook his head and said, "Honestly, your boy is still getting it in right now."

"For real, my nigga," Obi replied, "who have you been messing with?"

"This consultant that started working at my company about six months ago. She is a tall redhead with some big ass breasts and supple lips. Her sex game is so amazing that I am getting chills just thinking about it," Nnamdi said.

Obi shook his head. "I see that you got a '*Becky*' on the team. I ain't mad at you for that."

Nnamdi was a little surprised at his answer. "Damn, Obi, I thought your pro-black ass would be tripping about that shit."

"Nigga, I never said I wouldn't fuck a white girl, I just wouldn't marry one. Pussy is pussy at the end of the day."

They both shared a hearty laugh. "Bruh, once I started thinking about the idea of not having sex with anybody else for the rest of your life, that shit kind of shook me. I love Ogechi with all my heart and soul, but is a nigga ever ready to give up chasing women."

Obi shook his head. "The answer to that question is hell fucking no, bro. But you must choose between being a womanizer for the rest of your life or trying to build a life with one woman. The shit gets even more real when you have a kid."

Nnamdi smiled. "Damn, Obi, I see you dropping knowledge on folks. I see that this marriage thing is making you sound wiser. Anyway, enough about me, anything interesting happening in your life beyond work and the family?"

Obi paused for a moment before answering. "Man, beyond this awkward situation going on with Sade, I'm good."

"Oh really, I was thinking you were going to tell me that you were still entangled with some Tamika shit."

"Tamika and I engage in a little sexting here and there, but it is pretty harmless. She still sends me some naked pics from time to time, but I have that situation under control. But dealing with Sade is totally different."

"I know you guys were fucking around for a minute, but after Adaorah passed away, didn't shit get weird and the relationship kind of fizzle away? Nnamdi asked Obi.

"Yea, but Sade is running for city council and Chi Chi is working on her campaign. I told her Sade and I were just friends and that nothing happened between us. I wanted to tell her the truth, but after the incident that happened with Tamika on New Year's Day, I don't want to reveal any more of the skeletons in my closet. Also, to make matters even crazier, Chi Chi invited Sade to her graduation ceremony this weekend."

Nnamdi shook his head and said, "My nigga, you are stuck like chuck. I don't know how you get out of this situation without fucking yourself up. I have no words of advice to handle this situation at all. But this does remind me of that scene from The Best Man, where Harper has to tell his girl Robin, that he was about to fuck his homegirl Jordan after Lance's bachelor party."

Obi chuckled. He loved that movie, The Best Man, and he knew the scene Nnamdi was talking about. "Yea, I never understood the ending of that movie. All Harper had to do was propose to his girl and everything is forgotten. That shit never works out that smoothly in real life though."

By the time they knew it, they had arrived at Obi's place. As soon as they entered the house, Nkechi ran to Nnamdi and gave him a big bear hug.

"Dang, honey, you never get that excited when I enter the house," Obi said to Nkechi, teasing her. "I'm starting to feel neglected."

Nkechi playfully slapped Obi on his arm and said, "I see somebody is a little jealous. Anyway, I don't get to see my brother, Nnamdi, every day. But if he hadn't put a ring on my girl Ogechi's finger, I would have greeted him very differently."

A few minutes later, they all congregated in the living room. Ike came from the bedroom and jumped onto Nnamdi's lap. Nnamdi held him. "Ike is getting big, for real. You guys must be feeding him steaks or something."

Nkechi laughed. "Most of his weight is in his head, he can blame his father for that problem."

They all laughed before Nnamdi said to Obi and Nkechi. "Chi Chi always knows how to put a cap on you Obi. Man, I am so happy to be out here with you guys." Then he pulled a fifty-dollar bill from his wallet and handed it to Nkechi.

"What is this for?" she asked, looking at the bill in her hand.

"It is for Ike, buy him some clothes or toys or something from his Uncle Zik. I have to spoil my godson a little bit while I am here."

"Bro, you do a lot for Ike. You send him money for his birthday and Christmas every year." Obi said.

Nnamdi simply shrugged.

Not too long after Nnamdi arrived, Nkechi got up and went into the kitchen and brought out a plate of rice and stew with a glass of water for Nnamdi.

"My sister, thank you for the food. But can you bring me a bottle of Heineken as well?" he asked, taking the food from Nkechi.

Nkechi laughed and said, "Ogechi sent me a text message to tell me not to let you drink anymore Heineken. But based on your stomach, you may have to lay off the farina with egusi soup as well."

"I guess we are a long way from our days of making late-night study break runs to Ben's Chili Bowl, Nnamdi said, laughing. "I miss the times of eating whatever we wanted and not worrying about the repercussions. I ain't going to lie, getting older sucks."

The three of them shook their heads in agreement. Later, Obi went into the kitchen and fixed himself a plate of food and went back into the living room to eat.

He and Nnamdi ate in silence while Nkechi held Ike on the couch.

"So, Chi Chi, when are you and Obi going to give Ike another brother or sister to play with?" Nnamdi broke the silence. "I know your parents will ask you this same question when they come down tomorrow."

Obi attempted to answer the question at first, but he decided to see how Nkechi would respond.

Nkechi could feel their eyes on her, she took a minute to respond. "That is the million-dollar question for most married couples. How many kids do you want to have? I have always thought that I wanted to have like four kids. But now, I hope we can have at least one more child. If not, adoption is always an option."

Obi had a stunned look on his face hearing that. They had never discussed adoption. He would have preferred that he and Nkechi could have at least discussed this before sharing it with other people. Obi tried to play off his displeasure by saying to Nnamdi, "Well, marriage is all about compromises. You will quickly learn that this is how most issues are resolved."

Nnamdi could sense the tension between Obi and Nkechi, so he decided to change the subject. "Chi Chi, any big plans beyond the graduation ceremony this weekend?"

"Nothing major beyond going to Obi's parents' house to eat, why do you ask?"

"You know that I have to check out the nightlife out here as always. I am just trying to get all this clubbing out of my system before I get hitched."

Nkechi laughed. "That is not a problem at all, but remember that I have Ogechi on voice command on my phone, so if I hear about you acting a fool, she will know about it immediately."

Nnamdi laughed. "Damn, Chi Chi, you have been my homegirl for over eight years, you can't be diming me out like that."

Obi just shook his head without saying a word.

Nkechi responded, "I know how you Naija men get down. Zik, I love you like my own brother, but you are a dog. Out of all the women that you have dated since I have known you, Ogechi is the best one you have been with. I am not about to let you do anything foolish while you are in my city."

Then she looked at Obi sternly and said, "I also don't want you giving him any ideas either. I know how you married men tell your single friends how boring marriage is and how they should enjoy all of their freedom till the very end."

Nnamdi's mouth was wide open. "Is my reputation that bad?"

Nkechi and Obi laughed uncontrollably, and Nnamdi responded with a smirk, "I guess that answers my question."

The three of them talked for a little while longer before Nnamdi looked at the time and said it was time for him to check into his hotel room.

Nkechi took Ike in her arms and walked the men outside to the car. "I hope I wasn't too rough on you today, Zik," she said as he was about to open the car door.

"Chi Chi, you are so you. If you had acted otherwise, I would have thought something was wrong with you."

Nkechi covered Ike's ears and said to Nnamdi playfully, "Fuck you, nigga. If I were a different type of woman, I would have made you take a taxi to your hotel."

Nnamdi smiled and looked at Obi. "I know Obi wouldn't do his boy like that."

Nkechi looked at Obi and said, "Oh really? What do you have to say about all of this, honey?"

Obi smiled and said, "Chi Chi, I love you like no other. But I can't leave my boy Zik out like that. I would just have to take my tongue lashing when I got back home."

Nnamdi started pumping his fist in the air and said, "My nigga, Obi. You are a true Naija man. The first round of drinks is on me when we go out."

Before they got onto the car, Obi tried to give Nkechi a kiss on the cheek, but she just side-eyed him.

"What is wrong Chi Chi?" he asked.

"You answered the hypothetical question wrong. You are lucky my parents are coming into town or I would have had you pack a suitcase and stay with Zik for the weekend."

The men laughed and drove off.

"Are you really ready for this shit bro?" Obi asked Nnamdi jokingly.

"I have officially accepted that all women are bi-polar. You can do everything right and they will still find a reason to be mad at something that you did." Nnamdi responded with a chuckle.

"And don't let it be that time of the month for them either," Obi interjected, "that makes them crazier than they usually are."

Obi shook his head. "Women, are hard as hell to live with, but you would have no sex life without them. I guess that makes them essential to a man's life." He said.

"Obi, you are an absolute fool, bro. You sound like a cave man right about now."

Obi responded, "I know that I can be a Neanderthal at times, but I am an Igbo man, so what do you expect? On another note, what church are you guys having the wedding at? I know that you are Catholic and Ogechi is Anglican."

Nnamdi didn't say anything for a while as he was trying to get his story together. Then finally, he said, "Bro, we are going to have it at her church. It is a long story."

Obi was shocked to hear that. In law school, he remembered how Nnamdi never missed Sunday mass for anything."

Obi responded, "So you mean to tell me that "Deacon Okafor" will not be getting married in a Catholic church. The world might truly be coming to an end now."

Nnamdi laughed and said, "Obi, you are being extra dramatic right about now. But to be honest, I barely go to church anymore."

Obi got serious and asked, "Why, what has caused that change? I know that your faith always meant a lot to you."

Nnamdi cleared his thought and said, "Man, I was going to church because that is how my family programmed us to be. I always thought that if I didn't go, something bad might happen in my life. But lately, the whole idea of practicing a certain religion is something I don't know if I believe in anymore. So am I supposed to believe that some friends of mine who practice Islam won't get into quote on quote "heaven" because their religion doesn't believe that Jesus Christ is the Messiah of the world?"

Obi shook his head and said, "Zik, it seems like you and Chi Chi are reading from the same playbook. She and my mom got into it earlier this year about Ike getting baptized and stuff like that."

Nnamdi responded, "Obi, your wife was born a radical, so what you are saying isn't news to me. I guess the real question is whether you are worried that somebody might label her to be an atheist."

Obi hesitated for a minute and then responded, "I am not going to lie to you, that idea has crossed my mind. I guess I am not as open-minded as I thought I was."

"Don't be too hard on yourself, bro. We live in a world that puts a label on everything, especially when it comes to our faith. If you tell people that you believe in God, but don't believe in religion, they don't know what category to put you in."

"So you don't believe in a supreme God who has dominion over us?"

"If you want to ask me if I believe some guy with white hair and a beard is up beyond the skies directing what is happening to billions of people here on this earth, my answer to that is no. But I do believe that we as humans were created and designed by a creator and we have evolved since we have inhabited this planet."

By this time, Obi had pulled into the parking lot of Nnamdi's hotel.

"I have enjoyed our discussion on spirituality, but let us talk about more pressing issues now," Nnamdi said after Obi switched off the engine. "Whether or not I go to heaven and hell has already been determined, so I am not worried about that aspect of my life. What is up with you and Chi Chi? I know she threw you for a loop with the whole adoption thing."

Obi was trying to avoid having this conversation with Nnamdi, but he knew that he couldn't wiggle his way out of it. "I am not totally against adoption, but I figured I would have some more kids before that would take place. But Chi Chi's comment does make sense now because every time we talked about having more kids, she was always hesitant. I guess I misread her switching careers as a signal that she wanted to have more kids."

"Obi, I think the fault lies with us as men. We expect women to drop everything they are doing in their life and start a family once they are married. But we as men don't have to change our lives at all. Sometimes I think that we expect them to be superwomen when they are not. Chi Chi just wants to have a life outside of being your wife and Ike's mom. She wants to reclaim her individuality."

Obi pondered what Nnamdi was saying and he did have a point. Chi Chi was ready to get back into the working world and he was seeing if she wanted to have another baby.

"Damn, bro, I guess I have been a tad bit self-centered and not thinking about how Chi Chi would feel about the idea."

Nnamdi laughed and said, "Don't be too hard on yourself man. I know what I know from Ogechi ranting on me concerning things that she felt that I wasn't sensitive enough about."

Nnamdi looked at his watch, it was already 8 p.m. "Bro, I have enjoyed our convo, but I am tired as hell. We will catch up tomorrow, man."

On the drive home, Obi thought long and hard about his conversation with Nnamdi. Even though he accepted what Nnamdi had to say, it still hadn't eased his feelings on the matter. Obi didn't know any Nigerians who came from a one-child family. It was crazy to think that regardless of how modern Nigerians thought they were, they still clung to the idea that having multiple children was a sign of wealth and accomplishment for a man. It was the same concept that the men during his grandfather's time had about having multiple wives. Obi also knew that his mother would be even more disappointed about them not having any more kids. If she asked if it was a decision that both he and Chi Chi agreed upon, Obi would have to tell her that it was. But he knew that his mother would keep prodding and ask him how his wife convinced him to make this decision. Obi always thought that his mother would have been a great prosecutor.

It took Obi fifteen minutes to get back home from Nnamdi's hotel. Nkechi met him at the front door. She hugged him tightly and asked, "Honey, is everything ok with you? I just sent you a text to see where you were. I was starting to get worried."

When she pulled away, Obi noticed the tears in her eyes. "Chi Chi, are you ok?" he asked, concerned. "Why have you been crying?"

She wiped the tears from her face and said, "I am just so emotional right now. I didn't mean to blurt out my feelings about having children to Nnamdi. I just hope that you aren't mad at me and that this doesn't put any distance between us."

"Babe, don't worry about it at all. We both could have been better at communicating our thoughts and concerns to one another."

Nkechi was surprised at his response. She thought Obi would be upset with her, but his calm demeanor was throwing her for a loop. Obi walked to the kitchen and poured himself a glass of wine. Then he joined Nkechi on the sofa in the living room.

"I was pretty ticked off when I left the house with Nnamdi this evening. But Nnamdi gave me a couple of golden nuggets of knowledge to chew on and made me see the whole situation differently."

Nkechi was thinking about asking Obi what Nnamdi told him, but she didn't want to belabor the point any further. "Well, I will have to send him a thank you text later."

Right after they laid the issue to rest, there was a knock at the front door. Obi went to see who it was, it was Chinwe, Obi's sister. She said she was just driving by and decided to stop in and say hello.

Obi let her in. Once they were all seated in the living room, Chinwe began excitedly talking about the Fela concert.

"Man, I can't wait to go see this FELA musical on Sunday. Uncle Ugo has been more excited than anybody else," Chinwe said.

"Weezy, you know Fela represents the music of his era. I can't even imagine him with a big Afro, dark-rimmed glasses, and bell bottoms."

Nkechi chimed in, "Everybody gets old and wants to find some way to cling on to their youth, even if it is for a couple hours or so. Heck, I have seen a return to the 1990s with some of these young dudes sporting hi-top fades like Kid N Play."

"Chi Chi, please don't get Obi started on this nostalgia stuff. He still watches House Party every time it comes on like it just came out. The movie is over twenty years old or something like that," Chinwe said.

Obi chuckled. "Weezy, it is a classic movie. I remember me and Chike trying to mimic Kid N Play's dance moves. Life was mad fun and so carefree back then."

Chinwe sighed and said to Obi, "I never understand why men cling to their late teens and early 20s as being the best times of their lives. It is almost like you guys feel everything beyond the age of 25 is all downhill."

"Weezy, there is some truth to what you have said. But it is also knowing that once you have a family, you are now living for your wife and kids. Your personal pursuits must be put on the back burner. It is hard going from being totally selfish to being totally selfless with the snap of your fingers," Obi explained.

"Dang, bro marriage can't be that tough," Chinwe said with a chuckle.

Nkechi jumped in. "Weezy, you might find this hard to believe, but I agree with Obi. I have always told you that you need to enjoy and embrace your single life. Just simple things like trying to catch up with your homegirls or going to that author's book reading aren't as easy when you have a child. It is definitely a different world in and of itself."

Chinwe shook her head and said, "That is why I need to marry a man in his mid to late forties who already has grown children. I would be a great stepmother."

"So you don't want to have any children of your own?" Obi asked his sister. "You are mama's only daughter, she will surely die if you don't have kids."

Chinwe laughed. "Bro, I am just being silly right now, but the thought has crossed my mind though. At the end of the day, there is only so much traveling any one person can do. Also having kids is a blessing. I wouldn't want to miss out on that part of the life experience."

"Speaking of author's doing readings," Chinwe said, as if she had just remembered, "Chimamanda Adichie will be in town for an event next month discussing her book, *Half of A Yellow Sun.* I heard that they will be making the book into a movie."

"I have a huge woman crush on her," Nkechi replied. "She wears her feminism on her sleeves and doesn't care what people think about her. She is this generation's version of Chinua Achebe"

"What is this book about?" Obi asked.

"It is a love story that takes place in Nigeria during the Biafra War," Nkechi told him.

Obi's eyes widened. "Wow, that seems pretty interesting. That is a bold time in history to fictionalize, in my opinion. Most Nigerians really don't discuss Biafra outside of the privacy of their family and friends."

Nkechi responded, "Every time I bring it up with my parents, they go into this long tirade about how Igbos don't trust the Yoruba's because Awolowo sided with the Hausas after promising to align with the Biafrans."

"So many Igbos were killed and many lost their homes because of the war," Obi explained. "My mother always says she wonders if God will ever forgive Nigeria for all of the lives that were taken.

Chinwe chimed in, "I remember telling mom about the book and she patted me on the face and said, "*Ada,* my daughter, I don't need any book to tell me about Biafra. I saw everything with my own two eyes. But read it so you can understand the suffering that your people endured."

"So, Chi Chi, what is the plan for this weekend?" Obi said, switching the topic. "Is there any particular place that you want to eat at on Saturday after the graduation?"

Nkechi paused for a moment and said, "Honestly, I haven't even thought about that. But you know I am not picky about food so it doesn't matter to me."

Chinwe added, "Obi, where are you and Nnamdi going tomorrow night?"

Obi looked at his sister with a smirk on his face and said, "Weezy, what are you talking about? I never told you that I was going out anywhere."

Chinwe laughed. "Brother, everybody knows that when you and Nnamdi get together, you guys are definitely going to hit the streets."

Nkechi looked at Obi with a stern look on her face before smiling. "Obi, you and Zik can hang out tomorrow night. I already know that you guys will be at Club 1960 which is the Nigerian hotspot on Friday. You know I have eyes and ears all over the place, so I don't wanna hear that Nnamdi was trying to get any phone numbers from available women."

Obi wanted to argue about how Nnamdi wasn't like that, but Nkechi knew Nnamdi well, so Obi decided to direct his attention towards his sister instead. "Weezy, will this mystery guy you have been seeing be coming to Chi Chi's graduation? I know that mom is dying to meet him."

Chi Chi chuckled and said, "Hell no. First, we are just friends right now. Secondly, I don't want him to encounter the family during this event. I am not trying to intimidate him or have you guys scare him off."

"So, what is his name?" Nkechi asked Chinwe.

"His name is Ola."

Obi chimed in and said, "So you went and got yourself a Yoruba guy? That is cool, I won't take offense that you are rejecting your Igbo lineage."

Nkechi looked at Obi and said, "Honey, put a sock in it for a minute." Then looking at Chinwe, she asked, "Where did the two of you meet?"

"We met at this spot that was having a spoken word event. He was performing one of his poems when I first got there. It was pretty good so I went up to him after he was done and started a conversation about the meaning of his words."

Nkechi looked at Obi and said, "Why don't you ever write any poetry for me?"

Obi responded, "Chi Chi, you know that I don't do that type of stuff. Weezy has gone ahead and gotten herself the Nigerian version of Darius Lovehall from Love Jones."

"Obi, I am too tired to go back and forth with you about this matter. Anyway, it is getting late and I am about to head back home."

Nkechi and Chinwe hugged each other before Obi walked his sister to her car. Obi's demeanor turned serious once they were outside.

"Weezy, I am really happy that you came over here today. There was a lot of tension between me and Chi Chi before you came."

"What is going on between you guys?" she asked.

Obi responded, "When Zik was over here earlier, Chi Chi said that she wasn't sure about having another child. She was talking about the possibility of adopting."

Chinwe could tell by her brother's body language that this wasn't sitting well with him. She was about to tell him that Nkechi had mentioned that to her as well. But she didn't want to make him feel that she was withholding information from him. So, she said instead, "Well, I know that you guys will figure out some type of compromise to this situation."

Obi sighed. "We don't have any choice but to figure something out. Life is always so much easier when you plan things in your head."

She responded, "Yea, bro, everything is more complicated the older we get. But in the end, John Legend said that we are just ordinary people, we don't know which way to go."

Obi laughed. "I see that Ola has turned you into a wordsmith now."

Chinwe shook her head and said, "Obi, you are a lost cause. Have a good night, my dear brother."

They both laughed before Chinwe got into her car and left. By the time he got back into the house, Nkechi was already asleep. Obi was too mentally drained to do anything and just went straight to sleep himself.

When he woke up the next morning, Nkechi had already left for the airport to pick up her parents. She took Ike along with her, so Obi had the house to himself for a little while before they came back home. He took a shower and ate a bowl of cereal while watching his favorite ESPN show, *First Take* with Stephen A. Smith and Skip Bayless.

Forty-five minutes later, Nkechi arrived home with her parents. Obi went outside to meet them and to help them with their luggage. He did not want to be branded by Nkechi's parents as useless and lazy.

As he was heading toward them, Nkechi's mother saw Obi first and hugged him. "Obi, how are you doing? You still look in very good shape."

Obi responded, "I am doing well, mama. I hope that you guys had a pleasant trip down here from New York."

She responded, "It was a smooth journey. We thank *Chineke* for his grace and mercy."

Nkechi's father was carrying Ike in his arms and said to Obi, "My son, how are you doing? I finally got around to reading Obama's first book, *Dreams of My Father.* It was a fascinating read, to say the least. I have a newfound respect for him as a man."

Obi was surprised to hear his father-in-law's comments. Nkechi's father was a diehard Hillary Clinton supporter and, like most folks in 2007 and 2008, he wasn't sure if America was ready to elect a black man as president."

Obi responded with a laugh, "Sir, I am doing well. I see that it took four years for you to be converted to an Obamanite. Don't worry though, you will be able to support Clinton again in 2016 when she runs for the presidency."

Nkechi jumped in and said, "Obi, you know that isn't going to happen because Obama is going to suspend the Constitution and run for a third term."

All of them had a good laugh about Nkechi's conspiracy theory that the right-wing media always tagged to Obama. As they got into the house, Nkechi continued the conversation, "Obi, I was surprised by my father's comments about Obama. I still remember him not understanding why we made Ike's middle name Barack."

Nkechi's father laughed. "As these American politicians would say: my position has evolved."

The framework of Obi and Nkechi's idea came from *The Cosby Show.* The Huxtables oldest daughter, Sandra, had a twin boy and girl. Her and her husband, Elvin, named them Nelson and Winnie in respect to the Mandelas. As everybody was getting settled in, Nkechi led her mother and father into the guest bedroom. Obi called his parents to let them know that Nkechi's parents had arrived and would be staying with them as agreed. Although Obi's parents had agreed to have the Okoyes stay over at their house, Nkechi's parents had insisted on staying with Obi and Nkechi. They said they wanted to spend as much time as possible with their grandson, during their short visit.

Obi had just hung up the phone when Nkechi's father came back into the living room to watch television. Obi changed the channel to CNBC for him since he knew that he followed the stock market. Even though he was currently an economics professor at Columbia University, Nkechi's father used to be an investment banker on Wall Street for almost fifteen years.

Nkechi's father shook his head and said to Obi, "I don't know how Obama will win this election against Romney with the unemployment rate at almost eight percent. He was given a tough situation in 2009 and has managed the best he can in my opinion. These types of economic turnarounds take four to five years to correct. Unfortunately, the political calendar doesn't know or care about this process."

Obi nodded his head in agreement at what his father-in-law had said. Nkechi's father continued, "Nkechi has been talking about this political campaign she has been working on. I think she mentioned that the woman's mom is black American and the father is Nigerian. She seems pretty excited about the whole thing."

Obi responded, "Yes, sir. Sade is a woman whose father is a friend of my uncle's. I used to be in an organization with her when I moved back down here from law school."

Nkechi's father shook his head and said, "I used to tell all of my kids not to get involved in politics, but Nkechi was the one who fought me against that notion. Honestly, I am happy that she didn't listen to my advice. We need Nigerians to be involved in the political arena in this country. I never thought like this until Obama won the presidency. He has really changed the game for all immigrants, but, especially, for Africans."

Obi could see that the conversation was getting a bit emotional for his father-in-law. It was interesting because Obi had always seen him as this stoic man who showed very little emotion if any at all.

Obi responded, "Sir, I did find it interesting how a guy who has a Kenyan father is the first black president of America."

Nkechi's father responded, "Obi, God sometimes works in mysterious ways."

Shortly thereafter, Nkechi and her mother came back downstairs and headed to the kitchen to cook while the men continued debating politics and sports. Nnamdi had texted Obi earlier to find out what the plans were for the evening. He had gone ahead and got himself a rental car so he could get around the city by himself. When Obi told him that Nkechi's parents had arrived, he decided to come over and see them. As soon as he got off of the phone, Nkechi's mother yelled at him from the kitchen, "So when will you and my daughter be having another child? Ike is getting lonely. He needs a sibling to play with."

Out of all the conversations to have, this wasn't the one that either Obi or Nkechi wanted to have at this moment. Both Obi and Nkechi locked eyes with each other from across the room, trying to figure out how to respond to her statement.

But Nkechi's father jumped in and said to his wife, "Nneka, we are here to celebrate our daughter's graduation. Let us not discuss this matter at this very moment."

Mrs. Okoye felt a bit scolded by her husband, but she dropped the issue. Nkechi breathed a sigh of relief. She didn't want to hear her mother go into a long diatribe about how having kids gave a woman more value than the profession she had. Mrs. Okoye would always say she chose the nursing profession because it gave her more options to be available to her children as they grew up. Even though Nkechi was a very smart and ambitious woman growing up, her mother often worried how that would affect her chances of settling down and getting married. She knew that Nigerian men would be intimidated by a woman who was as independent and assertive as her daughter.

When Nkechi had discussed interest in pursuing her master's degree, her mother was very hesitant about this decision. It was only when Nkechi and Obi started dating that her mother's fears subsided.

Nkechi asked her mom, "So when is Chinedu going to produce you and daddy a grandchild?"

Her mother responded, "Nkechi, even though your brother is 31 years old, you know that he doesn't have any sense of direction in his life. I warned him about going to NYU film school, I thought he would find himself a steady job after he finished college. Now that degree has been useless for him, and your father and I have to help him cover his bills."

Nkechi's father shook his head and said, "Every time I ask Chinedu when something will materialize from these movies he is working on, he always says, "Dad, you know things take time to pan out in show business."

Mrs. Okoye said, "He wanted to come down for your graduation, but he wanted us to buy him a plane ticket and we refused."

Chinedu was more of a free spirit than Nkechi. He rejected the morals of corporate America. He believed that success could come from getting fulfillment from doing what you are passionate about, even if that passion brought little to no money. Unfortunately, he hadn't found too many women who were in their 30s who shared his ideology.

"I wish Chinedu would have followed the same path as his older brother, Kelechi," Nkechi's father said.

Nkechi responded, "Daddy, nobody will ever be able to live up to Kelechi's standards. He was an all-state quarterback in high school, went to Rutgers for undergrad, and is now married with a child while being a lobbyist for the pharmaceutical industry. But you guys always forget that he and his ex-girlfriend, Annalisa, had Uzo during his junior year of college."

"My daughter, that situation can happen to anyone, to be honest," her father said.

"I forgot that we live in a world of double standards for men and women," Nkechi said, looking from her father to her mother, and finally landing on Obi. "If I had gotten pregnant in college, everybody would have been disappointed in me and I would have been labeled as an ashawo."

Nkechi always felt that deep down she had to be almost perfect for her parents while her brothers were always given a lot of flexibility. She had always felt restricted in her actions.

Nkechi's father responded, "Obi, this is what me and my father had to deal with since she was a child. Nkechi has always had a very fiery personality. I am happy she married a calm man like yourself to balance her out."

Nkechi laughed and said, "Mom, Dad, Obi isn't the choir boy that you guys make him out to be. When he gets upset with me, he definitely lets me know about it."

By this time Nkechi was standing next to Obi and she playfully kissed him on the cheek.

Obi checked his phone and saw that Nnamdi had sent him a text message stating that he was in the parking lot. Obi went outside and brought him up. Once Nnamdi got into the house, he was greeted by Nkechi's mother and father.

"Nnamdi, how you are doing?" Nkechi's mother asked him. "I hope everything is going well with you. Where is Ogechi? I thought she would have come down here with you."

He responded, "Madam, I am doing well. Ogechi has been so overwhelmed with the wedding and work-related stuff that she couldn't come. I will let her know that you asked about her though."

"I can imagine how that moment is for her. Mrs. Okoye had grown fond of Nnamdi since Nkechi's time in law school. He also closely resembled one of her male cousins. She also played matchmaker with Nnamdi and Ogechi through a mutual friend she shared with one of Ogechi's aunts. Mrs. Okoye had hooked up so many other people that everybody started to label her the *Godmother of Love.* Even though she always downplayed her title, she secretly loved the status that it gave her.

Unfortunately, her husband didn't like it because he was always stuck going to a bunch of weddings for people he really didn't know. By this time, Nkechi and her mother had finished cooking rice and stew with plantains. While they were at the table eating Nnamdi said, "Mrs. Okoye, I haven't had your stew in a long time. I remember it was always very good."

Nkechi looked at him and sarcastically said, "Zik, you don't have to try and keep kissing butt. My mom likes you already, chill out homie."

Mrs. Okoye shook her head while laughing and said, "Nkechi and Nnamdi, you guys must have been brother and sister in another life or something. Nkechi doesn't even fuss with her real brothers like this. I always thought you guys might end up dating each other."

Obi said, "Mrs. Okoye, imagine I had to put up with them together for three years."

Nkechi responded to Obi, "Well honey, now you get to deal with me only for the rest of your life."

Nnamdi patted Obi on the shoulders and said, "My brotha, you are a better man than me."

Everybody started laughing profusely after that. Nkechi responded, "So Zik, how many women are you going to get at when you and Obi go out tonight?"

Mr. and Mrs. Okoye looked at Nnamdi with a stern look.

Nnamdi responded, "Chi Chi, first, I am not talking to any women when I go out. Secondly, you don't have to be a hater all of your life."

Nkechi's father said, "I love the fun that you guys share amongst yourselves. Life is too short, you got to enjoy the times that you have with friends and family."

Everybody said amen to that as they continued talking and eating. After they finished eating, Obi headed to the bathroom to take a quick shower before he and Nnamdi headed out. While her mother, father, and Ike were all in the living room watching TV, Nkechi asked Nnamdi to speak with her outside.

When they got there, she said, "Zik, what is the real deal with Ogechi? I am not buying this bullshit story that you are selling to me and everybody else. I hope that you didn't do some stupid shit and get caught cheating or something."

"Chi Chi, I am telling you the truth. I am not sure why you don't believe what I am saying."

She responded, "Ok, I am just checking. Because it seems that lately, Ogechi is always sounding weird when I talk to her over the phone. I am not sure if something is bothering her or something."

"I am happy to see that you are concerned. But I think it is all this wedding shit. You already know the stress of getting everything in place, then making sure folks from Nigeria can get their visas to travel out here, et cetera. I love being Nigerian, but why the hell do we have to do a traditional wedding and white wedding, all in the same weekend. Sis, I can't wait for this thing to be over with."

"You guys will be fine. It will be here and over with by the time you know it."

"Thanks for the reassuring words. Is everything cool with you and Obi? I know things got a bit awkward yesterday when I left."

She responded, "Yea, just some marriage stuff, bro. Get ready for this shit. Everything is cool until you guys have a kid. A child changes the dynamics of your marriage overnight. Anyway, let us go back into the house before folks start thinking we are making out or something like that."

Nnamdi responded, "They don't have to worry, you are definitely not my type."

Nkechi slapped him on the arm before they walked into the house. Once they walked back in, Obi was in the living room ready to go. Nkechi looked at him and said, "Honey, you are looking very nice. I hope you and Nnamdi have fun, but not too much fun tonight. You know my graduation starts at noon tomorrow."

"Don't worry Chi Chi, I will keep my eyes on Obi," Nnamdi responded.

Nkechi laughed. "Who will be keeping tabs on you then? You ain't slick, my brotha."

Nnamdi shook his head and he and Obi said their goodbyes to Nkechi and her parents. Obi drove them to the club.

"Have you been listening to any new music lately?" Nnamdi asked Obi during the drive. "I have been jamming this new cat, Kendrick Lamar's debut album, *Good Kid, M.A.A.D City*. My joints on there are *Bitch Don't Kill My Vibe* and *Real*. The lyrical content is nice. Honestly, I haven't liked an album this much since Kanye West's, Graduation album."

Obi responded, "Yea, Kendrick is really nice, I can't lie about that. But I have been jamming this Robert Glasper, Black Radio album of late," Obi said.

Before he could continue, Nnamdi jumped in. "Bro, that Glasper cat is fire right now. Ogechi and I and some friends saw him and his band about a month ago at this lounge. Erykah Badu was also there and they performed *Afro Blue*. The whole club got turned up when they played that song. I have never been into jazz that much, but the way he infuses it with hip-hop and R&B is real smooth."

Obi said, "Man, that is what I miss about the culture of D.C., it was just very eclectic. You could also go to Busboys and Poets and catch your favorite authors talking about their new books. We don't have anything resembling that out here."

Nnamdi laughed. "It is funny how folks up there want to move out here for the nice weather and low cost of living. I guess in life, nobody is ever truly satisfied with their situation."

They arrived at the club about twenty minutes later. Once they stepped out of the car and started walking toward the front of the club, Nnamdi said to Obi, "Damn, the women in H-town always have an extra level of thickness to them. If I lived out here, I would definitely be getting into all types of trouble."

They stood in line to enter the club. It was not a very long line, and Obi was hoping that they would get in soon. While they were waiting, they heard a woman yell out, "Nnamdi, is that you?"

Obi and Nnamdi turned around at the same time to see a five-foot five-inch curvy, light skin woman walking up to them.

"Amaka, how are you? What are you doing out in Houston?" Nnamdi asked, obviously not expecting to see her there.

"I am doing fine, thanks for asking. My cousin is having her bachelorette party this weekend, so I came down to celebrate with her. What are you doing out here?"

"Well, I am out here for a friend's graduation, which is tomorrow afternoon."

She asked, "So who is this guy that you are with?"

"This is my best friend from law school, Obi," Nnamdi said, introducing Obi.

Amaka shook Obi's hand. Her friends had since joined them.

"I was telling my homegirls how we met each other on *Black Planet* back in the day. Wow, I guess that we are showing our age by mentioning that site. I still remember my screen name was SexyNaijachick19 or something like that."

They all laughed. Obi looked at Amaka's friends and he could tell that they were ready to go into the club. "Zik, let's go inside and get this party started," Obi said to Nnamdi. They were now next in line to get into the club. Obi remembered how Nnamdi always said that Amaka was the woman that got away. They dated on again, off again, while they were in undergrad at Hampton University. They first met when he was a junior and she was a sophomore.

Once inside, Nnamdi and Amaka started carrying on with each other. Some of Amaka's single friends tried to push up on Obi, but he made his wedding ring visible so they wouldn't get any ideas. As Obi was walking around the club, he noticed that Nnamdi and Amaka were sitting in the corner of the club kissing up on each other. As Obi was about to walk over towards them, the DJ started playing P-Square's hit single, *Chop My Money*. The club erupted as everybody started heading toward the dance floor. He was standing around watching everyone dancing when this random woman came up to him and started dancing with him. At first, he was reluctant to do anything with her, but after he scanned the crowd and didn't see anybody that he and Nkechi might know, he decided 'what the hell' and started dancing with her.

When the song finally ended, the random woman turned and said to Obi, "I see you were acting scared in the beginning, but you did your thing after some time. Anyway, my name is Abisola."

"My name is Obi."

She responded, "Ok, that is cool. I really don't act this forward. I just graduated from college today and I'm celebrating with my friends."

Obi laughed and said, "Don't worry about it. Everybody has to let loose occasionally."

By this time, Abisola's friends had come around to see what was going on. "Well, it was nice meeting you, Obi," she said. "Do you think that we can talk sometime?"

Obi responded, "I would love to, but I am married so that isn't going to be possible. But, congrats again and good luck with everything down the line."

She responded, "I definitely understand that. Some of these Nigerian guys will have a wife and still try and get other women's phone numbers. Anyway, my celebration time will be short lived. I will be starting law school in August at Howard University."

At first, Obi didn't want to reveal to her that he and Nnamdi both graduated from Howard as well. But he decided that he would tell her. "It is a small world, me, my homeboy, and my wife all went to law school at Howard a few years ago."

Abisola started shaking her head and said, "No way. Tell me that you are lying to me right now. This is too cool. I know I can't get your phone number, but do you think we can be Facebook friends?"

"Yea, no problem. I live in Houston, but my boy Nnamdi still lives there so he can help you out as well."

Abisola said, "Yea, I hope that his girlfriend over there doesn't mind that I hit him up."

Obi turned to look at Nnamdi and saw Amaka caressing his face. He grimaced and turned back around to Abisola and got her information so that he could send her a friend request. Obi spent the rest of the night chatting with Amaka's homegirls. Some of her friends were upset that she had abandoned them for Nnamdi, but her cousin, Ifeoma, was more sympathetic to her situation.

"You guys know that Amaka just finalized the paperwork on her divorce only a few weeks ago. I guess she is just trying to enjoy herself and is getting caught up in seeing her old flame."

Obi said, "I can understand where she is coming from. But Nnamdi is engaged to be married."

All the women started shaking their heads in disgust.

Then Ifeoma said, "My cousin will be disappointed when she finds out about his situation. But that is how life plays out most of the time."

As the night finally came to an end, Nnamdi and Amaka were still being playful with each other when the time came for them to walk out of the club. Nnamdi didn't seem to want the night to end. When he saw Obi and Amaka's people outside he said, "Do you guys want to go grab some food at IHOP or something like that? It will be my treat."

The nonchalant body language displayed by everybody showed that nobody was in favor of doing that. Amaka and Nnamdi gave each other a big hug as they both made plans to try and catch up before the weekend was over. Once they got to the car, Nnamdi said, "Bro, this was one hell of a night. I haven't had this much fun in a long time. That young tender who was dancing on you looked nice. She looked like that fine ass Nollywood actress, Genevieve Nnaji."

Obi responded, "She was straight, bro, I ain't even going to lie. She is going to Howard for law school in August. Anyway, it seems like you and Amaka were getting pretty hot and heavy in the club."

Nnamdi responded, "We were just having a little fun. I haven't seen her since she got married about five years ago."

Obi responded, "Yea, her cousin said that Amaka is recently divorced."

Nnamdi was a little bit surprised. "She never mentioned that to me. She only said that she and her husband were going through a rough patch or something like that. But hell, I can't even front, I didn't mention that I was engaged either." Nnamdi let out a big sigh and said, "If only I could turn back the hands of time, I would have handled the situation with Amaka differently. But when you are young, you naively think that when you break up with somebody that you guys will magically find your way back to each other. Unfortunately, most of those scenarios only take place in books and the movies."

Obi wanted to ask Nnamdi why he was feeling that way. But he felt that nostalgia mixed with alcohol was the reason, so he didn't say anything to him.

By the time they got back to Obi's house, it was already 2 a.m. Nnamdi was in no position to drive, so he just crashed on the sofa for the night. Before Obi went to his room, Nnamdi whispered to him, "Hey, bro don't tell Chi Chi about what happened tonight."

Obi nodded and left Nnamdi on the couch to sleep. When he got into bed, Obi leaned over and told Nkechi that Nnamdi was sleeping on the couch. She happened to be half asleep and able to say to him, "I guess you guys had too much fun."

She rolled over to her side of the bed and went back to sleep. Obi quickly drifted off to sleep and when he opened his eyes again, it was already 8 a.m. After getting himself together, he went to the living room to check on Nnamdi, but he had already left. Nkechi was in the kitchen making breakfast. "Nnamdi just walked out of here about 15 minutes ago. He said he will come back here to follow us to the graduation." Obi went back upstairs to take a shower and got dressed. Then he came back to the kitchen to eat breakfast with Nkechi, Ike, and her parents. Nnamdi called him to say that he was outside, they all decided to leave the house at the same time. Obi and Nnamdi would drive in one car, while Nkechi, Ike, and her parents would ride in the other. Nnamdi wore a pair of sunglasses with his suit because his eyes were bloodshot from the night before. Once the two of them got into Obi's car, Nnamdi said, "Bro, last night was mad crazy. Amaka sent me a text message saying that she wanted to have sex with me. I just read it this morning. Even if I wanted to, I was too wasted to do anything with her anyway."

Obi responded, "Zik, you were in rare form yesterday. Did Chi Chi ask you anything about last night?"

"Not really, she just asked if I had a good time. I told her that it was all good and that you had a little bit too much to drink."

Obi nodded his head.

"Is Sade going to be at the graduation?" Nnamdi asked.

Obi responded, "As far as I know, she said she will be there."

"Hey, do you think that I should meet up with Amaka before I head back to D.C.?"

"I don't think it will be a big deal. But it depends on what your intentions are. If you are trying to have sex with her, I wouldn't advise it because you would be reopening up Pandora's Box. Especially with her being newly divorced, she is probably pretty vulnerable right now and wants to gravitate towards somebody like yourself who she feels safe and comfortable with." Obi advised Nnamdi.

He sighed in response and said, "Yea, bro, you are probably right. But I still wouldn't mind fucking her one last time for old time's sake though. I can't even lie, Amaka's sex game was good back college. Anyway, let me switch the topic of our conversation. What is Chi Chi's plan in terms of job prospects after she walks the stage today?"

"That is the million-dollar question. Right now, she is working on Sade's campaign, so depending on if she wins this election, maybe she will have a role on her staff or something like that. We will see what happens."

Nnamdi said, "So how is everything going with your job situation? What is your next move?"

Obi responded, "Shit bro, I am just hoping to become a permanent employee very soon to get these company benefits. Even though Obamacare has been a God-send, I could get even lower deductibles and premiums through my job."

Nnamdi chuckled. "Obi, you went from a dude who was trying to change the world to now having the big decision of picking between a PPO or HMO plan."

Obi said, "Bro that is how life is right now. You go from being an idealist to being a realist. But I know one thing is for certain, I will never buy a minivan. I gotta keep my swag game at a high level. You can't be cool bumping your music in a Nissan Quest."

Both men laughed as they finally pulled up to the University of Houston campus to park. Once there, they linked back up with Nkechi and her parents. Nkechi left the group as she headed towards another entrance at Hofheinz Pavilion where the graduates were meeting at. Obi started looking at how much his alma mater had changed. There were new buildings, parking garages, and a bunch of new places for the students to eat that didn't exist when he was a student there. But even with the new facelift that the school had received, for Obi, every time he stepped onto campus, it reminded him of how far he had come from being that skinny 18-year-old kid who was searching for himself. This was where he had grown up and had some of the best years of his life.

Nnamdi finally interrupted his daydreaming, "Dang, Obi, I didn't know U of H had all of this money. The school looks nice as hell."

Obi laughed and said, "Yea, hopefully, the football and basketball teams can follow suit and get good by the time Ike gets into elementary school, so I can take him to some games occasionally."

They walked towards the main entrance of the pavilion where Obi's parents and his sister were waiting for them. Both sets of parents gave each other hugs and greetings before they all went in to find seats. Just as they were about to head inside to find places to sit, Obi heard someone shout his name. He turned around to find Sade walking very quickly towards him. While everybody went inside, Obi stayed outside so he could meet up with her.

Nnamdi went inside but came back because he wanted to get a glimpse of what Sade looked like in person. He had only seen pictures that Obi had shown him of her.

When Obi saw Nnamdi coming towards him, he shook his head with a smile and said, "Zik, you just couldn't resist could you?"

Nnamdi tried to act like he didn't know what Obi was talking about at first. But finally said to Obi, "A brotha taking in some eye candy ain't never hurt anybody, did it?"

When Sade finally reached them, she was wearing a pair of Gucci sunglasses to go along with her black dress pants and blue blouse. Sade immediately gave Obi a hug and then introduced herself to Nnamdi. As they were walking inside, Sade went in first, followed by Nnamdi and then Obi. Nnamdi was checking out Sade's booty while giving Obi a thumbs-up for approval.

Obi laughed. Then whispering to Nnamdi, he said, "Bro, you are all the way clowning right now man. How would you be acting if Ogechi was here?"

Nnamdi smiled and said, "I would be doing the same thing, just more discreetly."

Once they got inside, Obi sent Chinwe a text message to see what section they were sitting in. She stated that there weren't any empty seats near them. As they were walking around trying to look for some available seats, Nnamdi and Sade struck up a conversation.

"Obi tells me that you, him, and Nkechi rolled pretty thick back in your law school days. Any embarrassing stories about them that you would like to share?"

Nnamdi glanced at Obi with a smile and said to Sade, "Well, there was that one time when Obi and Nkechi..." Nnamdi caught himself from saying what he was going to say and said, "I think I will save that story for another time."

Sade laughed and said, "Obi, your boy must have a whole bunch of dirt on you."

Obi responded, "Sade, don't let Nnamdi mess with you. He just likes to draw attention to himself."

Sade continued talking to Nnamdi, "I hear that you are about to get married at the beginning of next year. Congratulations on that, are you ready to take the big plunge?"

Nnamdi quickly responded, "Definitely, I have had a great run, but it's time to hang up my bachelor jersey."

"That is good to hear because there are a lot of single, attractive, and educated black women in the D.C. area and a man can get caught up if he doesn't have his head screwed on right."

"You are 100% correct on that matter. I know some cats who have lost good women because of what you just said. The excessive pursuit of women is the downfall of most men."

Before anybody could respond, it was announced that Nkechi's group would be next to cross the stage. By this time, they had gone back to the section where Obi and Nkechi's family was seated and found some empty seats.

The ceremony did not last as long as they had expected it to. It was over in about two hours. They all exited the commencement venue together and found a gathering spot and waited for Nkechi to join them. While they waited, Sade and Nkechi's father were engaged in conversation, as was everybody else.

"Sade, my daughter, and my son-in-law have been singing your praises for quite some time. I have been quite impressed with the conversation that I have been having with you. I feel like I am talking with the potential first Nigerian American president of the U.S. right now."

Sade blushed. "Sir, thank you for seeing me in that light. But right now, I am just hoping to win this city council election in November."

"I am very sure that you will win. I will be donating to your campaign as well. Also, when I get back to New York I am going to talk with my friends about donating too. I strongly believe that when a Nigerian happens to be running for political office, we have to rally around that person with our votes and our wallets."

"Mr. Okoye, thank you so much for your support. These campaigns aren't cheap to run by any stretch of the imagination."

After that, everybody was just talking amongst themselves waiting for Nkechi to come out. Nkechi's mother approached Sade and asked her, "So my dear, you are a very beautiful and smart woman, I know you are dating somebody I assume?"

"Unfortunately, Mrs. Okoye, the love bug hasn't struck me yet. But I am always open to meeting a nice guy. If only there were more guys like Obi to go around, then I would be in a good situation."

Chinwe was talking with her parents when she overheard Sade's comment.

"Sade, I know that you mean well, but please don't pump my brother's head up any further, if it gets any bigger it might explode."

Nkechi's father said, "Sade, I am very happy to have a son-in-law like Obi. I can sleep well knowing that my daughter and grandson are in good hands."

After that exchange, Obi and Sade locked eyes for only a moment. She smiled and tried to be respectful, but she couldn't help undressing him with her eyes. Obi looked out of the corner of his eye to make sure nobody else was noticing what was going on. He quickly raised his eyebrows up to signify to her that he knew what she was doing. Shortly after that Nkechi appeared, still wearing her graduation gown and cap. She was quickly mobbed with hugs and congratulations by her parents, then Obi and Ike, followed by Obi's parents, Chinwe, Nnamdi, and then Sade.

"Let's get these pictures out of the way. It is too hot out here and my feet are hurting from being in these heels all day."

Everybody took their turn with taking pictures with Nkechi. Once that was finished they started to plan their next move.

Obi's mother said, "Everybody will be heading back to our house to eat and to continue the celebration of Nkechi's big accomplishment." As they started to disperse, Nkechi said to Sade, "You are welcome to come if you want."

Sade nervously responded, "Are you sure that would be fine? I don't want to interrupt you guys' family time or anything like that."

Nkechi responded to her, "Yes, I would love for you to come hang out."

Obi's parents felt a little bit awkward when they were around Sade because of her past dealings with their son. But they didn't want to make the situation weird, so they didn't object to Nkechi's invite to Sade. As Obi and Nnamdi were walking back to the car, Obi asked him about how Ogechi was doing.

"I spoke with her this morning when I got back to my hotel. She is doing well and sends her regards to everyone. She said she will call Chi Chi later this evening."

Once they got into the car, Obi asked him, "So what is up with the situation with her dad? Will he be at the wedding or not?"

Nnamdi shook his head and said, "Bro that is the million-dollar question right now. Ogechi has been on some G-classified status towards me about the situation with her father. Hell, I still don't even know her dad's name or what state he lives in."

Obi responded, "Hopefully, you will learn some more information about him before the wedding."

"Yea, I think he will be coming up to visit her in the next month or so. I will probably finally meet him this time around."

"Well, all I know is that it will be a very interesting exchange when it does happen between you and her dad. I couldn't even imagine being in that type of situation," Obi said.

Nnamdi responded, "Yea, but I know this whole thing has been very tough on Ogechi. She really doesn't have anybody that can relate to what she is going through."

"So anyway, your girl Sade was looking sexy as hell today. I ain't even going to lie to you, her booty had me in a daze on the real."

Obi started laughing and said, "Zik, you are ignorant, you know that, right? But that is Sade being Sade. I can't even lie, outside of Nkechi, I haven't enjoyed another woman's company more than I did Sade's.

Nnamdi was quiet for a moment after that. He later said, "Obi, that is deep bro. You guys really had a strong connection back then. Anyway, I am thinking about meeting up Amaka for lunch tomorrow, but I don't know if that would be a good idea. One thing can lead to another and we will start having sex."

"Just tell her that you are engaged," Obi suggested to Nnamdi. "Once you say that, she won't want to do anything to mess up your situation. But you should still try and catch up with her. Life is short, bro, who knows when your paths will cross again."

Nnamdi nodded in agreement. They decided to make a quick stop at the liquor store. While they were in there, Obi picked up two 12 packs of Heineken along with a bottle of Crown Royal and Hennessey. Then they headed over to Obi's parents' house. When Obi and Nnamdi walked inside, they saw that everybody was carrying along with one another. Obi noticed that Ugo, Nkechi's dad, and Sade were in the living room talking with each other. When Uncle Ugo saw Obi headed toward the kitchen with the drinks, he yelled in his direction,

"Obi, did I ever tell you that I helped Sade's father on his first campaign for municipal judge many years ago?"

Even though Obi already knew the answer was yes, he didn't want to make his uncle look bad. "Really? I didn't know that."

Soon, lunch was ready and everyone was busy coming in and out of the kitchen, fixing themselves a plate to eat.

Obi was walking past the bathroom when he saw Nkechi changing Ike's diaper. She laughed when she saw him. "This is my graduation day, I am not supposed to do this. But a mother's work never ends."

"I am happy that you are doing it, because you know I am terrible at changing diapers."

"It is my fault, I have spoiled you by not letting you in on this. But best believe that when Ike gets ready to potty train, you will not be getting off that easy."

Obi walked with Nkechi to Obi's old bedroom to lay Ike down so he could take a nap. As Nkechi was trying to leave the room, Obi blocked the doorway.

"Obi, stop playing and move out of the way."

"I was thinking that maybe we could get a quickie in before Ike wakes up."

Nkechi laughed and said, "Honey, are you out of your mind right now? Do you know how bad it would be if somebody caught us having sex in the house?"

Obi smirked, "Yep, doesn't it sound fun and daring. Let's be spontaneous for once in our marriage. I did some research and quite a few couples have had sex in their parents' or in-laws' house."

She thought about it for a minute and leaned toward Obi and started kissing him on his neck and then on his lips. Obi was caught off guard by Nkechi's aggressiveness, but he soon gathered himself and started taking off her clothes.

They tried to be as quiet as possible so as not to wake the baby. At one point, Obi had to put his hand over Nkechi's mouth when she started moaning too loudly. After about thirty minutes, Nkechi had an orgasm. While they both lay on the floor naked, Obi asked Nkechi whether she was surprised at what they had just done.

"I usually would never do anything like this, but I graduated today and I was horny," Nkechi said, giggling. "Also, with my parents staying with us, we barely have a free moment to ourselves, so I decided to just do it."

Obi smiled and said, "You won't get any complaints out of me."

Obi got dressed and left the room while Nkechi stayed with Ike. They didn't think anyone else in the house knew what they were doing, but they didn't want to look too suspicious. When he got into the living room, he saw that everybody was still talking. By this time Nnamdi and Chinwe had joined the conversation with Uncle Ugo, Sade, and Nkechi's father.

"I can't wait for the Fela show tomorrow. I heard that they have made the stage to resemble *The Shrine*, the place where he used to perform in Lagos."

Obi's mother and mother-in-law were talking in the kitchen. His father was dosing off in his bedroom. After some time, Nkechi came out for the bedroom. Everybody chatted for a little while longer before Sade asked for permission to leave. Obi and Nkechi walked her to her car.

"I really appreciate you spending the day with me, Sade," Nkechi said to Sade who was opening her car door.

She reached into the passenger seat for a package and handed it to Nkechi. Nkechi hugged her. "Thanks, Sade. Now that I am finished with school, my next goal is to find you a man. You deserve to have somebody to spend your time with."

Sade laughed and said, "Yea, I wouldn't mind having some company besides my dog. I usually don't let folks playing matchmaker for me, but I will let you give it a shot."

Sade gave Obi a quick friendly hug before she got into her car to leave. She had to resist the urge of giving an intimate hug in Nkechi's presence. After she drove off, Obi and Nkechi walked back into the house and Nkechi said: "If I happen to die or go batshit crazy, I give you full permission to mess with Sade."

Obi laughed off her comment and said, "Chi Chi, stop being silly."

"Honey, I am dead ass serious. Honestly, if you told me that you had sex with her back in the day it wouldn't bother me at all."

Obi wasn't going to fall for that stunt. "What about me and Tamika being together?"

Nkechi gave a devilish laugh and said, "I will come back from the dead and haunt your dreams if that shit ever happens."

When it was time for everyone to start leaving, Obi and Nnamdi headed out to Obi's car. Again, Nkechi would drive home in her car with her parents and Ike.

"Obi, I strongly believe that Chi Chi knows you and Sade had sex before," Nnamdi said to Obi when they were a few minutes into their journey. She is just waiting for you to come out and tell her. Women have a sixth sense about shit like this."

"Bro, we will see how it turns out in due time. So, what's up with you and Amaka?"

"She was texting me the whole time we were at your folks' house. I will probably meet up with her for lunch tomorrow. She is bringing her cousin along so that saves a nigga from fucking up."

Obi laughed. "This might be the first time where having a third wheel is actually a good thing."

When they arrived at Obi's place, Nnamdi hung around for a few minutes before heading back to his hotel. Everyone soon called it a night, it had been a long and busy day.

"Hey, I forgot to mention to you that Sade wants me to go with her to the Democratic National Convention in September. I think it will be held in Charlotte, North Carolina," Nkechi said to Obi while they were lying in bed.

"That is cool. It will be a great thing for you to check out."

"You are the best," Nkechi said. "Also, don't worry about the cost, I will find a way to pay for it."

"Chi Chi, don't worry about the money. We will get everything figured out before then."

Nkechi eventually drifted off the sleep. Obi started to realize that his mother and father didn't really interact with each other for pretty much the whole day. He was a bit concerned by it, but he wasn't going to inquire about their issues. He decided to just chalk it up to the highs and lows of being married for over thirty-five years.

CHAPTER EIGHT

Thank you for applying with our company, the computer-generated email began. *We have reviewed your qualifications and even though they are highly impressive, unfortunately, you were not selected for a face to face interview with us at this time. We wish you the very best in your job search.* Nkechi read and felt deflated all over again.

It was the middle of August and she was now three months removed from graduation, but no closer to landing a job. Even though Nkechi tried to stay positive about the situation, pessimism started to creep slowly into her mind. On this day, Obi had just arrived home from work. By the look on Nkechi's face, he knew that something was bothering her.

"How was your day today, honey?" Obi asked after giving her a hug and a kiss.

Nkechi sighed. "If you want me to be honest, it has been horrible. Another company has sent me a rejection email. I know that I am setting some type of record for the number of rejections sent to a prospective employee."

"Chi Chi, don't be too hard on yourself. We just have to continue to have faith that something will open up for you soon."

Nkechi was silent for a moment before responding, "I guess you are right. Anyway, I still need to go to the mall and buy some new clothes and shoes for this Charlotte trip."

Obi was happy that the Democratic Convention was approaching so Nkechi could at least get away for a couple of days and preoccupy her mind with other things beyond her dismal job prospects.

Later that evening, Obi and Nkechi were both watching CNN as they showed a clip of Obama's 2004 keynote speech that he gave at the Democratic National Convention. Obi laughed and said, "Wow, I can't believe it has been eight years since Obama became an instant overnight celebrity."

"I still remember calling you and Nnamdi on a three-way call during the speech and saying that God had revealed to us who the first black president of the U.S. will be. But even still who could have imagined that Obama would be the nominee of the Democratic Party four short years later," Nkechi said.

"I remember going to The Chill Spot with Chike, Chinwe, and Uncle Ugo to watch Obama give his nomination speech from Denver in 2008. The place was standing room only by the time we arrived, "Obi said. "As I was feeling in awe at that moment, my uncle was glued to every word that Obama was delivering. During the speech, I remember Uncle Ugo blurting out something to the effect of, "I can't believe what I am watching on this television. After I worked on Jesse Jackson's campaign in 1988, I didn't believe that this country would give a black man a shot to be their president." Another older black man who was standing next to my uncle patted him on the shoulder and said, "My brotha, I never thought I would live to see this moment." The man took off his glasses as tears started flowing down his face.

Uncle Ugo had handed the man a napkin to dry up his face. The two men talked amongst themselves for about five minutes or so. Once the speech was over, everybody headed for the exits. While we were walking toward the car, Uncle Ugo said to us, "When I first came to this country, if you had told me that a man who had a Kenyan father might become America's first black president, I would have laughed at the person mercilessly. For Obama to rise at the time that he has, it can only be God's doing."

Uncle Ugo was very much wrapped up in the idealism of Obama because it made him harken back to his younger self. As he looked upon his son, niece, and nephew, he had this big smile on his face. When Chike asked him why he was so happy, Uncle Ugo had said something like, "I should admit my son, that for the first time in my life, I feel optimistic about the future. You guys must understand that if Obama wins this election in November, America will be forced to look at itself differently. The image of a black family in the White House will be very symbolic. When you guys become parents, you will be able to tell your kids with all honesty that every opportunity they ever dreamed of pursuing is available to them, and not have to be lying when you say it."

Obi's mind finally drifted back into the present, and he was reminded of how rough the last four years had been for the Obama presidency.

"All of the slogans, like *Yes We Can* and *Hope and Change,* which defined that 2008 campaign, are now a thing of the past. The sober reality right now is that Obama is an embattled president who is trying to eke out an election victory over Mitt Romney to uphold his legacy. The post-racial America that some people in the media were saying Obama was going to usher in never happened. We still can't have an honest conversation with white people about race right now. Even the new political discourse that Obama was supposed to bring to the country never happened because the Republicans were fiercely against any policy agenda that his administration presented to them," Nkechi said somberly.

"Well, the one thing that nobody can take away from Barack and Michelle Obama is their lasting impact on black people in this country. I am not a political prognosticator by any means, but I know black people will be voting in droves to help make sure Obama gets another term in office. Regardless of whether we agreed with him on all his policies or not, we are too emotionally invested as a people to not stay the course."

"That's true. So, how are things going for Sade with election day being under three months away?" Obi asked Nkechi.

"Everything is going well so far. Just trying to help with fund-raising and policy stuff. I have to respect Sade, running for political office is way harder than I would have ever thought. You have to meet so many various groups and constituencies."

"Yea, the shit is no joke on the real. How is the outreach with the Nigerian community? Hopefully, she has hit some of our churches and social organizations."

"I remember at our last meeting talking about how to approach our people. I told them to try and put up posters in Nigerian grocery stores and businesses in the city along with running commercials on the local Nigerian television station. They also need to try and do some town hall meetings with the various Nigerian social organizations. I also suggested that she get in contact with the Nigerian Student Association at University of Houston as well."

Obi nodded his head in agreement to everything she was saying. "Chi Chi, you are giving her some great advice. The Nigerian vote is a hidden gem that is waiting to be tapped. Sade could mobilize a good amount of our people who never paid too much attention to local politics to get excited about her campaign solely based on her being Nigerian," Obi said.

"Only time will tell how everything turns out. I know that a few young Nigerian professionals are planning a fundraiser for Sade at the end of September."

Obi laughed and said, "That event is exactly two weeks before Nnamdi's bachelor party in Atlanta."

Nkechi sighed. "Don't remind me of all the debauchery you guys will be getting into out there. I know that you guys are going to have strippers, so I don't even have to ask you about that."

Obi tried to downplay Nkechi's comment. "Chi Chi, what type of man do you take me for? The only woman's body I lust after is yours."

"Honey, I have seen your porn collection that you try to hide under this special folder on your laptop. You are very fond of lusting after other women's bodies beyond mine. So, what you just said earlier is total bullshit. But you are a man, so what am I really supposed to expect?"

Obi knew he was fighting a losing battle, so he did not respond. Nkechi continued: "Speaking of Zik, how is everything going with him? Have you talked to him about meeting up with Ogechi's father?"

"I have been texting back and forth with him during the last month or so, but I haven't had a phone conversation with him yet about the situation you are talking about."

"Why don't we call him right now to see what he has to say about it?"

Obi said to her, "I see that somebody is really nosey suddenly. Since you are so eager, I will go ahead and give Zik a call later this evening."

They watched television for a few more minutes before heading to the kitchen to eat dinner. Nkechi had made spaghetti and pork chops with a side of tossed salad. As much as Obi loved eating Nigerian food, he was happy for a change every once in a while. While they were at the table, the conversation soon turned to Obi's sister.

Obi asked Nkechi between chewing a pork chop, "How are things going with Chinwe and this Ola guy? I know that she shares more information with you than she does with me."

She rubbed his hand softly and said sarcastically, "Ah, I see you trying to be such a concerned big brother. I love it when you show your sensitive side. Anyway, dude seems like a keeper. She is planning on inviting him to your parents' house for dinner one of these weekends."

"Damn Chi Chi, I was supposed to screen this dude before he meets my folks. Weezy is breaking all types of protocol right now."

Nkechi sighed and said, "So instead of being excited about your sister's happiness, I see you have made everything all about you like most men usually do. Honestly, the only real question that you want to know is if Ola is having sex with your sister. Am I right or am I wrong?"

In the back of Obi's mind, he knew that his sister was probably having sex with this dude and probably had sex with other guys she dated. But most men found it hard to fathom the thought of their own sisters or daughters having sex with anybody. Even though these same men didn't have a problem having sex with someone else's sister or daughter. Obi slyly dodged the question and said, "I am just trying to see if this dude got any womanizing traits in him. You know that I have a sixth sense for spotting these types of things."

Nkechi laughed and said, "Obi, please stop trying to flatter yourself. Anyway, let's give Zik a call before it gets too late."

Obi got his phone and made the call. Ogechi picked up the phone.

"Hey, Obi how are you doing?"

"I am doing well, just relaxing at home with Chi Chi."

Nkechi turned Obi's phone to speaker mode and said to Ogechi, "My sister, I hope everything is well with you."

Ogechi responded by saying, "Wow, it is great to hear from the both of you at the same time. Zik is in the bathroom and will be out in a minute."

Ogechi and Nkechi started talking about wedding stuff and plans for the bachelorette party and bridal shower. As the two women were finishing up their conversation, Nnamdi came on the line, "Hey Chi Chi, hey Obi, I see my woman has been keeping you guys preoccupied while I was away from my phone."

Obi laughed and said to Nnamdi, "Bro, you saved me from all of this woman talk. I thank God every day that he made me a man."

Ogechi laughed and said, "Chi Chi, you better straighten out your man real quick. I got his boy on a tight leash."

Obi blurted out, "Dang Zik, your woman has already put the clamps down on you? I guess I need to ask her for your permission to go to ATL for our guys' trip then."

"Obi, stop being silly. Nnamdi is a grown ass Naija man. He can come and go as he pleases. But I better not find out any extra foolishness is going on during his bachelor party weekend. If I do, it won't be pretty for either you or Zik."

Nkechi jumped in and said, "Ogechi, I had the same talk with Obi. You know these men go out of town and start trying to relive their 20s forgetting that they aren't in college anymore."

"Thanks for your support, Chi Chi," Ogechi said to Nkechi. "Anyway, I have some stuff to take care of so I will let you guys finish your conversation."

Nnamdi, Obi, and Nkechi continued talking amongst themselves until the discussion finally turned to Nnamdi's meeting with Ogechi's father. "Did you win over her dad with your charming personality yet?"

"I see you got jokes, Obi," Nnamdi said, laughing. "But in all seriousness, I didn't get to meet him. He had to cancel his trip at the last minute."

"Damn, this is a crazy ass situation. The way things are going you might not see him until the weekend of the wedding. How is Ogechi handling this whole thing?"

"I guess she is handling it the best way that she can. I know her mom isn't too thrilled about having him come around, but she knows that it is Ogechi's decision to try and build a relationship with her father."

Nkechi said, "Well, I know that everything will work itself out at the end of the day."

"Only time will tell on that matter," Nnamdi said softly. "Anyway, I will get back with you guys later. Chi Chi, I will hit you up in the next couple of weeks about trying to meet up with you in Charlotte."

Once they got off the phone, Nkechi went to get Ike ready for bed. Obi was in the living room when he received a text message from Tamika.

"Hey, Obi. How are you doing, I haven't heard from u in a minute? I hope all is well with u."

"I am doing well. Just living life and doing the family thing."

"That is great to hear. You have been in my thoughts for the last couple of days, so I decided to reach out to you."

"Ok, no problem."

Then a few minutes later, Tamika wrote back.

"Well, I am over here wearing nothing but my t-shirt and panties drinking some red wine and feeling really horny right now."

Obi was about to reply when Nkechi came back into the room and sat right next to him. Obi calmly put his phone on the table.

"Who were you on the phone with?" she asked.

"I was just sending a message to my brother over Facebook to see what he was doing. We were just chatting for the most part."

Nkechi smiled and said, "Oh ok, I thought you might have been talking to one of your side chicks."

Obi snapped his fingers and said, "Dang, I forgot to tell you that Crystal said hello and wants to know if you would grant me permission to see her next week."

Nkechi shoved Obi roughly and said, "You play way too much, honey. I don't even like the thought of another woman messing with you even if you are just joking around."

"So, speaking of other women, has Sade been receptive to some of your advice on dating?"

"I will just say this; President Obama may not be good enough to meet Sade's standards. Sometimes I get the feeling that she will be one of those very successful women who never gets married. I think that she wants to date and marry the male version of herself," Nkechi said.

Obi smiled. "Chi Chi, I will say this about Sade, at the end of the day she respects people who are completely honest with her. Because she is smart and attractive, a lot of people rarely challenge her on her views. I feel that she likes you because you will tell her about herself and not be afraid to say so."

Nkechi responded, "Obi, all I can say is that I hope she comes across some guys she might be interested in at the convention. Anyway, I am about to take a shower and get ready for bed. I will see you in the bedroom in a little bit."

Obi waited for Nkechi to get into the bedroom before looking at his phone again. Tamika had sent another message.

> *"Have a good night sleep. Hopefully, you make it into my dreams tonight."*

Obi smiled but did not respond. Instead, he turned his attention to the television where ESPN was showing sports news. About thirty minutes later, he headed to bed.

The next couple of weeks went by very quickly on the lead up to Nkechi's trip to Charlotte for the convention. Sade let Nkechi know beforehand that she could share a room with her and not have to worry about the hotel expenses. On the day that Nkechi was to travel, Ike sensed that she would be leaving and started clinging on to her more than he usually did. This was going to be the first time since Ike was born that Nkechi would be away from him for more than a couple of hours. As Nkechi carried Ike in her arms, Obi said, "I see my son is a mama's boy."

"Your sister says that you and your brother were mama's boys growing up. I guess it runs in your family. But don't feel bad, if we have a girl, she will have you wrapped around her little finger."

Obi was surprised to hear her talk about the possibility of having more kids. Neither one of them had mentioned kids in the last three months or so. Obi wanted to try and get her to expound on her answer, but he felt that it wasn't the right time to have that discussion, so instead, he said, "Chi Chi, I have seen the way your father goes out of his way for you and the way my father has treated Chinwe, and I have to agree with you on what you have said."

Obi loaded Nkechi's suitcases into the trunk of the car and the three of them headed to the airport. Before they set off, Obi received a text message from Nnamdi asking Obi to call him when he had a moment. Once they got on the road, Nkechi immediately put the AC on.

"I hope the weather in Charlotte is not as humid as it is out here," she said. "Even though I have lived in Houston for almost three years, the summer heat continues to be hard for me to deal with."

While they were still driving, Kanye West's song, *Through the Wire* came on the radio. Obi and Nkechi started singing the verses to the song in unison. Once the song was over, Obi said, "Damn that was the joint back in the day. I remember listening to this on *The College Dropout* album almost every day for almost a month straight."

Nkechi responded, "Obi, I do have to give you credit for convincing me to give Kanye's album a chance. I wasn't a huge fan of his in the beginning, but his sound wore on me over time. I still remember guys started wearing a blazer with their jeans because of Kanye."

Obi smiled and said, "Sometimes I wish we could go back to that period in our lives if only for one day."

Nkechi patted Obi on his lap as a sign of her agreement. After about five minutes she said, "That is why I tell some of my younger cousins to enjoy being young and free. Sometimes, we get so caught up in this race to reach a certain status in our lives that when we finally achieve our goal, it never feels the way we thought it would. But then again, I also realize that you have to do some things that you don't like to do to eventually find out what you really love to do."

Obi was about to respond, but Nkechi's phone started ringing. When she picked it up it was Sade on the line. Sade wanted to know how far Nkechi and Obi were from the airport. They were scheduled to be on the same flight to Charlotte. Nkechi told her that she was about to pull into the airport entrance in a couple of minutes and hung up the phone.

Then Nkechi glanced at Ike in the back seat as he was in his own world playing with his toys. After that, she glanced at Obi who was bobbing his head to another song on the radio. Even though she still felt at a crossroads in her life, Nkechi took solace in the fact that she had her son and husband to give her the strength that she needed. Having someone to share the ups and downs of life with was very important.

At the airport, Nkechi checked in one of her suitcases, and the three of them sat down for a while before Nkechi had to go through the security line. While she was playing with Ike on her lap, Nkechi said, "I am going to miss my two favorite guys in the world. I hope that you guys don't miss me too much now."

Obi laughed and said, "Chi Chi, stop being overdramatic. You are only going to be gone for a few days."

Nkechi shook her head and said, "Obi, you really know how to make a woman feel wanted I see."

"Honey, you are too gullible. You know damn well that I am going to miss the heck out of you. I thank God that my mom and Chinwe have volunteered to help me out with Ike."

Fifteen minutes passed before it was time for Nkechi to get going. Obi kissed her on the cheek as they said their goodbyes to each other. Then Nkechi looked at Ike and said, "Honey, mommy is going to be leaving you now, but I will be back soon."

As Obi tried to take Ike from Nkechi's lap, he started clutching onto her chest and refused to let go. Once Obi got Ike in his arms, Ike began to wail. Nkechi couldn't help herself as tears welled up in her eyes. This was more difficult than she had expected. Eventually, she started walking away from Obi and Ike.

An older black woman who was observing the family dynamics said to Nkechi once they were in the security line, "It never gets easy leaving our kids, no matter how old they are."

Nkechi looked in the direction of Obi and Ike one last time and saw that Ike had stopped and was now waving at her. Once she saw that, Nkechi started to feel a little bit better and waved back at them. Obi took one look at Ike and finally realized that he would be taking care of his son by himself for a week. He started to feel a knot in his stomach as he carried Ike out of the airport and back to the car.

It also didn't help that Ike was very emotional when Nkechi was about to leave him. Even though Obi was a nonchalant guy, for the most part, he did want Ike to feel the same level of emotion about him when he wasn't around. The car ride was quiet without Nkechi's conversation to keep Obi preoccupied. Once he got home, Obi carried Ike to the bedroom and laid him down for his nap. A few minutes after that he received a text message from

Nkechi stating that the plane was about to take off for Charlotte. Obi texted back that he loved her and wished her a safe trip.

A few minutes later Obi nodded off and slept for about half an hour. When he woke up, he checked his phone and saw that he had received another text message from Nnamdi asking him if he could talk. Once he got himself together, Obi called Nnamdi.

"Bro, you won't believe who I crossed paths with a few days ago," Nnamdi said to Obi.

Obi threw out some random names of people that Nnamdi said weren't correct. "Does the name Abisola ring a bell to you?"

As Obi was wracking his brain trying to remember who the person was, Nnamdi finally said to him, "Bro, it's that chick you met at the club when I was out there in May. She is cool with one of Ogechi's cousins."

Obi's eyes widened once he started visualizing Abisola. He said, "Damn Zik, I remember exactly who she is now. She saw you all hugged up on Amaka that night and thought that was your girl."

"Dude, I can't even front, I was a little shook when they showed up at the house. Abisola could have called me out fair and square, but she just played it off like she didn't even know me."

"Bro, she showed mad love by not snitching on you."

Nnamdi said, "You ain't never lied about that. I wanted to get her phone number to straighten out things with her and see how I could help her out, but Ogechi is kind of jealous on the low, so I didn't want to start any wahala. Especially with the wedding coming up, she is starting to turn into a mad woman."

"Yea, I feel you on that. I think I still have Abisola's contact information so I will text it to you later."

"Bro, do you think God intended for man to only be with one woman for the rest of his life?" Nnamdi asked Obi out of the blue.

Obi thought about the question for a minute before saying to Nnamdi, "In my humble opinion, I don't think that men were ever designed to be in monogamous relationships, but over time we have been conditioned to accept that lifestyle by society. Also, if guys would be honest with themselves, we just fantasize about the sexual elements of polygamy. But if I had to come home every day and deal with the emotional elements of Chi Chi and another woman, I would lose my God damn mind."

Nnamdi laughed uncontrollably. "Obi, you are crazy as hell. I still don't know how our great grandfathers were able to have multiple wives back in the day. But in retrospect, they lived in a far different world and culture than the one we live in today."

"Bro, I am just keeping it real. I advise every dude to take their time before they get married," Obi said. "On one hand, I can personally say that being a father and husband is probably one of the most rewarding experiences of my life. But I also see how easy it is for folks to get a divorced as well. Sometimes you want to just say "fuck it" and think another woman will understand you better than your wife does. But then you realize that all women expect too much from men and that it is better to make it work with the one that you already have."

"My nigga, you sound like this old school white guy from my job. He always complains about how he should have made it work with his ex-wife and now he is paying her child support for their two kids. It is sad to see how a man can go from seeing his children every day in his house to only being able to see them every other weekend, and for two months or so during the summer, after a divorce."

Obi responded, "Zik, that is the world that we live in, unfortunately. Anyway, I need to check on Ike. I will hit you up later in the week."

For the rest of the day, Obi spent time with Ike and talked with Nkechi once she landed in Charlotte later in the evening.

As the rest of the week progressed, Obi would occasionally watch some of the Democratic Convention on television when he got home from work. Nkechi was also updating him with all the things she and Sade were doing. She even got to meet some of Sade's friends who were working for the Obama administration. Nkechi also told Obi how much she and Sade were bonding with each other on a personal level. Even though Obi was happy that she was enjoying herself, he wondered if Sade would disclose their previous relationship to Nkechi. He began to wonder if the idea of not telling Nkechi about the matter was now the right decision.

As Obi was pondering the situation, he heard a knock on his door. At first, he wasn't sure who it was, but then he realized that Chinwe told him she would be stopping by to see him and Ike. When he opened the door and she came in, Ike came running off the couch to embrace her.

Obi laughed and said, "Well, I know one thing for sure, my son loves his auntie a whole lot."

Chinwe responded, "I love him immensely as well. He will always unofficially be my first child."

She also brought some food that she had cooked for them. She placed it in the fridge in the kitchen and came back out to the living room.

"What did you bring over," Obi asked her when she sat down. "I am starving for real."

Chinwe said, "I made some plantain and moi moi. I hope you like it, hopefully, it meets your level of expectation. I know that you are a tough critic of everybody's cooking except for our mother's. Only God knows how Chi Chi puts up with you. All I can say is that you are lucky you aren't married to a woman like me."

Obi smiled, "Aren't you still single though?"

Chinwe threw the throw pillow at him as he got up and made his way into the kitchen. He brought out plates for them to eat. Chinwe followed with Ike.

"I always know that bringing up your singlehood gets under your skin," Obi said. "Anyway, I appreciate you looking out for me as you always do." Obi gave her a playful peck on the cheek.

While they were eating, Obama was giving his re-nomination speech at the convention.

Chinwe said, "I wonder; if black women had to choose between Michelle or Barack who would they pick?"

Obi shook his head and said, "That is an easy question to answer, they would take Michelle easily. Black women love her more than they do him."

"Yea, I agree with you. I appreciate everything that Barack has done for the country and black people in general, but having a black First Lady is just utter worldly to me. She is his secret weapon, to be honest. Even though Michelle has two Ivy League degrees, she comes across as so down to Earth. I read in one magazine that she still buys her clothes from Target and the Gap."

Obi responded, "Mrs. Obama wears her blackness on her sleeves, which I feel is a great thing. She has elevated the status of black women not just in this country, but all over the world."

Chinwe said, "I can honestly say that I am happy to have been born during this time in world history. We have gotten a chance to witness the Obama era with our own eyes."

Obi looked down at Ike who was eating and watching television without a care in the world. "Weezy, I agree with you. That is why making Ike's middle name Barack was so important to me and Chi Chi. When he gets older we will be able to tell him the significance and power behind both of his names."

"I know one thing for sure, whenever I have kids I am not giving them a European name. Also, I am going to make sure that their teachers pronounce their names right. If we have to know how to say some of these German and Russian names, then they need to learn ours as well."

"Dang, Weezy, I see that you have a Pan African streak running through you. Don't let mom find out or she will start calling you a radical."

Chinwe sighed, "Don't get me started on her. Since she and dad met Ola, all that she keeps bringing up is to be mindful of Yoruba men. I keep telling her that he was born in Chicago and has been to Nigeria less than five times in his whole life. I thought she would be happy that I was dating a Nigerian guy at least."

Obi shook his head and said, "Weezy, you will soon find out that parents want you to be with the person that they think is the right fit for you. I know mom be tripping because Chi Chi isn't into church and religion like she is. Sometimes she feels like I should be bothered by it, but the truth of the matter is that I really don't care about it too much. In the end, do what makes you happy, because mom will grudgingly deal with whatever relationship that you are in."

Chinwe responded, "Obi, I hear where you are coming from. Speaking of which, how is Nkechi doing in Charlotte? I know she is meeting a lot of influential people out there."

"Yes, she is. I know Nkechi told me that she and Sade have done some partying while they have been out there as well."

"Dang, I see that she and Sade seem like they are growing closer by the day. You might want to tell Nkechi about you and Sade before she finds out from her. No woman wants to be blindsided by this kind of secret from their husband."

Obi hesitated for a while and then said, "Weezy, I was going to ask for your opinion on that matter, but it seems like you have already given it to me. I just have to find the right way to tell Chi Chi about it."

Chinwe laughed and said, "Well if things take a turn for the worst between you guys because of it, I will try and negotiate with Nkechi to get visitation rights to see Ike."

Obi shook his head and said, "Weezy, you play around too damn much."

Once the speech was over, Obi and Chinwe continued talking while sipping on a few bottles of red wine. When Chinwe tried to leave, Obi could look at her and tell that she was drunk and in no condition to drive. He ended up convincing her to spend the night at his place. Not too long afterward, Chinwe fell asleep on the couch.

Obi put Ike to sleep and went to bed. During the night, he woke up feeling kind of horny. It had been a few weeks since him and Nkechi had had sex. He got up to get his computer so he could masturbate quickly. He was about to start when he heard a sound coming from the living room.

He thought it might be Chinwe moving around so he paid it no mind. Once he finished jacking off, he heard the sound he had heard earlier, this time it was louder. Obi decided to see what was going on. When he turned on the lights, Obi saw his sister with no clothes on and a vibrator next to her. Chinwe quickly threw on her shirt and underwear and said, "Obi, I am so embarrassed right now. I didn't know that I had gotten so loud."

Obi was at a loss for words and just said, "Nah, it's cool. Good night." As Obi went back to his bed, he was a bit taken aback. He wasn't under some illusion that his sister wasn't having sex, but to catch her playing with herself was crazy. He knew that it was sometimes easy to forget that women had the same level of sexual urges that men did. As Obi finally settled back into sleep mode, he thought about how he would tease Chinwe about this incident in the morning.

CHAPTER NINE

The first day of October marked a month and a few days before Election Day. The polls were showing that Obama had a 3-point lead over Romney, but it was really anyone's guess who would win.

In Sade's contest against current city council member, David Jackson, things were also tight. She was running a great campaign and doing better than most people would have suspected her to do because this was her first time running for public office. The date also represented Nigeria's Independence Day.

Obi decided to write a post on Facebook to commemorate the occasion.

> *"Nigeria is like a fine ass woman that got a lot of issues. You have every intention of leaving her, but she got that thing that keeps you coming back for more. Even though her potential is great, she will disappoint you most of the time. But by the time you realize it, you are in too deep and your love for her is too strong. At the end of the day, we are all married to this idea called Nigeria."*

Unfortunately, Nigerian Independence Day was a time when most people reflected on the failures of the country and wondered if it would ever become free of systemic corruption by the government. Regardless of the matter, Nigerians were still going to celebrate for celebration sake.

Obi and Nkechi were going to be attending a campaign fundraiser for Sade put on by some young Nigerian American professionals later that evening. Obi saw this a sign that Nigerian millennials were becoming more engaged and involved in what was happening in the politics in the United States at a greater level than their parents had been. But Obi also realized that Sade couldn't be boxed into being the black or Nigerian candidate. She had to have an appeal outside of those groups as well. Sade's Ivy League education was lauded as a huge plus to many college-educated white liberals. They felt like she was a safe pick who they could trust to make the right decisions from their point of view.

Most black people didn't have a problem with white people liking black candidates. But many were always concerned when up and coming black politicians would try so hard to immerse themselves with the white power structure, such that they would forget about the needs and concerns of their own people.

Sadly, that was the price of success that most ambitious black people had to deal with not only in the field of politics but also in the corporate world as well. Obi and Nkechi discussed this matter on the drive to the event.

"Chi Chi, I hope that Sade is ready for her crowd tonight. Hopefully, she will wear traditional Nigerian attire and speak a little pidgin English. I know a lot of people will appreciate the symbolism at the very least."

Nkechi responded, "I hate to agree with you but you are right. But Sade is different because she is one of our own. She doesn't have to pander like most politicians would have to do."

"Chi Chi, I always told myself that if I ever come back to this world in another lifetime, I hope that God makes me a Nigerian again."

Nkechi laughed and said, "Honey, I agree with you 100%. My only request is that I can be born in Southern California near the beach so I can wear flip flops everywhere I go."

A few minutes later, they arrived at the hall. As they were getting out of the car, they saw that the place was jam-packed. As they were walking toward the entrance, Obi said, "Damn, I hope we can find a place to sit."

"We don't have to worry about that. Sade reserved a few tables for her guests," Nkechi told him.

Once they got inside, they saw everybody was wearing their traditional attire and dancing to Dbanj's song, *Igwe.*

Obi shouted, "Chi Chi, you know this is my jam, lets hit the dance floor for a little bit before we go sit down."

Nkechi wasn't in the mood to dance, but when she saw the glee on Obi's face, she decided to go along with it. "I guess so, but no grinding on my booty. I know how nosey and judgmental our people can be sometimes."

Obi said, "I see where you are coming from. The crazy thing is some of these guys in here got mistresses and side chicks, but then want to play the overly moral role in public with their wives."

As the two of them continued dancing to the next song, Nkechi asked Obi, "If you saw a guy in here that you knew was cheating on his wife, would you tell me?"

He laughed. "The answer to the question is hell no, honey. I can't break the "G" code."

Nkechi sighed and said, "Men kill me with their no snitch policy when it comes to infidelity. Don't you think the man's wife deserves the right to know what is happening in her marriage?"

Obi responded, "Babe, you are absolutely right. But the issue is that it isn't my obligation to tell her. Unless it is Chinwe or my female cousins, my lips are sealed. Anyway, let me flip the question. If you knew your homegirl was dipping out on her husband would you tell me about it?"

Nkechi took a long pause while thinking of her response. Obi finally came in and said, "Your silence on the matter says it all."

Nkechi was annoyed by Obi's comment and said, "My feet are starting to hurt, and I need to go sit down."

As they were walking to their table, Sade came up to them. She was wearing a light green dress with a white head-tie to go with it. She was trying to represent the colors of the Nigerian flag.

She said to them, "I saw you guys doing your thing on the dance floor and didn't want to interrupt."

Nkechi embraced Sade and complimented her attire. Sade gave Obi an awkward hug as she always did when she was around Nkechi.

"I am about to say a few words in about 15 minutes or so."

The three of them got seated, and Obi realized that Sade's mother was sitting next to them. He greeted her: "Mrs. Olufemi, how are you doing?"

The woman turned around and said, "Obi, I can't believe that it is you. I haven't seen you in ages. She got up and gave him a hug. Obi introduced her to his wife. Even though Sade's mother was in her early 60s, she was still in great shape. Sade had inherited her looks and body figure from her mother.

Mrs. Olufemi said, "Sade tells me you have a little boy."

Obi responded nervously, "Yes ma'am I do. He is about two years old."

"That is great to hear. Kids are such a blessing from God. Anyway, I hope that your parents are doing well also."

"Thanks for asking ma'am. Everybody is doing well. I know that you and your husband are so excited about everything that Sade is doing with this campaign."

Mrs. Olufemi laughed and said, "Obi, you already know that my daughter is the biggest overachiever that you will ever meet.

But as happy as I am for her jumping into this new endeavor in her life, I would remiss to say that I wish you could find a nice man to meet and settle down with. Sade's brother and sister are married with kids and she is now the only one who is single. I just hope she can find a man by the time she reaches the age of forty because after that, it will be very hard for her to get married."

Obi was surprised by her very honest remarks about Sade. He quietly said to her, "I know Sade will find a good guy one of these days."

Mrs. Olufemi glanced over in the direction of Nkechi and said to her, "Obi is a very good man and you are lucky to have him."

Nkechi looked at him and said back to her with a smirk, "Thank you, ma'am. But don't pump him up too much, he already has an over-inflated ego as it is."

Sade had been talking with some other people but decided to jump into the conversation with Obi, and Nkechi, and her mom.

"Nkechi and Obi, I hope my mom isn't talking your ears off about my lackluster love life,' Sade said with a smile while looking at her mother.

"Sade, my dear, I am just expressing some motherly concern that is all. Your father and I have tried to introduce you to different men, but every single time you find something wrong with them. Sometimes I wonder if Barack Obama would have been able to meet your standards."

Sade got a bit sensitive when her mother talked about her personal life in public. She responded sarcastically, "Don't worry too much mom. I have hired Nkechi to be my dating coach as well."

Sade whispered in Nkechi's ear, "You are lucky that your mother lives a thousand miles away from you. I love my mom, but I can't stand her being up in my business all the time."

Nkechi put her hand on top of Sade's hands and said, "Moms will always be moms. Hell, my mom still tries to give me advice on how to raise Ike all of the time even when I don't ask her."

Sade thought about it for a minute and knew that Nkechi was right. She said, "Nkechi, I guess this whole campaign is just wearing on me. I wish my Dad was here tonight, he always knows how to calm me down and bring a sense of levity into my life."

While this was going on, the emcee of the event finally called Sade to the stage to speak. Once Sade got that microphone in her hands, she flipped back into politician mode instantly. She told the crowd about how proud she was to be a Nigerian woman, what her plans were to make Nigerians more influential within the city, and lastly how much she would appreciate them donating money to her campaign. Even though the speech lacked substantive policy proposals, Sade got a rousing applause from the crowd as people lined up to write checks and bring cash to her as soon as her speech ended.

The after party lasted for two hours. On the drive home, Obi and Nkechi were discussing what had taken place during the fundraiser.

"Damn, Sade did her thing tonight Chi Chi," Obi said, obviously impressed with Sade's performance. "She got a lot of Nigerians pumped up about her candidacy."

Nkechi responded, "I agree she did well. I also think her play to go light on policy was good as well. She needed to make an emotional connection with people and she did just that. I also noticed that Sade's mom really likes you a lot. I guess that you made a lasting impression on her back in the day. I got the feeling that she wishes that Sade was dating somebody like you."

Obi smiled at Nkechi and said, "I can't help it that I am the type of brotha who is in demand."

"I forgot that I can't give you a compliment. When I give you an inch you take a mile," Nkechi said, smiling.

They both laughed.

The Atlanta trip was finally here! Obi kissed Nkechi and Ike goodbye at the airport. But before he walked off, Nkechi gave him one last warning, "Honey, you guys have a great time. But don't have too much fun. I have friends in ATL who know you, but you don't know about them."

Obi smiled. "Chi Chi, I love you and I will call you when our flight touches down in Atlanta."

Obi's flight arrived in Atlanta two hours later. When Obi arrived at the airport he got into his rental car and drove to the hotel. Obi decided to get some rest before everybody else started heading into town later that evening. He checked his phone when he woke up and saw that he had missed calls and text messages from Nnamdi and some of the other groomsmen.

He was about to call Nnamdi when Nnamdi called him.

"My nigga, where have you been? I have been trying to get in touch with you for a minute. Have you gotten to ATL yet?"

Obi responded, "Yea, I am actually checked into the hotel right now. I took a nice power nap once I got here. The drinks on the plane caught up with your boy."

"Obi, I hope you came ready to play hard this weekend. We are going to be keeping some late hours these next couple of days. I hope you brought your vitamins with you to maintain your energy."

Obi laughed. "Zik, I see you trying me right now. Anyway, what is the move for this evening?"

"I spoke with my cousin and he was thinking about hitting up a lounge to drink and smoke some cigars. We will keep it low-key tonight and tear the city up tomorrow."

Obi liked the idea. "That sounds fine with me. Were any of the guys trying to meet up for dinner before we go out?"

"It will probably be just me and you," Nnamdi said. "We can meet in the hotel lobby for dinner around 8:00 p.m. if that works for you."

Obi called Nkechi after he was done with Nnamdi. She told him that everything was fine back at home and that she missed him. When they were done talking, Obi took a shower and then started to get dressed. When Obi finally headed downstairs to meet up with Nnamdi, he noticed that the place was jumping. He walked up on Nnamdi at the bar.

"Bro, I guess we picked the right hotel for the weekend. There is nothing but women in here."

"I talked with some folks at the front desk and they said that Morehouse and Spelman's homecoming is this weekend," Nnamdi said.

Obi smiled broadly. It sounded like they were about to have even more fun. "Zik, this weekend was already going to be nice, but now it might turn into the black version of *The Hangover.*

They ordered their food and started eating as soon as it arrived. They noticed a couple of women sitting close by and checking them out.

Obi told Nnamdi about his earlier experience on the flight with a flight attendant called Tamara.

"Bro, some women just toss all caution to the wind and go for what they want. I know that she had to see your wedding ring was on."

"Zik, the chick was no more than 25 with some nice perky titties with an apple shaped booty. She also had a honey brown skin tone, slim shape, and she was around five feet four in height."

"Damn, that sounds like a good look. Unfortunately, there isn't too much either of us can do beyond enjoy the attention we get from women at this point in our lives," Nnamdi said, defeated.

"Zik, wouldn't it be cool if dudes could get a one-day hall pass from their wives to have sex with any women they wanted to?" Obi said.

"Obi, you know good and well that dudes would never be satisfied with just one day. Once we open Pandora's box, that shit ain't ever closing back up."

Obi thought about it for a minute and then nodded his head in agreement. After they finished eating Obi and Nnamdi drove a couple of blocks to the lounge where they met up with some of the other groomsmen. Once Obi and Nnamdi got inside, Nnamdi's cousin, Ejike, came up to them and said, "Zik, we have been waiting for you to get here. It's time for you and Obi to catch up to us on these Patron shots."

At the bar, Nnamdi and Obi were greeted by Jamal, Nnamdi's old roommate from Hampton and Chidi, Nnamdi's older brother. Chidi said to Obi, "Bro, how have you been? I haven't seen you in a minute. How is the married life treating you?"

Obi responded, "I have been good, just maintaining for the most part."

Chidi responded, "The real question is whether you and your wife are still fucking or just having sex. There is a difference between the two."

Obi said, "My nigga, Chidi stay dropping dimes on us."

"Even though I have been married for six years and have two kids, my knowledge of understanding the game hasn't changed," Chidi said, braggingly. "I am like Michael Jordan when he came back out of retirement the first time. He couldn't go to the basket and straight dunk on dudes anymore, so he started hitting that turnaround jumper from the low block."

Obi remembered how hard he and Nnamdi partied whenever they went out with Chidi when they were in law school. Chidi would always get the VIP section at the club and pick up the tab for the drinks. During that time, Chidi was playing professional basketball in Europe, so he was just happy to hang with his family and friends and see some black women whenever he was in town.

As they were ordering another round of drinks at the bar, Chidi started giving the toast. "I hope all you guys took your vitamins and got plenty of rest because we are going hard in the paint this weekend for Nnamdi. Also, whatever happens here, stays amongst the fellas."

As the five of them were still drinking and smoking on their cigars, a woman walked up to them.

"Nnamdi, is that you?" she asked, looking directly at Nnamdi. "What are you doing out here?"

"Jemele, it is great to see you. It's been a minute since we have seen each other. I am actually out here for my bachelor party weekend."

Jemele gave him a hug and said, "Congratulations to you. I am so happy that you have found true love. I guess I am still waiting for my prince charming to come into my life. Anyway, I am just celebrating Homecoming with my homegirls from Spelman."

Nnamdi and Jemele dated during their junior and senior years of high school. They wrote in one another's yearbooks that they would be married with two kids by their 10-year class reunion. Unfortunately, their relationship had fizzled during their first year of college because Jemele went to college in Atlanta and Nnamdi stayed in Virginia and attended Hampton University. Even though she went on to become a successful TV producer at NBC, Jemele sometimes wondered how her life would have been with Nnamdi. As the two of them continued talking Jemele said to Nnamdi.

"When are you heading back to D.C.? I was hoping we could catch up for lunch on Sunday."

Nnamdi hesitated for a moment and then said, "I will be leaving on Monday, but I might be catching up with my uncle and aunt on Sunday. I will keep you posted if I can fit in some time for you if possible."

"Well, definitely let me know. Anyway, I need to get back to my girls." Before she left, Jemele gave Zik a tight hug and a quick peck on the cheek.

As soon as she walked off, Chidi came up to Zik and said, "I know that isn't who I think it is."

Nnamdi laughed and said, “Bro, it is Jemele Williams.”

Chidi shook his head. “I still remember catching you and her having sex at my apartment back in the day. I had to stockpile you with condoms, the way you guys were fucking.”

Nnamdi responded, “Bro, I was being real reckless during that time. I remember the first time me and Jemele had sex without a condom and I didn’t pull out quick enough.”

Chidi started laughing and said, “This nigga Zik called me with a low tone in his voice telling me he came inside of Jemele. Dude was scared that he would have to tell our parents that he got his girl pregnant. I was trying my best to contain my laughter when he was telling me everything. I told him about the day after pill and then I told him that I would go to Planned Parenthood to pick it up for him.”

Obi chimed in. “I can’t lie, having sex with no condom is a euphoric feeling. But it can be addictive at the same time.”

Chidi said, “Zik, I can’t front though, Jemele has filled out nicely over the years. When you guys were dating, she was slim. Now she has a grown woman’s booty on her.”

Nnamdi said, “I can’t believe that in the last few months, I have randomly run into Amaka and Jemele.”

Chidi said, “Bro, it is probably the universe trying to see if you are going to slip up and have sex with one of them. Before I got married, all types of women from my past were hitting me up out of the blue to have one last fling. Unfortunately, I failed and had sex with a couple of them.”

Obi jumped in, “I can’t front, I had sex with Tamika before Nkechi moved down from D.C.”

“I already have some dirt on my hands, I can’t afford to add more chaos to my life. Anyway, where is Jamal at? I haven’t seen that dude for a minute.”

“I saw him heading toward the bathroom and he didn’t look in good shape,” Ejike said.

They decided to go and check on him. Once they opened the bathroom door, Nnamdi saw Jamal sitting down on the floor looking dazed and confused. Chidi smirked and said, "I guess J is the first casualty of the evening."

Nnamdi said, "Jamal was always a lightweight in the drinking department, even when we were in undergrad."

Nnamdi and Obi helped Jamal to his feet and started walking him towards the exit to the car. Once they got him into the car, Chidi came outside with a bottle of water and handed it to Jamal.

"Make sure that J throws up before you guys leave. If he throws up in the rental car that will be a horrible look and will force Obi to get an expensive detail on the inside of the car."

Obi and Nnamdi drove Jamal back to his hotel and got him to his room before heading back to the lounge. When they walked back in to join the rest of the guys, they saw that Chidi and Ejike had about five women around them, and lots of drinks. Chidi looked at Obi and Nnamdi with a big smile on his face and said to the women, "I told you that my brother and his homeboy would be back."

One of the women said, "So who is the bachelor?"

Nnamdi raised his hand. Suddenly, the woman who asked him, along with another woman, started dancing on Nnamdi. After that, another woman from that same group started dancing on Obi."

"Didn't I tell you guys that we were going to have a good time? Jamal is going to hate that he missed out on this," Chidi said while grinding against the backside of one of the women. The plan was to go to another spot after the lounge, but with all the drinking and dancing, time got away from them and they ended up leaving the lounge at about 1 a.m. Obi drove Chidi, Nnamdi, and Ejike back to the hotel.

The next day, everybody, except for Obi, woke up with terrible hangovers. Obi didn't meet up with Nnamdi until around 2 p.m. to grab lunch in the hotel restaurant.

"Are you good bro?" Obi asked Nnamdi when he spotted him.

Nnamdi responded, "I am fine man. I took some aspirin to deal with a headache I have from all of that drinking we did."

Obi laughed, "Zik you know that your brother likes to do everything at a level of 10. What is the game plan for tonight?"

Zik said, "I know he wanted to go to the strip club around 11 p.m or so. He got us a section."

Obi responded, "Boys better get some rest before this evening. How is Jamal doing?"

Nnamdi said, "Actually, he is doing pretty well. He told me that he grabbed breakfast and I think he caught up with some of his friends that he knows out here."

As their conversation continued, Nnamdi said to Obi, "I forget to tell you that Ogechi and I were thinking about coming to Houston for Thanksgiving this year. We wanted to try and be somewhere that is warmer than D.C. for at least one of these holidays."

Obi responded, "That is what's up man. I know that Chi Chi would definitely love to have you guys around." Obi had thought about asking about Ogechi's situation with her dad, but he decided to leave it alone, at least for this weekend.

Nnamdi said, "Jemele texted me this morning. I can't lie, she has been on my mind since last night. She was the first woman to whom I said I love you. I guess in some regards she will always have a small piece of my heart."

Obi said, "I believe that all of our past relationships leave a profound and definite mark on us. Each experience makes us learn about the good and bad things about ourselves."

Nnamdi responded, "You are 100% right my friend. Anyway, this food really hit the spot for me. I think I am going to head back to my room and get some sleep before we get back at it this evening." Once Nnamdi left the table, Obi ordered another drink while he was checking his phone. He had seen that Nkechi had sent him a text message, it read, *"I hope that you guys are having fun doing God knows what. LOL. Anyway, hit me back when you get a free moment. Thanks, and I love you."* Just as Obi was about to respond, Chidi also sent him a text message. He said, *"Bro, I am going to need to get about $200 dollars from you and Jamal for the section and bottles tonight. Can you swing it?"* Obi texted back, *"No doubt man."*

Chidi responded, *"Cool. We gotta send my brother out with a bang man."*

Obi responded, *"LOL. Bro, everything will be fine."*

After he finished texting Chidi, Obi sent a text to Nkechi. He wrote, *"We are doing ok so far. The devil hasn't gotten a hold of us yet. LOL. Anyway, I miss you and Ike and I will call you later this evening."*

Obi went back to his room and watched a college football game and without knowing it dozed off. Zik called him a couple of hours later around 6 p.m. Obi picked up his phone while still half asleep and Zik said, "Bro, we are going to meet up in the lobby in about an hour to head out to a Jamaican restaurant for dinner. Are you down?"

Obi told Zik that it was cool and then the phone conversation was over. Obi decided to give Nkechi a call because he knew this would probably be the last chance he would get for the rest of the evening.

When Nkechi answered she said, "Wow, I am happy you remembered that you have a family to think about."

Obi laughed and said, "Chi Chi, stop being overly dramatic for no reason. How is everything going with you?"

"Everything is going well. Sade is over at the house with me. We are going over some campaign stuff while drinking wine and listening to Beyoncé."

"It sounds like you guys are enjoying yourselves. What is Ike up to?"

"I took him to your parents' house for the evening. I needed to be able to concentrate on what we are doing. So, what are you and fellas about to get into tonight?"

Obi said, "Probably grab something to eat and maybe hit up a club or something."

Nkechi sarcastically said, "Oh ok. I guess that is the story that you are sticking with. I know Zik already told you, but I talked with Ogechi and they will be in town for Thanksgiving. Did he give you any particular details about why they would be coming?"

"Yea, he told me, but maybe it's just a getaway before the holidays and the wedding."

"Yea, I have been in Ogechi's position and can certainly relate. Anyway, let me get back to Sade. She told me to tell you hello and to enjoy your trip. I will talk to you later and I love you."

"I love you too."

After the phone call, Obi took a shower and got ready for the evening. He was on his way to the elevator when he got a text message from Sade. It said, *"Hey, I hope you are having fun in ATL. I know what I am about to say is random, but I finally realized that I don't know if I could have ever loved you the way Nkechi loves you. I guess I have always been so much into my own personal ambition that I rarely tried to have a deeper relationship with anybody."*

Obi didn't know how he was going to respond to the message at first. He texted back, *"You aren't giving yourself enough credit. I enjoyed what we had going on back in the day."*

She responded, *"Thanks, I really needed to hear that. I know that I shouldn't be telling you this, but I have always tried to find another guy who was like you. But judging from my single status, I haven't found that person."*

Obi responded, *"You are a great catch, you just have to be patient."*

Sade responded, *"Thanks, anyway enjoy yourself tonight. I still care about you more than you will ever know."*

Obi texted back, *"Same to you."*

Obi took a deep breath as he put his phone back into his pocket. He finally met with Nnamdi and Chidi in the lobby and then they drove to the restaurant. While they were in the car, Chidi said, "Fellas, I just wanted to tell you guys that I seriously needed this trip. I have to be honest me and my wife are going through a rough patch in our marriage. Honestly, I don't know if we are going to make it or not."

Obi said, "Dang, Chidi I hate to hear that news. I will keep you guys in prayers."

Chidi responded, "Thanks, Obi, but my faith in God is waning. Sometimes I don't understand how people can just pray about their problems, but don't want to discuss them with each other or with a counselor."

Nnamdi said, "Big bro, people have been bred to believe that only a supernatural force who has powers greater than them will help intervene into various problems in their lives."

Chidi said, "In my opinion, every single human being on this planet has control over their own individual life."

Obi said, "So Chidi what is the reasoning that you guys aren't working out?"

Chidi responded, "We really don't know either that well. Oluchi and I dated for like 6 months before she got pregnant with Chijoke. At the time, I was 33 and not sure if I was ready to get married to her. But I also didn't want to pay child support and just see my son every other weekend if that. I decided to propose to her after Chijoke was born and the rest is history. Since we have been married I found out that we really don't have too much to talk about beyond the kids and household issues. I don't feel like I can share my hopes and dreams with her."

Nnamdi said to Chidi, "Damn, bro I didn't know things had gotten that bad. I guess I have been so wrapped up in this wedding that I haven't asked you how things are going on your end."

Chidi responded, "Zik, don't worry about it, man. When you get married, some things you must deal with on your own. I know Obi can relate to me on that notion."

Obi nodded his head in agreement to what Chidi said."

As they arrived at the restaurant, Chidi said, "Fellas, I am hungry as hell and ready to make it drizzle in this strip club later tonight. Thanks for allowing me to vent real quick, but let's get back into party mode."

Once they got into the place they ordered their food and the conversation switched back to Nnamdi. Chidi said, "Ogechi is a great woman. My kids love her and my mom adores her. All I know is that my brother bet not fuck it up or he will have a lot of people mad at him."

Nnamdi smiled and said, "Since she is a nurse, Ogechi brings a warm sense of understanding in how she interacts with people. But don't get it twisted, when she gets really mad she can go from zero to one hundred in an instant."

Obi responded, "Zik, that is a trait most women all share with each other."

"Zik I am not sure how often you and Ogechi have sex, but get ready for it to drop once you guys get married."

Nnamdi sighed, "You guys are making this marriage thing really depressing."

Obi laughed and said, "Bro, me and Chidi are just trying to be real with you. Even with all the bullshit, I'd rather be married than single again."

Once they got their food and started eating, Nnamdi got a text message from Jemele. She asked him what he was doing for the rest of the night?" He responded saying that he was not sure yet. She texted back and asked him to keep her posted. She and her girls wanted to come out and hang out with them.

After some time, he told Chidi and Obi that Jemele had hit him up.

Chidi asked, "Did you tell her that we are hitting up Magic City?"

Nnamdi responded, "I didn't tell her about our plans."

Obi jumped in, "Bro, it looks like Jemele might be trying to give up the ass."

Nnamdi responded, "Honestly, that is what I am afraid of. If we did end up having sex, Jemele would think it means more than just having sex. I am not ready to deal with her emotions right now."

Chidi said, "Bro, I agree with you. But don't front like you haven't thought about having sex with her one last time."

Obi decided to switch up the conversation. "What is up with Jamal and Ejike?"

Nnamdi said they would be meeting up with them at the club later in the evening.

After they finished eating, the three of them left the restaurant and headed back to the hotel to have drinks at the bar. They stayed there for about an hour and then started on their way to Magic City at around 10 p.m. Once they got inside, they were escorted to the VIP section. A few minutes later, the waitress brought them two bottles of Cîroc Vodka.

Chidi shouted out, "Let the fun commence gentlemen."

As they were drinking, two strippers came toward their section. One of them was dark skinned and the other was light skinned. Both had big breasts and huge behinds.

Zik said, "There is a God somewhere. Man, can't make it like this."

Obi and Chidi started laughing.

Obi responded, "Zik, you sound like the preacher from the movie *Coming to America* right now. But I have to agree with your assessment."

While the three of them were getting lap dances, Jamal and Ejike finally arrived and joined the lap dancing party. Nnamdi was the center of attention since he was the groom-to-be. The ladies moved seductively and fluidly and the guys were losing their minds.

"Hold my phone for me, man. I don't need to be answering it by mistake, in case it's Ogechi," Nnamdi said to Obi, handing over his phone.

Obi laughed and took the phone from Nnamdi and Nnamdi went back to focusing on the girl who now had her behind in his face. Obi was about to put the phone in his pocket when he noticed the light flashing. He looked at the flashing notification and saw that it was a message from Jemele.

> *"Hey, me and my girls are about to leave this lounge and are heading up to Magic City. Let me know if you are up there."*

When Nnamdi finally came up for air, Obi handed the phone back to him and pointed to the message.

"Damn, my worst fears are coming true," Nnamdi said, looking at the message and shaking his head. While Nnamdi was thinking about how to act when Jemele arrived, Chidi was still drinking and getting more lap dances.

"Little bro, you are messing up everybody's vibe right now," Chidi said to Nnamdi while a girl was grinding on his groin. "Why are you stressing this hard over Jemele? If you don't want to mess with her, just let her know that when she comes up here. Hell, she might end up buying you some drinks and lap dances while you're bullshitting."

"Bro, I am just not trying to get caught up on some foolishness, "Nnamdi said. "We all know that alcohol always impairs a person's judgment."

Nnamdi looked at his phone and saw that Jemele had sent him another message. The message said that she was taking a rain check on Magic City because one of her homegirls got her car towed, and another one was drunk as hell. She ended the message by saying that she hoped to see him before he left Atlanta.

The five of them stayed at the club for a couple of hours and left at around 3 a.m., stopping over at Waffle House to eat before they all headed back to the hotel.

The following afternoon, Obi, Chidi, and Nnamdi met in the hotel lobby to watch the Atlanta Falcons play the Washington

Redskins at 4 p.m. They order a few drinks and chicken wings and reminisced about the previous night in between plays.

"Last night was epic," Obi said, not taking his eyes off the television screen. "I got so many lap dances that I can't even remember."

Chidi and Nnamdi nodded and smiled.

"Obi, I had a great time too," Chidi said. "The funniest part of the whole night goes to that boy Jamal. He was damn near falling in love with them strippers and shit."

"Bro, I give Jamal a pass, to be honest," Nnamdi said. "His girlfriend broke up with him a few weeks ago and the dude is just lonely and looking for some companionship."

Chidi laughed. "Zik, these ain't the women to be crying your sorrows to. Neither their time or them lap dances are free."

"Well the real question of the day is whether Zik will be meeting up with Jemele today," Obi chipped in.

Nnamdi smirked. "She already texted me this morning. She will be meeting me for dinner this evening."

Chidi took a sip of his drink and smiled. "Let me know how it goes, my brother. You might get lucky tonight."

"Jemele indirectly said she is on her period. So absolutely nothing sexual is about to go down."

"Zik, that is probably for your own good you know," Obi said.

Nnamdi then asked Obi, "So have you talked with Chi Chi about your previous situation with Sade yet?"

"Dang, I always thought that I was the only one with issues in my marriage, but I see you guys have some skeletons in your closets as well," Chidi teased.

After the game, they headed back to the individual rooms. Obi spent the rest of the evening in his room talking on the phone with Nkechi and his sister. The next morning, Obi and Nnamdi met up for breakfast before they checked out of the hotel. It turned out that Nnamdi and Jemele had spent a relaxed evening together as old friends. According to Nnamdi, they had spent the evening catching up on each other's lives. Jemele had told Nnamdi all about her dating life, wanting kids, and how she felt like she had hit a glass ceiling in her career. There was a little bit of sexual innuendo on both sides, but that was about it.

"So, do you think that she still loves you?" Obi asked when Nnamdi was done telling him about his date.

Nnamdi thought about how to respond. "I feel that she will always have love for me, but isn't in love with me."

"Well sounds like a great way to end this weekend. Anyway, bro, I gotta hit the road to the airport. I really appreciate this weekend. It was fun, man. Tell Jamal, Chidi, and Ejike I said what's up."

"No problem, hit me up when you touch down in Houston."

Nkechi and Ike were waiting for Obi when he stepped out of the arrival terminal. He did not realize just how much he had missed them until he saw them. He ran up to them and hugged them tightly before they got in the car and drove off towards home.

"I see somebody is excited to see his family," Nkechi said once they merged onto the interstate.

"It's just good to see my two favorite people in the world," Obi said excitedly.

"It is good to know that you missed us with all of the fun you and the fellas were having in ATL."

Obi smiled as he lowered the window on his side and took in the warm breeze. Then out of the blue, Nkechi said to Obi, "Did you know that Sade was pregnant before?" Obi was taken aback by Nkechi's revelation. While he tried to gather himself, he realized that he was going to have to face the facts of his past quicker than he thought he would have to.

CHAPTER TEN

Nkechi was glued to the television when Obi came home to pick her up to go to Sade's election night watch party. After all the hoopla and intrigue, Election Day 2012 had finally arrived. Obi had voted early, so he spent most of his time that day at work following the exit poll results on his phone. It was quite an interesting day. Even though he rarely discussed politics besides talking with his co-worker, Keisha, Obi knew that most of the people at his job were pulling for Romney.

"Honey, the lines at these polling places are ridiculous," Nkechi said when Obi walked into the living room. "The media didn't think that black folks would be as enthused as they were in 2008. The Republicans are trying to use every voter suppression tool in the book to hold some of us back, but they can't stop us from showing up for Obama. As Obama used to say on the campaign trail, *"I am still fired up and ready to go."*"

"Chi Chi, I love your energy right now. On another note, how confident are you in Sade winning her city council race?"

Nkechi sighed and said, "Based on some projections we have received from early voting, we are hanging in with the incumbent.

But I don't know how things will turn out. All I can say is that we are hoping for the best and bracing for the worst. Regardless of whether we win or lose, this whole experience of working on a campaign has been great for me."

Obi smiled. "I am very happy for you, Chi Chi. At the end of the day, sometimes what we have learned from a situation is more valuable than the actual results. Anyway, I am going to take a quick shower before we leave."

While Obi was in the shower, Nkechi was in the bedroom getting dressed. She was going toward the dresser to grab her earrings when Obi received a text message notification on his phone. Nkechi picked up the phone to turn off the alert when she noticed that the message was from Sade. She usually didn't check Obi's phone at all, but she was a bit intrigued to see what the message said.

> *"I feel the spirit of Adaorah is with me tonight. I can still feel the softness of her little hands grazing my face."*

Nkechi tried to read some more, but she could hear Obi turning the doorknob to the bathroom and quickly put the phone back down. She didn't mention the incident on the car ride to the watch party, but she did have all types of thoughts running through her mind about why Sade had sent the message to Obi and who this Adaorah was.

During the drive, Obi was in his own world. He bobbed along to Stevie Wonder's *Signed, Sealed, Delivered* on his iPod. Nkechi sat silently beside him.

"I have a feeling that tonight is going to be a victorious night, Chi Chi."

Nkechi smiled and placed her hand on his thigh. She wanted to ask him about everything that she was thinking, but the words couldn't come out of her mouth.

Obi continued talking. "I can't believe that I cast my ballot for Barack Obama as president, twice. I never thought he had a shot until he won the Iowa Caucus in 2008. I remember thinking that if a state that is over 90% white can vote for him, then he has a chance to be president. I can't front though, it will be tough for the Democrats to win in 2016 even if Obama wins tonight. They don't have anybody that excites folks like Obama."

"I guess that means you aren't sold on Hillary Clinton then?" Nkechi asked him.

"I like Hillary, but I feel that 2008 was her time. She could probably run again in 2016 and win the Democratic nomination and presidency, but it depends on the mood of the country. Hell, Donald Trump might run and become president."

They both laughed until they had tears in their eyes.

Then Nkechi said, "If that dude ever becomes president, you will know that hell has frozen over."

They finally pulled up to the lounge where Sade was having her watch party. Obi got out of the car and walked over to open the door for Nkechi, and they both walked in. The moment they were inside, they could tell that the mood wasn't quite the same as it had been in 2008. The festive atmosphere from four years before was tame.

Obi went to the bar to order a drink and overheard a random black guy say, "Even if Obama does win, he hasn't done anything for the black community, to be honest."

The guy's friend then asked him, "What do you want him to do in particular? The Republicans control the House of Representatives, so there isn't anything he can really do."

The guy responded back, "He is the president, he just needs to do something."

Obi shook his head and walked away with his drink. What was it with some of these black folks and their unrealistic expectations of the president. Some folks only saw his presidency as either completely wiping out systemic racism altogether or bust. Even Obi had to accept that politics is a game of incrementalism. He knew that Obama wasn't going to follow through on every campaign promise that he made. But he began to wonder if the blame should be laid on the shoulders of the voters who had crazy expectations of what politicians can accomplish during their term in office.

Obi joined Nkechi, Sade, and other friends and supporters of Sade, in their section of the lounge. CNN had just announced that Obama had won the state of Ohio. Everybody clapped and high-fived each other and clinked their glasses. But the joy of the group was dampened by the news that Sade had lost her bid to get onto the city council. Sade had gone to the bar to get a drink, so Obi and Nkechi followed her over there.

"How are you feeling about everything?" Obi asked Sade when they caught up to her.

"Pretty damn good, honestly. I would have loved to win, but it is what it is. The one thing that I can take from this whole journey was my ability to step out on faith and believe in myself."

"Sade, I love your attitude. You have nothing to hang your head over. You will get them next time," Nkechi said.

Sade shrugged her shoulders and said, "We will see how things go. I need some *me* time to figure out my next move in life. I will probably do some traveling and give online dating a chance."

The three of them laughed. They ordered drinks and hung out by the bar for a little bit before Sade went over and gave a speech to her supporters. By the time she was finished talking, Obama had been declared the winner of the election. The DJ played Young Jeezy's *My President is Black* to set the mood. And everybody started shouting, Four More Years!

Even with all the excitement in the air, Obi had been so far removed from the 2008 celebrations surrounding Obama's win that this time felt different. He had spent that day celebrating his birthday and having sex with Tamika the following day. He remembered the rush of emotions that intoxicated the country for the two months leading up to the record-setting inauguration crowd that came to see President Obama get sworn into office in 2009.

Obi and Nkechi partied till about 11 p.m. and finally left the spot to go pick up Ike from his grandparents' house. During the drive, they were both quiet for the most part. Even though they were excited about Obama winning, they felt bad that Sade hadn't won her election.

"I can't lie, Sade held herself together pretty well tonight," Nkechi finally said. "I know that she is completely devastated. She put her heart and soul into this campaign."

"Yea, I can only imagine. Sade wants to succeed at everything that she does. But I know she will bounce back from this disappointment."

"I agree with you. Now I have to figure out what my plans for 2013 will be," Nkechi said. "It's crazy how our life's decisions aren't as clear-cut as they were when we were younger. Sometimes I want to crawl underneath a rock and just hide from the world for a little bit."

"Chi Chi, I have come to the realization that life is really about trial and error. Most great people have failed their way to success. We still have time to figure out our path in life." Obi said reassuringly.

Nkechi always appreciated Obi giving her a sense of calmness whenever she felt her world was getting too chaotic.

At home, Nkechi put Ike to sleep while Obi was up watching the election results.

When Nkechi came back downstairs, she said to him, "I thought you were going to bed as soon as we got home."

Obi smiled at her and said, "Chi Chi, I have to soak in this moment for as long as I can. Who knows if we will ever see another black family in the White House in our lifetime."

Nkechi shook her head and said, "I already see that you might fall into a mini-depression in 2016 when Obama won't be on the ballot."

"Honey, I love you, but please don't steal my joy right now. I am anticipating all the fake smiles some of my co-workers will be giving me tomorrow in the office. I will be enjoying every minute of it."

Nkechi wanted to wait up to see if she could talk with Obi about his situation with Sade, but she fell asleep before she could have that conversation with him. She decided it was probably best to have that talk with him maybe sometime in 2013 after the holidays and after Ogechi and Nnamdi's wedding.

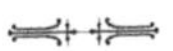

The weeks leading up to Thanksgiving were humdrum. Nkechi spent most of her time preparing the house for the arrival of Ogechi and Nnamdi. It was going to be a much-needed distraction from everything that was going on in her mind, even if only for a few days or so.

Ogechi and Nnamdi arrived on the Wednesday before Thanksgiving. Obi picked them up from the airport and brought them to the house. Nkechi was finishing up dinner when they arrived. They excitedly greeted Nnamdi and Ogechi with warm embraces and welcomed them into their home.

Ike ran directly into Ogechi's arms even though he didn't really know her. Nnamdi took this in and smiled, "Obi, I see your son is going to be a ladies' man. I can't lie, I would want to be held by Ogechi any day of the week."

Nkechi sighed, "Zik, you are a trip. I hope that you don't try and have sex with Ogechi in our house. I can hear everything."

"Chi Chi, I hope you have your ears wide open because you will be hearing a lot of bumping and grinding these next few days." Nnamdi teased.

Ogechi sighed and said to Nnamdi, "Babe, I can't take you anywhere."

They hung around the kitchen for a little while, the men pouring and sipping glasses of wine while the women set out plates and cutlery. Soon, the conversation switched back to the wedding.

Nnamdi started it when he said, "I can't wait for this wedding to come on already. All I know is that I am only having one of these," he said, pointing at Ike who was playing in his highchair. "If Ogechi and I don't work out, the next time I get married I am going to the Justice of the Peace."

Nkechi looked at Nnamdi with a side-eye and said, "Bro, it better work out."

"Chi Chi, thanks for your concern. It is very much appreciated."

"Let me know if Obi's mom and aunt will need our assistance in cooking tomorrow," Ogechi said, changing the topic. "I am ready to help in any way that I can."

Nkechi smiled at her and said, "We will have to head over there around 8 a.m. to get things going. It is going to be a full house of people. Obi's brother, Okey, will be in town along with a woman that he has brought along with him."

Nnamdi looked at Obi and asked, "Does anybody know anything about Okey's new chick?"

"I asked Chinwe about her, but she said Okey was keeping this one under wraps."

"I can't blame him for that. Sometimes your family doesn't need to know about every move that you make," Nnamdi said.

"So what is the situation with your father coming for the wedding?" Nkechi asked Ogechi out of the blue.

Ogechi's eyes drifted in the direction of Nnamdi as if she was waiting for him to give her some sort of cue. When that did not come, she burst into tears.

"What's wrong, Ogechi," Nkechi asked, genuinely concerned. The men exchanged glances at each other.

"I am sorry, you guys. I can't do this anymore," Ogechi said between sobs. Then looking directly at Obi, she said, "Your dad is my father."

Obi looked at her like she was crazy. He couldn't utter the words that were trying to come out of his mouth. Nkechi looked at Obi, wondering if he was going to say something, but then she realized that he was in a state of shock.

"Ogechi, are you for real about this. There must be some type of mix-up."

Ogechi looked at Nnamdi and he responded, "Sis, it is all true."

Everybody in the room turned their attention to Obi. He looked and sounded calm when he finally spoke, "I guess Thanksgiving dinner has gotten a whole lot more interesting."

Nkechi walked over to Obi and gave him a big hug and kiss on the cheeks. "Honey, I don't know what to say."

Ogechi gently walked up to Obi and put her arm around him and said, "I am so sorry to do this to you. I never meant any harm by it. My mother always told me that my stepfather was my biological father for most of my life. It wasn't until last year that she finally told me the truth. I blame myself for pressing her to tell me who he was."

As Ogechi continued talking, Obi put his hand on her face and said, "Sis, you don't have anything to apologize for. You didn't do anything wrong."

Obi looked at Nnamdi and said, "So how did my father react when he found out that you were Ogechi's fiancé?"

"He was very shocked and told me not to tell you anything. He didn't plan to reveal any of this until after our wedding," Nnamdi said to Obi.

"So, does he know that you and Zik are down here?" Nkechi asked Ogechi.

"I told him that I was coming and he wasn't very pleased about it. But I can't worry about his feelings, I have to find my own truth."

The four of them spent the next hour or so talking about the situation. Ogechi explained to them how her mother and father met each other while attending Howard University for undergrad. While they were dating, her father got a job at Shell and moved back to Nigeria. Ogechi's mother thought he would ask her to marry him, but he didn't. She later found out that he had married somebody else, Obi's mother. The two of them kept in contact and saw each other from time to time whenever he came to the U.S. for business. Eventually, one of their sexual encounters led to Ogechi's mother becoming pregnant.

"Wow. I can't imagine my husband getting another woman pregnant while we are still married. I don't know how I would react in that situation," Nkechi said, contemplatively.

Obi was also contemplating how all this had happened. He was leaning against the island with his hand on his chin and listening to the conversation. He was stunned because he never took his father as someone who would be a cheater. But Obi also realized that he only knew his father as his dad. He didn't know or think of him outside of that context.

"This is a lot to digest in one night. I think we need to continue this conversation tomorrow," Obi finally said.

They ate dinner, Obi barely touching his food, and then dispersed for the night. Ogechi and Nnamdi went into their bedroom and watched some television while Obi and Nkechi decided to take Ike to his bedroom and get him ready for bed. Afterwards, Obi took a long shower before getting into bed. Nkechi tried to figure out what to say to Obi while he was in the bathroom, but she couldn't think of anything.

Once they were both lying in the bed, Nkechi leaned over and asked Obi, "So what do you think about this situation?"

Obi sighed and said, "Chi Chi, I really don't know what to say. Honestly, the people that I feel the most for are my mom and Ogechi. I couldn't imagine being them right now."

Nkechi was surprised that Obi wasn't more upset about the actions and coverup of his father. Obi on the other hand still had the guilt of not telling Nkechi about his previous relationship with Sade and them having had a child together. In retrospect, he wasn't really in the right place to play the holier than thou role. Before falling asleep, Obi started to think about how he was going to tell his brother and sister about their father's transgressions.

Obi woke up around 9 a.m. the next morning. Nkechi was already eating breakfast with Ogechi when he walked into the kitchen. They were busy discussing what dishes to prepare for Thanksgiving.

"Good morning, big brother," Ogechi said to Obi with a big smile on her face once they realized he was there. "I guess I have to get used to saying that from now on."

Obi smiled back and said, "The same to you little sister. I can't believe that I have two sisters right now."

"I think that we are all still trying to navigate our way through this new terrain," Nkechi said.

"Chi Chi, you ain't never lied about that."

Obi decided to call his sister, Chinwe. She was silent on the other end of the line the whole time Obi was explaining things to her. She did not speak for a full minute after Obi was done. When she finally spoke, all she said was, "I guess this explains all of the weirdness and fighting that has been going on between mom and dad. I love my father with all of my heart, but he is a man, which still doesn't excuse him from being deeply flawed."

"I thought you would be a little angrier, Weezy," Obi said, trying to make sense of his sister's reaction.

"What is done is done, bro. Right now, we need to try to heal the family and establish a connection with Ogechi."

"How do you think Okey will take the news?" Obi asked her.

"I don't know how he is going to take it. But in other news, which will make Thanksgiving dinner more interesting, Okey's new girlfriend grew up Christian but is not 100% sure Jesus really existed."

Obi sighed. "Does mom know about it yet? She is going to explode when she finds out about this."

"Mom doesn't know yet."

"I guess Okey will lose his title as the perfect child who always does everything the way our parents taught him to do things. Anyway, what is up with you and Ola?" Obi said.

"I don't know about us right now. Dude is seriously considering quitting his job to pursue his passion, spoken word, and full-time acting. I can't knock what he is trying to do, but I am thirty years old and I am not looking to be with someone like that at this stage in my life. I want to get married and have kids in the next few years."

"Weezy, life is complicated as fuck the older that you get. Anyway, I will see you at mom and dad's house in a little bit."

After he got off the phone with Chinwe, Obi was in deep thought about everything going on within his family. A few minutes later, Nkechi walked into the room and said, "Just wanted to let you know that I will be heading to your mom's house in the next twenty minutes to help her and your aunt out with the cooking. Should I bring up the situation involving Ogechi with your mom?"

Obi pondered the thought for a moment and then said, "That is a great question. You can go ahead and do it. I want to see how much information she will divulge to you."

"That is cool. So what time will you guys be coming over?"

"Probably around 3 p.m. or so, Obi said. "Hopefully that will give you guys enough time to get the food close to being ready."

After Nkechi left, Obi went downstairs to eat breakfast. Nnamdi joined him a few minutes later.

"So how are you holding up with everything, bro?" Nnamdi asked Obi as they ate.

"I am actually doing well. I am just disappointed that I couldn't find out about Ogechi from my own father's mouth. I feel that me and my siblings deserved that much at least."

Nnamdi nodded in agreement. "Obi, you are 1000% correct. But maybe your father feared how you guys would react. Maybe he felt that you guys would lose respect for him. We all know that men, especially Nigerians, are very prideful. They rarely admit when they do something wrong. I am not excusing his behavior but just trying to get you to see things from his vantage point."

Obi just shrugged his shoulders. Nnamdi took that to mean that Obi was not too intrigued to discuss the issue surrounding his father. A little while later, Ogechi walked into the dining room carrying Ike. Obi looked at them with a smile and said, "I see that Ike is bonding very nicely with his aunt."

Ogechi paused for a minute and said, "Ike is so adorable."

Obi responded, "He is playing nice with you since he doesn't know you. But don't be fooled, Ike is a handful. He can go from quiet to tearing up shit in a heartbeat."

As they were continuing their conversation, Obi heard a knock at the door. It was his father. Obi opened the door. His father had a very nervous and unsure look about him. His father tried to give him a hug, but Obi gently patted him on the back instead. When Obi's father locked eyes with his daughter sitting on the couch with his grandson, he was at a loss for words.

Obi sat back down on another part of the couch and said to his father, "I could have saved you the trip and told you that Ogechi has already told me everything."

Chukwuemeka said to his son, "Obi, there aren't enough words to say how much I am sorry about how everything has transpired. I now realize that I was very selfish in trying to protect my own self-interest that I never thought about the pain that my transgressions would bring to my family."

Obi responded, "Father, with all due respect you never had any intention of discussing this manner. If not for me and Zik being close friends, you may have never felt compelled to even tell anybody that you had a daughter."

Before Obi could say another word, Ogechi jumped in and said, "Obi, I know that you are angry and disappointed with our father, which you have every right to be. But none of us can change the past, all we can do is to accept the present and see how to move forward from this situation." Then in a move that surprised everyone in the room, she stood up, walked over to her father, and gave him a big hug as tears streamed down her face. Obi stayed silent on the couch watching television. Ike was sitting on his grandfather's lap playing, oblivious to the distress around him.

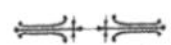

They arrived at Obi's parents' house about an hour after Obi's father's visit. Before he had left, Obi had assured his father that they will all be there for dinner and that nothing had changed. As they finally pulled up in the driveway, Obi said to Nnamdi and Ogechi, "We are here folks. I hope you guys have a big appetite. My mom always makes big portions of everything."

They laughed nervously. They all knew that this was not going to be an ordinary Thanksgiving dinner. Ogechi was especially nervous as she walked toward the house. Obi noticed this and asked her if she was okay.

"I am a little bit overwhelmed with everything," she said, shaking her head.

Obi walked over to her and took her hand in his. "Sis, don't worry about anything. I am here with you."

Nnamdi, who had Ike in his arms, nodded his assurance to both Obi and Ogechi right before they all walked into the house.

The first person to greet them was Ijeoma. She hugged Ogechi, surprising them all.

"My child, I hope all is well with you," she said, looking at Ogechi when the hug was over.

Obi looked on in dismay. He was waiting for his mother to flip, but it didn't come. After she was done welcoming Ogechi, she welcomed Nnamdi and Obi and gave Ike a kiss on his cheek. Ike squirmed and freed himself from Nnamdi's grip and ran to his mother whom he had just spotted in the kitchen.

Chinwe appeared from the living room to greet Ogechi. The two women sized each other up and down. Nkechi stretched her neck from the kitchen to see what was going on. Ike was now clinging to her, his tiny arms wrapped tightly around her neck. Obi saw her and gave her a questioning look that said, "I can't believe any of this is happening!" Nkechi responded by giving him the same look and they both smiled.

Ogechi asked Ijeoma if she needed any help in the kitchen.

"Of course, my dear. It is good to have a woman who wants to help. I usually have to drag Chinwe to do anything involving cooking for me."

Chinwe responded, "Mom, everybody doesn't aspire to be a master cook like you."

"I don't know any man who doesn't want a woman who can cook," her mother shot back. "You can't keep a man on microwave dinners and take-out food."

Chinwe rolled her eyes and walked back into the living room. Obi and Nnamdi followed. A few minutes after they had settled on the sofa watching TV, Okey arrived with his girlfriend, Yemi.

Yemi was a slender girl of five foot five and wore her hair in long dreadlocks with a scarf wrapped around her head. She talked easily about her family, so everyone soon got to know that even though her parents were Nigerian, she herself was born and raised in London. Yemi also talked about her love for Malcolm X, Angela

Davis, and Maya Angelou, and how they had helped her understand what it meant to be a black woman in this world. While Yemi was talking Obi looked at his brother to get his reaction to her comments and he could tell that Okey was very much into her. She made him think outside the box, which he rarely did in his job as an engineer. Although she grew up in a Christian household, Yemi also shared that she started reading the Koran when she went to college.

"Did you ever convert to Islam?" Obi asked her curiously

"The best answer to your question is that I dabbled in it for a little bit," she responded.

At that moment, Ijeoma walked into the living room to announce that dinner was ready, and it was obvious from the look of disapproval on her face that she had caught the tail-end of the conversation.

As everyone scurried to the kitchen to wash their hands and then made their way to the dining table, Chinwe went to wake up Chukwuemeka. He walked into the dining room a few minutes later and, taking one look at all his children gathered together in his house, he smiled. As usual, Ijeoma gave a long-winded prayer and they all settled down to eat.

"So, my dear, do you believe in God?" Ijeoma asked Yemi. All conversation ceased. Forks stopped scraping plates, mouths stopped chewing, and Okey may have stopped breathing. Yemi finished chewing her chicken before answering.

"Mrs. Ifeanyi, I believe we are the people we have been searching for. The faith that we have lies within us. Folks have gotten us to believe in the story of Jesus, even though some scholars say it resembles the narrative of the Egyptian God, Horus. Also in the Bible, they said Jesus had hair of wool and feet of bronze, but every depiction of him is a man with long blond hair with blue eyes."

Nkechi was smiling on the inside. Finally, she was not alone. She was not, and would no longer be, the only radical in the family.

Ijeoma put down her fork calmly and clutched her fingers together on the table. Then she said calmly, "You young people have your ways of seeing religion which is different from mine. All I know is that I will be seeing Jesus Christ in heaven when my time on this Earth comes to an end."

Everybody was surprised. That was it? But Ijeoma had other things on her mind, pressing things; this was not the time to be debating religion. As they continued eating, Obi looked at his father and saw that he was barely eating his food. Okey noticed the same thing and said, "Dad, is everything fine with you? You don't seem and sound like yourself right now."

"I am fine, my son, just enjoying listening to you guys talk amongst yourselves."

Ogechi was also quiet for the most part. She still felt awkward about the whole situation. Nnamdi was sitting next to her and would rub his hand on her thigh from time to time to make sure she was fine. As they continued eating, Obi's mother asked Nnamdi and Ogechi how their wedding preparations were coming along.

Nnamdi smiled. "Mrs. Ifeanyi, all I know is the time, date, and how much everything will cost. Ogechi is running the show and making most of the decisions for the most part."

The men nodded and the women laughed, then there was an awkward silence. Obi and Chinwe realized that their parents hadn't said two words to each other since they all gathered at the dinner table. They barely even looked at each other.

"I just wanted to say that I am happy to be in the company of my family," Ogechi said out of the blue, most likely in a desperate attempt to end the uncomfortable silence. Okey looked around with a confused look on his face. Chukwuemeka and Ijeoma locked eyes, it was then that Okey seemed to realize that something was amiss.

"What is going on?" he asked, looking from one person to the other.

Chukwuemeka cleared his throat and took a sip of water before saying, "My son, Ogechi is your sister. I didn't mean for you to find out about it like this. I am sorry and I hope you can forgive me." Then he abruptly got up from the table and headed to his bedroom.

Okey looked at his mother. Tears were now freely flowing down her face as she calmly walked away from the table. The rest of the evening was subdued as Ogechi explained things to Okey. She told him everything about the relationship between her mother and their father. Okey took the news very hard. He had always felt his dad was perfect, to find out that he was not, was crushing. To find out that he could withhold information about having another child from everybody...that hurt.

At the end of the evening, right before Obi was about to head out, Okey pulled him to the back of the house to talk.

"What do you think about all this shit with dad, bro?" Okey asked Obi.

Obi sighed. "Bro, I don't know if there is much to say about it. The shit came out of left field for real. Ogechi just told me about everything last night. I am still trying to process it all, to be honest with you. Anyway, how are things going with Yemi? She seems like she could be a keeper."

"You can say that again. We just found out that she is pregnant, so she will be around for a long while."

"Wow. Congrats, my brother. Why didn't you bring this up earlier while we were eating?" Obi asked.

"Yemi and I had planned on doing it, but with everything that transpired, I decided not to announce it right now. I will probably call mom when I get back to London."

"I feel you on that," Obi responded. "The only thing I will tell you is that your life will change when you and Yemi have that baby. Whether you guys stay together for a long time or not, you will forever be bound together because of your child."

"I can't lie, all of this happened so quickly. We started using condoms at first and then stopped."

Obi shook his head and said, "Going in raw gets dudes every time. Once you start down that road, you ain't going back to condoms ever again."

The two of them laughed as they headed back towards the front of the house. Everybody else was outside talking, except for Chukwuemeka. They said their goodbyes, and as Obi was saying goodbye to Yemi, he hugged her and whispered congratulations to her.

She looked puzzled for a minute and looked up to see Okey who was nodding his head with a smile on his face.

"Thanks, bro," Yemi finally said, "we all need to hang out again before we head back out of the country."

"No doubt, we will definitely get that worked out," Obi said.

Then he walked over to his mother. She was obviously trying to be strong despite everything that was going on. "Mama, everything will be fine," he said to her.

"My son, don't worry about me. I will be ok."

Obi gave his mom a big hug that lasted longer than usual and then headed to his car. When they got home, both couples went to their respective rooms to relax. Obi started contemplating more and more about telling Nkechi about his past dealings with Sade. Everybody had experienced enough excitement for one day and it was a good bet to hold off on that discussion until after Nnamdi and Ogechi headed back to Washington, D.C.

An hour later, Obi decided to watch television in the living room. Nnamdi was already there when he got there.

"Do you think Robert Griffin is going to guide your Redskins to a playoff run this year?" Obi asked Nnamdi after settling on the couch next to his friend.

"I hope so. We traded like five picks to move up in the draft to get him. He is playing well so far, so we will see what he will do."

Nnamdi responded. He could see that Obi was relieved to discuss something that did not involve his family's drama.

Obi got up to go to the kitchen for a glass when he heard his phone ringing. It was Chinwe. He sensed the panic in her voice the moment he answered the phone.

"Weezy, is everything ok?"

"No, you need to come quickly. Dad is having severe chest pains, me and mom are about to take him to the hospital."

CHAPTER ELEVEN

The year 2012 was quickly ending, and Obi was hoping to hear from his job about making him a permanent offer of employment. He was hoping for the best. Nkechi was also still searching for prospects. Unfortunately, things were not working out in her favor. Obi could tell that she was putting on a brave face even though deep down he knew that she was beyond frustrated with her current situation. Nkechi still met with Sade from time to time, she found Sade's presence to be comforting.

On their most recent outing, Sade had asked Nkechi if she had thought about moving back to Washington, D.C. because she knew of a job opportunity at the U.S. Department of Housing and Urban Development that would be a good fit for her. Nkechi had paused for a minute to think about it. She was not sure if she wanted to move back to Washington, D.C., she loved the weather in Houston, and she was not sure that Obi would be willing to uproot their family. However, Nkechi thought there was no harm in considering the opportunity. She got the contact information from Sade of the person she would need to talk to.

For the duration of their friendship, Nkechi had resisted the urge to ask Sade about her relationship with Obi. She sometimes wondered if Sade went out of her way to be helpful to her to cover up her guilt. But Nkechi knew that the real person she had to confront about the situation was Obi. She was starting to feel disappointed and betrayed by him. How could he keep this secret for this long without feeling bad about it? Nkechi's mind started to wonder if Obi was keeping any other secrets from her or if he was possibly cheating on her with somebody else. Her mother always used to tell her that nobody knows everything about their spouse. Her mother also said that sometimes when people go looking for dirt, they find it.

As these thoughts ran through her mind after leaving lunch with Sade that day, she saw a woman walking with her young daughter. She was surprised by her reaction to seeing them. Even though she told herself that she was not ready to have another child, that image made her begin to rethink her decision.

When she got home later that afternoon, Nkechi found Obi pacing around the living room.

Honey, is everything ok with you?" she asked him.

When he turned around to face her, she saw the tears.

"Obi, what is wrong, honey? Did something happen? Did someone die?" She rushed over to his side and guided him to the nearest couch.

Obi took a few minutes to respond, and when he did, he said, "Chi Chi, I just got off the phone with Chike. Uncle Ugo needs a heart transplant. He said the doctors said my uncle might only live a few more months if he doesn't get a new one." Obi paused for a minute and then continued. "I can't believe this is happening. We just got out of the woods with my father's health scare and now this? Life can be cruel as fuck sometimes!"

Nkechi wrapped her arms around Obi and tried to console him. But she had no words to tell him that would soothe his pain.

With Christmas and the New Year coming up, Obi wasn't in the mood to celebrate much of anything. His thoughts kept racing about his uncle's condition. A few days after the news of his uncle's need of a heart transplant, Uncle Ugo called Obi and asked if they could catch up for dinner alone the following night. Obi agreed.

The day they were supposed to meet was exceptionally hard on Obi. He was unsure of what to say to his uncle when they met. Nkechi told him to just stay positive and encouraging of his uncle's situation. She felt that surrounding Uncle Ugo with the right energy might have a certain effect on his mind and spirit.

When Obi picked his uncle up from his house, the first thing Uncle Ugo said was, "my nephew, how was Zik's bachelor party in Atlanta? I know you guys went to the strip club."

They both laughed. And just like that, the ice was broken. Obi was grateful for his uncle's sense of humor even amid what he was going through. On the drive to the restaurant where they were going to eat lunch at, they engaged in some light general conversation.

About twenty minutes later, they pulled into the parking lot of the restaurant. Uncle Ugo looked at Obi and smiled, patting his nephew on his thigh as if to assure him that everything was going to be okay.

"Did I ever tell you that your aunt Nkiru introduced your father to Ogechi's mother?" Uncle Ugo suddenly started, "your father was always studying his ass off in college, but the man never went to a party or rarely went on any dates with any women. I still think he was a tad bit socially awkward at the time and probably a virgin, but I digress."

Obi chuckled at the mention of his father's virginity.

His uncle continued, "I remember the first date that your father and Nkem went on was a double date with me and your aunt. The first time he laid eyes on her, he was in a daze, with his mouth wide open. I can't even lie, Nkem was very attractive. The two of them hit it off, they dated for your father's last two years of college, and then they started talking about getting married. This was right before your father got a job at Shell and went back to Nigeria."

"So why didn't he take her back with him?" Obi asked.

"Your dad wanted to save up some money to buy a ring and dowry and things of that sort. While he was in Nigeria, he and your mom started messing around, and one thing led to another and she became pregnant with you. Your father married your mom because he felt that was the right thing to do. But Nkem always had a big piece of his heart. I remember him telling me how much he cried over the phone when he had to tell Nkem the news."

Obi was quiet as he tried to take it all in. His uncle patted him on his leg again, this time, to get his attention.

"Let's not spend all our time in this parking lot. Once we get inside, I will tell you the rest."

Obi smiled and nodded his head. Once they got inside, they were greeted by a waitress and ushered to a corner booth that afforded them some privacy. The waitress took their drink order and left. Then they picked up their menus and began to scan the list.

A few seconds later, Obi put his menu down and asked Uncle Ugo, "So do you think my father was happy when he found out that Ogechi's mother was pregnant by him?"

Uncle Ugo pulled his menu away from his face and said, "Your father never expressed that sentiment to me, but I feel that even though he knew cheating was wrong, having a permanent connection with Nkem was something that he longed for. Love is a complicated thing..."

The waitress placed their drinks on the table and pulled out her pen and pad and took down their orders. When she left, Uncle Ugo continued, "... I only wish that your father had told you guys all of this sooner. You guys deserved to hear all of this from him, not Ogechi."

Obi was again quiet for a while, taking in all that his uncle had said. Having no other questions regarding his father's infidelity, he decided it was time to discuss the elephant at the table.

"Uncle, how are you processing your prognosis?"

Uncle Ugo smiled tensely. "I can't change the situation, so I just have to keep living my life. I can't afford to live in fear. After all, death is inevitable. We could leave this place and get into an accident and lose our lives right there on the spot."

The waitress returned with their food and placed it in front of them. They ate in silence for a few minutes before Obi spoke again.

"Uncle, do you think there is such a place called heaven?"

Uncle Ugo chewed on his food then drank some water before answering the question. "I really don't know, to be honest with you. I have always been believed that everybody should just live and enjoy their life to the fullest of their ability."

The drive back to Uncle Ugo's house was rather quiet. The food, along with the heart medicine that Uncle Ugo was taking, had drained a lot of his energy. He reclined in the passenger seat and relaxed the entire ride back to his house.

Once Obi dropped Uncle Ugo off, he called Nkechi to let her know that he was on his way back home. Then, alone with the silence and his thoughts, Obi began to think about some of the things Uncle Ugo had said during their time at the restaurant. *"People should make the most of the lives that they have..."* What would his life look like in the next five to ten years? Sometimes, he wished he could freeze time and keep everything just the way it. But, that was impossible, the world will keep spinning regardless of what we do.

When Obi got home, Nkechi was on the couch half-asleep with the television on. He woke her up and led her to the bedroom.

2013 was fast approaching, as was Ogechi and Nnamdi's wedding. Obi's father was given the okay from his doctor to make the trip to Washington, D.C. He was to be walking Ogechi down the aisle, along with her stepfather.

Nkechi was excited about the trip not just because of the wedding, but also because she had been in touch with Sade's contact at HUD and would be meeting her for lunch to discuss the job opportunity. She was hopeful that things would go well, even though she still had not told Obi about her plans. She knew she would have to tell him before they went out of town. The New Year would be the perfect time to tell him.

A week before the wedding, Obi came home frustrated. The company he worked for seemed hesitant to offer him a permanent position. Nkechi tried her best to assure him that things would work out, but Obi kept ranting about how tough it was being a black man working in corporate America. Nkechi decided to tell Obi about her opportunity after dinner. When she finally did, Obi's reaction was subdued. He wasn't sure what the right words were, to say.

"Wow. It sounds promising at the very least. I guess we will have to see how it plays out," was all he said to her.

Nkechi was expecting Obi to be a little more excited for her opportunity, but she knew that he had had a hard day and didn't hold it against him.

Obi found it difficult to fall asleep that night. He didn't want to leave Houston, but he couldn't tell Nkechi that. After all, she had moved to Houston for him, and because of that she rarely got to see her parents and siblings. It would be selfish of him to deny her the opportunity if it did present itself. For now, they just needed to focus on if she would get the job.

Obi and Nkechi spent their days, leading up to the wedding, getting themselves ready. On Friday night, they picked up their outfits for the traditional Nigerian ceremony, from the tailor. Then they went to the mall to buy an outfit for Ike.

Obi, Nkechi, and Ike arrived in Washington, D.C. the following Thursday morning. They rented a car and drove to the hotel. Nkechi and Obi observed the energy in the city as they rode through the city. It was different, they could tell. The buzz from 2009 was not in the air this time around. Things almost seemed too normal.

"I heard someone on television said that they were only expecting about a million people for the inauguration this year," Obi said to Nkechi. "I think almost two million were here four years ago."

"The first time for anything is always special. The buildup for how the first black president would govern and act in office was intriguing. Now we realize that even with all his charisma and uplifting speeches, Obama is still just another politician. I feel like too many people projected their own personal needs and desires onto him and expected him to take them on as his own."

Obi had a smirk on his face when he said, "Human beings will never be satisfied, even if you give them everything they want. In my opinion, being unfulfilled gives us the motivation to strive to do more and to find our own level of greatness."

They arrived at the hotel twenty minutes later and checked in. They were in the process of heading up to their room when they ran into Nnamdi, Ogechi, and Ogechi's mother in the lobby. As is typical of Nigerians in a celebratory mood, the greetings were loud and enthusiastic; except when it came to Ogechi's mother. There was an awkwardness when Ogechi introduced Obi to her mother as her brother. Ogechi's mother smiled tightly and tried to be polite, but her displeasure was apparent. It was obvious to Obi that she still had some bitter feelings toward his father.

After promising to meet with Ogechi and Nnamdi later, Obi and Nkechi finally went up to their room to get settled.

"Chi Chi, I got the feeling that Ogechi's mother didn't care for me too much, did you notice that too?" Obi asked Nkechi as he dragged their suitcase to the base of the king-sized bed.

"Honey, I wouldn't take it personally. It is hard for a woman to give her heart to a man and then have him betray her trust. You are a reminder of that betrayal. It doesn't matter how much time has passed, it still hurts."

At that moment, Nkechi's mind involuntarily drifted to her suspicions surrounding Obi and Sade. "I guess I can understand where Ogechi's mom is coming from," she added.

Obi looked at her, puzzled. "Babe, what are you talking about?"

Nkechi took a deep breath and said, "Obi, I know that you lied to me about your relationship with Sade. You had a child with her. How could you make me look like a fool this whole time?"

Obi looked at her, stunned. He crashed his body weight onto the couch to gather himself. What could he possibly say now? He decided that the truth would be best.

"How did you find out?"

Nkechi sat on the edge of the bed, Ike in her arms and tears in her eyes. "I saw a text message from Sade on your phone. Why didn't you tell me? I will never, for the life of me, understand why you feel like you couldn't tell me everything."

Obi took his time to respond. He knew he had to be careful what he said. "I'm sorry for not telling you. It didn't seem important until Sade resurfaced in my life. But then by that time, I just couldn't figure out how to tell you that we were once involved with each other."

"But I asked you and you said there was nothing between the two of you."

"I know, babe..."

"So you lied to me?"

"Yes, and I'm so sorry. I just didn't know how to go about talking about what she and I once shared. I thought if I said nothing happened, then it would all just go away. And the longer you guys hung out together, the harder it became to live with myself. And then this thing happened with my dad and I knew I had to tell you then –"

"So, what happened to this child the two of you had?" Nkechi asked, cutting him off.

"She died."

Nkechi was silent. Despite everything, she could not imagine what they must have gone through losing a child.

"I'm sorry," she finally said. "What happened?"

"She was born prematurely. Three months early. We thought the doctors would be able to save her, but she only lived for two weeks after she was born."

Nkechi saw what she thought were tears building up in Obi's eyes but she stayed on the edge of the bed, holding Ike.

"Was her name Adaorah?"

"Yes," Obi said, looking at her confused.

"It was in the text message," Nkechi explained. "What happened with you and Sade? Why did it end?"

Obi sighed. "Things with Sade went downhill after Adaorah died. I guess we were both processing our loss in different ways and we just drifted apart. I will always have love for Sade because of the bond we shared through the birth of our daughter, but that part of my life is over. I have you and Ike now." Obi fought back the tears. Nkechi allowed hers to freely flow.

"Chi Chi, I never meant to lie or deceive you. I guess in some way I was trying to move on with my life. Leave things in the past. But now, I realize that I was being selfish about my own feelings and not thinking about how you would feel about everything."

Nkechi didn't say anything to Obi as she laid down on the bed with Ike. After a few minutes of silence, Obi told her he was heading down to the bar to clear his head. He knew it would take time to earn back Nkechi's trust. He was willing to do the work, whatever it took to save his marriage.

When Obi got back to the room from the bar, Nkechi was watching television with Ike. She sat up when he walked in. "Obi, I don't want to spend my whole weekend dwelling and fussing over your past with Sade. We are here to celebrate the wedding of our friends, so let's just try and make it through this weekend. We can discuss our problems when we get back to Houston."

Obi nodded in agreement and they left it at that.

The next day, Nkechi met up with Ogechi for breakfast with the other bridesmaids while Obi headed to the airport to pick up his parents and Chinwe from the airport. After settling his parents in their hotel room, he headed down to the lobby with Chinwe for some food.

"You know mom is trying to play matchmaker with me this weekend," Chinwe said to Obi, once their food arrived. "I've already had two random guys call my phone saying they can't wait to meet me tonight. These guys sounded like they were in their early 40s."

"I take it that you and Ola are officially over?" Obi asked her, surprised.

Chinwe laughed. "That nigga is moving to LA to be an actor. I am back on the market, unfortunately."

Obi shook his head and said, "Damn, I really thought you guys might actually make it. All I can say is take your time before you jump back into another relationship."

"I am going to spend this year working on making myself happy. I feel women put too much value on either dating or being married to a man. This doesn't mean that I don't want to be someone's wife or mother one day, but I don't want my whole existence tied up in those titles. Meanwhile, men rarely have to sacrifice as much as women do when they get married and have kids. Guys don't have to give up their last names or be told to tame their career advancement because it might make them a bad father."

Obi paused for a moment and then said, "Sometimes, it is easy for men to forget how much male privilege still dominates our lives and society."

"Thank you," Chinwe said, "at least you get it."

Obi and Chinwe hung out in the lobby for a few more minutes before heading up to their various rooms to get ready for Nnamdi and Ogechi's traditional marriage ceremony.

The next day was Saturday. Nkechi met up with Sade's contact from HUD early that morning, while Obi and Chinwe met in the hotel lobby for breakfast. Chukwuemeka, who just happened to stop by the lobby bistro for something to eat, joined Obi and Chinwe at their table. It was obvious that something was bothering him.

"Is everything ok with you?" Obi asked his father.

"I am fine my son. Just a little nervous about this wedding on Sunday. I am working on the speech to give at the reception dinner. I honestly don't know what I'm supposed to say. I cheated Ogechi out of the opportunity to be a real father to her."

Chinwe placed a hand over her father's hand and said, "Daddy, you will do just fine. Just speak from your heart and everything else will flow."

Chukwuemeka started to get teary-eyed, but he quickly took a deep breath and said, "Weezy, a man couldn't ask for a better daughter than you. Thank you so much."

Chinwe came across the table and gave her dad a big hug."

Obi was about to mock his sister for being a daddy's girl but decided he didn't want to take away from their moment. So he sat back and watched his father have a moment with the daughter he had afforded the opportunity to be fathered by him.

CHAPTER TWELVE

"I can't believe my dad is really crying."

Those were the thoughts running through Obi's mind when he saw his father walking Ogechi down the aisle. Obi turned his head and saw Nnamdi was sweating and shaking a little bit. Obi always thought that Nnamdi was Mr. Cool, but this moment seemed to be getting the best of him. As if Chidi could read Obi's mind, he leaned over and told his brother to take a deep breath. The last thing anybody wanted was to see Nnamdi pass out today. All the elders would immediately start speculating that it was a sign that the marriage may be doomed from the start. Once Chukwuemeka got down the aisle with Ogechi and handed her to Nnamdi, Obi and Nkechi immediately locked eyes with each other. Obi used his mouth to say I love you to her. She just shook her head with a smile on her face. As Nnamdi and Ogechi were reciting their vows to each other, Nkechi began to get emotional as well. She started to think about the friendship that she forged with Nnamdi almost 10 years ago and how she was generally happy that he had found his queen.

At the same time, Obi glanced over at his mom to see how she was handling everything. She was holding her husband's hand the whole time. After Obi had taken stock of everything, the preacher said to Nnamdi, “You now may kiss your bride.”

“So how does it feel to be a married man?” Obi asked Nnamdi after the wedding. They were standing outside surrounded by many of the wedding guests.

“It is scary and exciting all at the same time. I will do my best to do right by your sister.”

Right then, Ijeoma walked up and congratulated Nnamdi and hugged him. “You and Ogechi look so perfect together. I pray that God gives you guys a long and fruitful marriage,” she said to Nnamdi, who thanked her for her kind words.

“I am sad that Okey wasn’t able to make it out here for the wedding. I wanted to see him and Yemi,” Ogechi said to Obi and Chinwe after the three of them had taken some photos together.

“I feel you, but we will try and visit them in the UK after Yemi gives birth to their baby.”

Nkechi looked over at the three siblings from where she was standing and saw the glow that Ogechi had on her face. She had finally found a level of peace in knowing who the other half of her family was.

The wedding reception took place a few blocks from the church about an hour later. It was an open bar, everybody danced and had a great time.

Nnamdi danced beautifully with his mother during the son and mother dance.

Meanwhile, Nkechi leaned over and whispered to Obi, “I don’t know if it is all this drinking or what, but I am horny as hell. Unfortunately, we can’t just leave the reception to go have sex. It wouldn’t look good.”

“I guess doing it in the bathroom in the reception hall is out of the question then,” Obi responded, looking longingly at the bathroom door.

Nkechi nudged him playfully. “Honey, what is wrong with you?”

The biggest moment of the night was the couple's first dance as a married couple. They danced to *Fortunate* by Maxwell. They were both very emotional during the dance and received a standing applause when the song ended.

As the night continued to wear on, all the drinking and dancing began to catch up with Obi and Nkechi. By the time they made it back to their hotel room, they were both too tired to have sex. Luckily, they were able to sneak in a quickie that morning before Ike woke up.

Later that morning, Obi was in the bathroom brushing his teeth when he noticed a bottle next to the sink. At first, he thought it was a bottle of vitamins. But upon looking closely, he realized that they were birth control pills. Obi was upset that Nkechi hadn't told him that she was taking them. This was the clearest message to him that Nkechi didn't want to have any more kids.

Back into the room, Nkechi smiled at him when he came in, and said, "Are you ready to watch the inauguration today? I can't wait to see my girl Beyoncé sing this National Anthem for President Obama."

Obi shrugged his shoulders and laid back on the bed.

"Obi, is everything ok with you?" Nkechi asked.

Obi responded, "I am fine. Just thinking about life. These last four years have gone by so quickly that I can't believe it sometimes."

Nkechi leaned over and gave Obi a kiss on the forehead and said, "I agree with you. Ike is about to turn three this year and I still haven't wrapped my head around that yet. In the end, you just have to enjoy each moment."

Ike was sitting on his mother's lap. Obi looked at him and said, "Do you see your namesake Barack on TV?" Ike looked at the TV, then at his father, and just laughed.

After the inauguration ended, Chinwe stopped by Obi and Nkechi's room to talk about the wedding.

"I saw you fighting over the bouquet yesterday," Nkechi teased her. I see someone wants to get married."

"Chi Chi, stop lying. I was camping out in the back as everything was going on. I wanted no part of that bouquet. Anyway, I have done a lot of thinking this weekend and I want to start a blog. I want to document the struggles of being a single, Nigerian American woman."

"Dang sis, that sounds interesting," Obi said. "Is there anything you want to address?"

"Oh absolutely! One of the topics I want to discuss is the double standard that we are held to. Nigerian men marry outside of their culture all the time and nobody says a word about it. But Nigerian women are always pressured to be loyal to their culture and marry a Nigerian guy." Nkechi started snapping her fingers in agreement. Obi smiled and said to his sister, "Weezy, you are sounding more and more like a Chimamanda Adichie disciple every day."

Chinwe smirked and said, "Fuck you, Obi. Don't be mad at me for speaking the truth."

Nkechi jumped in and said, "Not that I want to change the topic, but have you guys ever seen your dad as emotional as he was yesterday?"

"I was completely shocked," Obi said. "The most stoic man I have known was broken down in a way that I never thought was possible. When I got married, all I got from him was a stern handshake."

"Dad's speech to Ogechi and Nnamdi was so touching. I had goosebumps the whole time that he was talking," Chinwe said. "I remember looking at Ogechi's mother and she was tearing up the whole time too."

The three of them talked about their plans for 2013 and ordered some Chinese food. When they were done eating, Chinwe stretched out on the bed and said, "I can't remember the last time I just laid around and talked for hours on end. Oh well, I guess back to reality when we get on this plane back to Houston tomorrow. I swear these students are stressing me out. I notice my first strand of gray hair the other day and damn near cried when I saw it."

Nkechi laughed. "Chinwe, I felt like you do, the first time I saw a gray hair too. Now, I have come to embrace it slowly but surely."

Chinwe responded, "Where do you think our souls go to when we die?"

Obi looked at her and said, "Sis, you killed the whole mood with that question."

"My bad, I guess Uncle Ugo's condition has been on my mind a lot lately. It has me thinking about the afterlife more than ever."

Nkechi said, "Chinwe, in my opinion, the idea of heaven is something people use to keep human beings' minds at ease during our lifetime. Could we really deal with the notion that after we die there is a possibility that nothing happens after that? Also, heaven in some respects is simply an incentive for us to try and live a good and moral life while we are alive."

"Damn Chi Chi, your analysis was deep as hell. Anyway, I have enjoyed talking, but it's getting late and I need to head back to my room to finish packing my things," Chinwe said, getting up from the bed.

Later that night, Nkechi was in the bathroom getting ready for bed when she looked at the sink and saw the bottle of birth control pills. She grabbed it and put it away, but she wondered if, perhaps, Obi had seen it. She finally decided that even if he had seen it, she would worry about the fallout later.

The next day, Obi and Nkechi had breakfast with Chinwe, along with Obi's parents. They also caught up with Ogechi and Nnamdi as they were checking out of the hotel and heading to their honeymoon in Hawaii. It was a beautiful sendoff for the new couple.

Later, Obi went back to the room and brought down the rest of their luggage. They said their goodbyes to everyone and headed on their way to the airport with Chinwe. Obi drove while Nkechi and Chinwe talked and Ike slept.

"If Ike can sleep through the whole trip back to Houston, I will be happy as hell. I'm not ready to deal with him fussing for this three-and-a-half-hour flight."

Once onboard, Nkechi's mind was wondering how she was going to explain everything to Obi. She had *The Miseducation of Lauryn Hill* album on repeat on her iPod to help her search for clarity.

The weeks following the wedding, Obi and Nkechi carried on with their lives like everything was fine. Deep down, however, they both knew that the birth control issue needed to be talked about. Then one day, while Obi and Nkechi were eating dinner, Obi asked her, "Do you want to have any more kids?"

Nkechi chewed her food slowly and drank a glass of water before answering Obi's question. "At this very moment, no, I do not. But that answer can change in the future."

Obi responded, "So when were you going to tell me about the birth control pills?"

Nkechi breathed a big sigh and said, "Honey, I couldn't tell you because I know you wouldn't be fine with it. I just got the prescription when Sade told me about the HUD job in D.C. I just wanted to explore this opportunity and not worry about getting pregnant."

Obi didn't say anything while he finished eating his food. When he was done, he went into the living room to watch television. Nkechi came to join him after she was done cleaning up the kitchen.

"I am sorry for not telling you what I did. But I hope you aren't trying to be holier than thou. It seems like you have selective memory when it comes to hiding your secret relationship and baby with Sade. We have both made bad decisions that we have to own up to."

Nkechi went to the bathroom to give Ike a bath. While she was gone, Obi pondered what Nkechi had said. He was in the middle of processing his thoughts, his father called. Obi could tell that something wasn't right.

"Dad, is everything alright?" Obi asked his father, a little panicked.

"Obi, your Uncle Ugo had a relapse with his heart and is currently in ICU. The doctors don't know if he will make it another 48 hours."

Obi took about a minute or so to collect his thoughts before he responded to his father. "Dad, I thought he was on the list for a transplant."

Chukwuemeka said, "Son, right now they are just trying to keep him alive. A heart transplant isn't even a priority at this moment."

Chukwuemeka gave him the name of the hospital where Uncle Ugo was, along with his room number. Obi told him he would go and see his uncle in the morning. When Obi broke the news to Nkechi, they both started crying.

The car ride to the hospital the following morning was very silent. When they finally got there, they were met by Chike and his older brother and sister. All the cousins embraced each other. Once they got up to Uncle Ugo's room, Obi's Aunt, Nkiru, was sitting by her husband's bedside. Obi glanced at the ventilator that was the only thing keeping his uncle alive and he wanted to cry. But he fought the tears because he wanted to be strong for everybody else.

A few minutes later, they were joined by Chinwe and his mom. When Obi asked where his dad was, Chinwe said he was in the waiting room. Obi knew it was because this was too much for his father to deal with.

Obi and Nkechi stayed at the hospital for about an hour and a half before heading back home. Once they got home, Obi called Ogechi and Okey to bring them up to speed on everything concerning their uncle. After that, Obi listened to music while sitting on the couch staring blankly at the walls. Nkechi was going to come and talk to him after putting Ike to sleep but decided to give Obi his space. Obi ended up sleeping on the couch that night.

In a dream he had, Uncle Ugo was telling Obi not to worry about him and that everything would be ok. When Obi asked him if he was dead, Obi's eyes flew open. He looked down at his phone to see that it was 7 a.m. His first text message of the day arrived from Chike. It said,

> *"My dad is breathing on his own and responding to commands from the nurses. I thank God for answering our prayers."*

Obi breathed a huge sigh of relief and went to the bedroom to lie down. Only then was he able to sleep soundly.

The following week, Ijeoma came by the house to have dinner with them before Nkechi's trip to New York City to see her parents. His mother seemed to be in very good spirits as she and Nkechi cooked some jollof rice. Obi came home from work to the wonderful aroma of a well-prepared meal.

The three of them, along with Ike, sat down to eat a few minutes later. While they were eating, Ijeoma looked at her son, grandson, and daughter in law, with a big smile on her face.

"Obi, I have decided that I am going to separate from your father for some time," Ijeoma said to everyone's surprise. "I have been thinking about doing this for a while, but I decided to wait until after the wedding. Then Ugo had his health scare and I had to hold off yet again. But now, I have to think about myself for the first time in almost thirty years. I am going to Nigeria for about six weeks or so, and then, after that, go to the UK to see Okey and Yemi. From there I am not sure where the wind will carry me to."

Nkechi and Obi looked at each other with surprise. Before Obi could say a word, his mother said, "Son, I know what you are thinking, but I have made up my mind and I have already bought my plane ticket."

Ijeoma then looked at Nkechi and said, "My daughter, I know you understand where I am coming from. We, women, need to find ourselves sometimes, don't we?"

Nkechi simply nodded. Obi walked over to his mom and gave her a hug.

"I support you one hundred percent, mom," he said, meaning it in all truthfulness.

"Thank you, my son, I needed to hear that from you."

On her way out, Ijeoma kissed her grandson on the forehead and said a short prayer of blessing over his life. Once she walked out the door, Obi turned to Nkechi and said, "Damn, I got to call Chinwe."